ONE WOMAN'S TREASURE

What Reviewers Say
About Jean Copeland's Work

Spellbound—*Co-authored with Jackie D*

"The story is a mixture of history and present day, fantasy and real life, and is really well done. I especially liked the biting humor that pops up occasionally. The characters are vibrant and likable (except the bad guys who are really nasty). There is a good deal of angst with both romances, but a lot of 'aww' moments as well."
—*Rainbow Reflections*

"*Spellbound* is a very exciting read, fast-paced, thrilling, funny too… The authors mix politics and the fight against patriarchy with time travel and witch fights with brilliant results."—*Jude in the Stars*

The Ashford Place

"[A] charming story that I can recommend to anyone who likes a well-written mystery with a good dose of romance."—*Rainbow Reflections*

"Another enjoyable story from Jean Copeland with a bit of a difference. I think this book is definitely one to enjoy with a glass of wine near the warm fire."—*Les Rêveur*

The Revelation of Beatrice Darby

"*The Revelation of Beatrice Darby* at its epicentre is a story…of discovering oneself and learning to not only live with it but to also love it. This book is definitely worth a read."—*Lesbian Review*

"Debut author Jean Copeland has come out with a novel that is abnormally superb. The pace whirls like a hula-hoop; the plot is as textured as the fabric in a touch-and-feel board book. And, with more dimension than a stereoscopic flick, the girls in 3-D incite much pulp friction as they defy the torrid, florid, horrid outcomes to which they were formerly fated."—*Curve*

"This story of Bea and her struggle to accept her homosexuality and find a place in the world is absolutely wonderful. …Bea was such an interesting character and her life was that of many gay people of the time—hiding, shame, rejection. In the end though it was uplifting and an amazing first novel for Jean Copeland."—*Inked Rainbow Reads*

The Second Wave

"This is a must-read for anyone who enjoys romances and for those who like stories with a bit of a nostalgic or historic theme."—*Lesbian Review*

"Copeland shines a light on characters rarely depicted in romance, or in pop culture in general."—*The Lesbrary*

"The characters felt so real and I just couldn't stop reading. This is one of those books that will stay with me a long time."—*2017 Rainbow Awards Honorable Mention*

Summer Fling

"The love story between Kate and Jordan was one they make movies about, it was complex but you knew from the beginning these women had found their soul mates in each other."—*Les Rêveur*

Visit us at www.boldstrokesbooks.com

By the Author

Spellbound

The Ashford Place

Summer Fling

The Second Wave

The Revelation of Beatrice Darby

One Woman's Treasure

ONE WOMAN'S TREASURE

by

Jean Copeland

2020

ONE WOMAN'S TREASURE

ISBN 13: 978-1-63555-652-0

THIS TRADE PAPERBACK ORIGINAL IS PUBLISHED BY
BOLD STROKES BOOKS, INC.
P.O. BOX 249
VALLEY FALLS, NY 12185

FIRST EDITION: JULY 2020

CREDITS
EDITOR: SHELLEY THRASHER
PRODUCTION DESIGN: SUSAN RAMUNDO
COVER DESIGN BY TAMMY SEIDICK

Acknowledgments

First, I want to thank Sandy and Rad at Bold Strokes Books for always indulging my genre-hopping nature. It's wonderful to write for such a supportive publishing house. I'd like to give a special shout-out to Dana at Tri-State Vintage for helping me create and authenticate Daphne's world of antiques, and to Jamie, who's always there to answer medical questions whenever I make a poor character suffer some ghastly health crisis. And as always, I need to thank the readers, without whom I wouldn't have a platform to share what I create. Thank you. Lastly, thank you to my friends and family for their tireless support and dedication to my dream, and my author friends Jackie D and Erin Zak, who I lean on throughout the writing process. Love you all.

CHAPTER ONE

Daphne Carsen's thirty-eight years on the planet had been generally unremarkable—with the exception of that time she decided to slip into the back pew at the Unitarian church to watch her ex get remarried. Definitely not ranked among her top five best life choices, but rarely does anything good come from combining impetuosity with working through abandonment issues.

She'd made a noble effort to go incognito, but her last-minute dollar-store disguise of gossamer leopard-print scarf tied under her chin and a pair of round, white sunglasses left her looking more like an aging 1950s Hollywood starlet than an agent of espionage. But surprisingly, it had worked—at least until she'd decided to pursue the procession of limos and infiltrate the reception.

Her original intention had been to skulk over to the open bar for a free drink, catch a morbid glimpse of the happy couple, and be out of there. When the DJ introduced Savannah and her new wife, Francesca, as "partners for life" upon their entry into the lavish room overlooking the Sound, Daphne pretended to gag into her perfectly crafted lemon drop.

The bartender pursed her lips. "Something wrong with the drink?"

Daphne flinched, spilling some of the sticky liquid on her hand. "Oh, uh, no, no. It's actually pretty great. I was, uh, just thinking back to my own marriage," she stammered. "I'm divorced now so…"

As the bartender's face contorted with judgment, Daphne shrank into her awkwardness even more. *What in the hell am I doing?* She tilted her head back and dumped the rest of her drink into her mouth. Instead of leaving with her tail between her legs and a morsel of dignity, she signaled the bartender for another.

Savannah Locke, a voluptuous brunette with prairie-green eyes, was tucked into a curve-hugging, off-white dress and had never looked better. The scars from her surgeries to remove the excess skin were virtually undetectable. But none of this surprised Daphne. Ever since her ex, Ann Marie Cronk, as she used to be known, had morphed into Savannah Locke, all vestiges of the introvert self-conscious of her weight had vanished. Once she'd begun documenting her dramatic weight-loss journey for all of social media's hungry eyes to devour, she'd become a verified YouTube star and influencer. Her inflated ego and income now allowed her to indulge in any and all pampering and medical and cosmetic procedures necessary to complete her transformation into the person she'd always hoped to be: popular.

Daphne skewered the couple from the bar with a scowl. She'd reveled in her brief life as Mrs. Savannah Locke. They'd paid off their small ranch in a shoreline town in Connecticut, Daphne's consolation prize in the divorce, and Savannah even purchased a vacation condo in South Florida, but Daphne had never adapted to the way Ann Marie's self-importance expanded as her waistline shrunk.

Queasy from the couple's first dance, she glanced away and stared at the array of liquor bottles lining the wall behind the bar, preparing to order her third cocktail. As she licked the remnants of her second lemon drop from the bottom of the martini glass, someone tapped her shoulder. She turned around and met the blinding glare of Savannah's shiny Caribbean spray tan.

"Daphne?" Savannah said. Her false eyelashes twitched as she seemed to process the disguise. "What the hell are you doing here?"

"You look stunning in ivory," Daphne said. "Is that Versace?"

"You have to leave," she replied through a clenched jaw. "Crashing your ex's wedding is bizarre even by your standards."

"I just needed some closure, that's all—to know that you and I really are over, and we'll never get back together."

"Getting served with divorce papers would provide most people with all the closure they need."

"What can I say?" Daphne shrugged. "I'm an optimist."

"That ship has sailed," Savannah said slowly, coldly. "And you burned the dock when you cheated on me."

"Again with the cheating?" Daphne rolled her eyes in frustration. "It was a little online diversion that filled the emptiness in my life when you became obsessed with your internet fame. I never even spoke to her in real time. For all I know, she really was some fifty-year-old mail bomber living in his mother's basement."

"Not the point." Savannah scanned their surroundings. "Please lower your voice. I have about three seconds before Francesca finds her way over here, and I have no idea how I'm supposed to explain this." She indicated Daphne's getup with a flourish of her arms.

"Speaking of your blushing bride, does she know how intense you are? How wrapped up you get in your Vlogs and responding to each and every one of your adoring followers? How she'll be enjoying your luxurious vacation property mostly by herself once you tire of her?"

Savannah regarded her with a jagged glare. "I want you to leave now before I have you thrown out."

Daphne exhaled. Despite the satisfaction in recognizing she'd struck a nerve, she feared she was about to burst into tears at the suffocating weight of finality in Savannah's loveless eyes. "Good-bye, Savannah. My best to you and the new Mrs. Cronk."

Her chin up, she marched away with authority in her stride until her heel slid on a wet spot on the floor. After regaining her footing, she pushed through the double doors into the parking lot and pictured the reception hall exploding behind her as she slipped on her sunglasses in the twilight.

Once inside her car, however, she permitted herself the meltdown she'd been holding in since she learned of this day. Leaning her head against the steering wheel, she wept until she flushed away the images of her former life as someone's favorite human.

After she emptied her tear ducts and exhausted her emotional reserve, she determined that she needed to make changes in her life, to transform the work-day fantasies she'd entertained for years into a workable, sustainable reality. After all, what was the point of keeping a vision board in the kitchen and having a "salvaged-treasure room" if not for her to act on their inspiration?

Wouldn't it be a nice change to take action in the world instead of always moving in reaction to something beyond her control?

❖

After leaving the wedding reception and making a drive-thru *I've hit rock-bottom* McNugget run, Daphne found herself in the familiar refuge of her eighty-two-year-old neighbor's dining room. She and Sophie dove into their second bottle of cabernet, and she reminded herself that she had not included the goal of becoming a binge-drinker on her vision board. But after her encounter with Savannah, getting drunker and eating too many homemade pierogies with an elderly widow would perhaps inspire the much-needed impetus for change.

"Tonight I'm officially swearing off relationships. One and done." Daphne clinked her wine glass against Sophie's.

She waved her off with a petite, wrinkled hand. "Oh, don't be ridiculous, Daphne."

"No, I'm serious," she said, her words starting to slur. "It's too painful. You fall in love, promise you'll be together forever, and then one day, bang! Someone wakes up and decides she's not in love anymore."

Sophie shook her head, but her perfectly-coiffed white hair didn't move. "I'm sure that's an awful feeling, honey, but just because things didn't work out with Ann Marie doesn't mean you won't ever find that special someone to grow old with."

"I'm in my late thirties, Sophie. You think I can meet someone just like that?" She tried to snap her fingers, but her motor functions had fallen victim to the wine.

Sophie sliced into a home-made marble Bundt cake. "I don't know how you gay folk go about meeting each other, but you shouldn't give up on yourself. I don't like hearing you talk like this."

Daphne sighed. "Believe me. I don't like saying it, but I'm having a moment. I need to process."

Sophie side-eyed her as if Daphne wasn't making sense. "Why don't you concentrate on opening that antique business you love talking about? It'll take your mind off your personal problems."

"It's a work in progress, Sophie."

"That's what you always say. Get off your ass and do something about it. You want coffee now?"

Daphne grabbed the bottle of wine before Sophie could whisk it away. "And ruin this delightful buzz? No, ma'am."

"That's not a buzz. You're three sheets to the wind."

"That may be so, but nevertheless…" She refilled her glass, careful to control her wavering arm. "You and William were a success story. What was your secret?"

"We didn't have a secret. We had fifty-seven years together, one son, and two grandkids." Sophie smiled fondly. "You know how we made it so long?"

"How?" Daphne said before shoving the last sour-cream-coated pierogi into her mouth. By that point, the lemon drops and a bottle and a half of wine had her seeing two of Sophie. Luckily, her hearing was as yet unaffected.

"He never made me feel like I was unimportant to him."

"Wow. What's that like?"

Sophie raised a coffee cup to her lips with a shaky hand. "It was wonderful, Daphne. We had our hard times, too. Don't get me wrong. But during our first big fight after we were married, Willie yelled, 'But I love you, goddamn it,' smack-dab in the middle of it. And suddenly, whatever we were fussing about wasn't so important. He said that during every tiff we had from then on. He knew it would always get me." Her smile receded as she seemed to drift off. "That's how I knew he was sick…that first fight when he didn't remember to say it."

Daphne stared at Sophie in awe, her heart ready to implode.

Sophie seemed to gather herself again. "I hope you find a woman who makes you feel that way—not just when times are good either, but also when they aren't so good."

Daphne put down her fork and pushed her plate away. "That's all I've ever wanted. I had it for a while…in the beginning with Ann Marie. Oh, I mean *Savannah*," she said with air quotes and a sneer. "She hates when I dead-name her."

"It's easy to feel that way in the beginning of a marriage," Sophie said. "But then what happened? She got fat and got skinny and suddenly became too big for us on Morningside Drive."

"Ironic, isn't it? She loses weight and becomes too big for her britches." She sipped her wine. "And her britches were big, believe me."

"I know," Sophie said, sliding the bottle away from Daphne. "I used to see them hanging on your clothesline."

Daphne snorted into her glass, and they shared a belly laugh that she'd desperately needed. It had been too long since she'd felt anything that deeply other than discontentment and then grief. She was grateful to Sophie for being the coolest old lady ever and acting like a second mother to her since her own mother and stepfather had retired to Florida several years earlier.

Unable to stand without leaning against something, Daphne helped Sophie clear the table and wrap up the leftovers as best she could.

"Uh, excuse me." Sophie intercepted her. "The pierogies go in the fridge, and the dirty dishes in the sink, not the other way around."

"I think I'm ready to go home," Daphne said through slits in her eyes.

"Yeah. I think so, too." Sophie cradled Daphne's face in her hands. "Now you call me as soon as you get in."

"Sophie, I live next door. You can literally watch me."

"Fine. Then I'll stand on my porch and do that."

"Okay." She gave Sophie two thumbs up. After staggering across the yard, she had the decency to wait until she was on her own property before puking into the azalea bush on the side of her porch.

"Daphne? Are you okay?" Sophie shouted from her railing. "You need me to unlock your door for you?"

She waved Sophie off, went inside, and collapsed facedown on her living-room sofa.

CHAPTER TWO

Nina Colombo looked over at her son, Noah, in the passenger seat playing his Mario game on his iPad. To her delight, but not her surprise—for Noah had always been a precocious kid— he was taking the upheaval to their lives a lot better than she was. Maybe it hadn't hit him yet. Maybe she should have him see a therapist that specialized in the delicate issues of a ten-year-old, only children whose parents had recently divorced. And whose mom had also recently begun the process of coming out as a lesbian. Poor kid. Behind that brave face, he must be so torn up inside.

She reached over and squeezed his knee. "I'm sorry we're spending your April vacation moving instead of going somewhere awesome."

"It's okay," he said, not looking up from his game.

"Noah. Hey." She shook his leg. "Is it really?"

"Aww, Mom. You killed me," he said, finally looking at her.

"I'm sorry, baby. But listen. I want to talk to you before we get to the house." She gently pulled the tablet from his hands.

"I was listening," he said. "I don't care that we're not going away this month. Honest. You said we're going on a Disney cruise in June."

"Yes. It's already booked," she said. "But I know you look forward to going to Disney World with Dad and your cousins on spring break each year."

"Yeah, but we do that every vacation. No biggie if we can't this year."

Nina sighed to ease the knot in her stomach. She assumed he wasn't grasping the big picture. "Noah, you realize you won't take any more vacations with me and your dad?"

He rifled through the glovebox until he found a pack of gum. "Duh. I know what divorce is, Mom."

"I know, honey, but now that it's done and we're moving... away from Dad, how are you feeling about it?"

Noah shrugged as he chewed a big wad of fresh gum.

Now it was Nina's heart that felt twisted in a knot. Noah was always an outgoing, outspoken kid. A shrug and a distant stare were not his typical reactions.

"Noah, how are you? Tell me an adjective, a word that describes what you're feeling."

"Shitty," he said after a moment. "Can I have my iPad back?"

"In a minute." Nina gripped the wheel tighter and looked up at the highway signs. Their new exit was coming up. "Well, I feel like that, too, so that's one thing we have in common."

"Why do you? Do you miss Dad, too?"

"I miss seeing you happy," she said.

"I am, I guess. It's just kinda weird how things are now."

Nina reached out to Noah and gave the back of his neck a comforting caress. "You know you can see your dad any time you want. Just because I have primary custody, we don't have to follow it down to the hour. Your dad and I may have had our differences, but we've always agreed that you are our number-one priority. You know that, don't you?"

"He told me that a bunch of times, too," he said. "Can I have my iPad back now? Please?"

She handed it to him with a smile. Feeling somewhat relieved, she allowed her mind to review the afternoon's agenda, which included organizing Noah's bedroom, unpacking the household essentials, and having the security system installed.

Out of the silence came Noah's voice. "Do you miss Lacey?"

She almost veered off the road. What exactly did he mean?

"I do...sometimes," she said, unsure if she should elaborate. She'd introduced Lacey to Noah as her new "friend," and that's how she'd labeled their year-long relationship while she was still married to Zack. How else could she have explained the woman who'd inspired her physical and emotional awakening and subsequent filing for divorce?

They'd broken up after a year of passion, confusion, and apprehension, and she'd told Noah that Lacey had moved away. That explanation seemed to satisfy him. Until now.

"Why doesn't she ever come to visit? She always did before."

"Well, she moved pretty far away," Nina lied. "And besides, we've been busy with our own move."

"Maybe she can come over after we're all moved in," Noah said.

She tried not to let her facial expression reveal her surprise. She simply hadn't considered Noah's attachment to Lacey even with only occasional interaction. "We'll see," she said reassuringly.

She hated using mother-speak on him, but she wanted to drop the topic of Lacey. She hated even more having to lie to her son. At some point in the near future, once the dust from the divorce settled, she would be honest with him about the full spectrum of who she was—for his sake and that of her next relationship.

She'd learned early on this uncharted journey that the "new friend" safety net didn't usually fly for long with women these days. Once she'd created order from the chaos of her family life, she would sort out her inner self so another good one wouldn't get away.

But where or how was she supposed to find another good one like Lacey?

CHAPTER THREE

In her cubby at Sky-Hi Airlines call center, Daphne adjusted her headset and prepared mentally for the second leg of her double shift she'd taken as a favor to a coworker and to earn extra cash for her "future business" envelope. Her timing couldn't have been more unfortunate. Still nursing a hangover from her ill-fated night of closure-seeking with Savannah and then the wine and ghastly food combining with Sophie, she eyed the microwave bean burrito challenging her from the paper plate. She blew the steam off a chunk and stuffed it into her mouth before facing the next irritated traveler that lit up her customer-service line.

"Ahhh! Poop." She grabbed for her bottled water and guzzled it when the lava-hot filling scalded the roof of her mouth. At precisely the same moment, her line began twinkling like Christmas bulbs. After one more swig, she answered. "Sky-Hi Airlines customer-care center. My name is Daphne. How may I serve you today?"

"Yeah, this is the fourth fucking time I've had to call this number for service today," the woman bellowed. "When are you getting these planes off the ground here in Texas?"

"I'm very sorry, ma'am. The Dallas-Fort Worth area has been experiencing severe weather all day—"

"I know it has," the woman growled. "My friends and I have been stuck here since this morning watching it. But the hail wasn't that big, and it's been over for a while. When the hell are you getting us to Vegas? We have tickets for Barry Manilow tonight."

"Again, I'm very sorry for the inconvenience, ma'am." Daphne tried to respond in the calm, soothing tone she'd been trained to use.

"I don't want any more apologies," the woman shrieked. "I want your major, overpriced airline to get us out of this airport now."

"I understand, ma'am, but flights are backed up because of the weather delays and the maintenance inspections we've had to—"

"Don't give me that garbage. The storm stopped hours ago."

"Yes, I know but—"

"Now you listen here, Daphne. If that's even your real name. Am I even calling America on this number? Let me talk to your supervisor. Hopefully, he won't have an accent like yours. I can barely understand you."

"Accent? I was born in Connecticut." Daphne's head spun from the customer's tirade.

"We've been trapped in this airport for nine hours now, and we can't sleep here. We have a woman on a CPAP machine with us who needs a power outlet to—"

Daphne put the customer on hold, closed her eyes, and inhaled slowly. *Your life could always be worse. At least you have a job.* She repeated her mantra once more, then called out to her supervisor.

"Galena, I have a Def-Con Five on my line."

"Another one?" she shouted back from the cubicle next to her. "You have to learn how to diffuse these situations yourself, Daphne. How long have you worked here?"

Daphne heard Galena grumble out a few more demoralizing statements before taking over the call. She sank into her chair and fought back tears of inferiority. She played with the antique fountain pen on her desk she'd bought for a steal at an estate sale and promised herself that tomorrow she'd treat herself to a day trolling for roadside goodies people had cleared out of their houses for spring cleaning.

Maybe tomorrow she could also think about putting that business plan together.

❖

The next morning Nina awaited the delivery of the rest of their furnishings and belongings to the new house. This time she expected a smaller truck from a company specializing in transporting breakables and other valuables that required extra care. She stepped out onto the large, wooden front porch with her coffee in hand, watching Noah ride his hover board around the driveway while recording himself on his new cell phone.

"Noah," she called out. "Watch out for the moving truck while you're on that thing. I don't need you to get run over our first weekend in town. "

"When is it coming?" he asked in the middle of a series of circles on the board.

"Soon. And stop getting fancy on that thing. I don't know where the nearest urgent-care walk-in is yet."

"Relax, Nina," he said with a devilish grin.

"I'll give you 'relax, Nina,'" she said. "I'm not kidding, Noah. I have some cleaning to do inside, so if you're bored, you can ask Dad to take you for the day."

"I'm fine, Mom."

"Okay. Call me when the truck comes. And don't leave this yard." She went inside, grabbed her bucket of cleaning supplies, and started on the downstairs half bathroom. She was relieved that Noah chose to stay home with her instead of going with his father for the day. Evidently he wasn't harboring any subconscious resentment toward her or being tempted to take the side of the spurned parent.

Although Zack had been decent to her during their divorce proceedings, he hadn't been when she'd first told him she was filing. He hadn't wanted the divorce and still hadn't seemed ready to let Nina go completely, even after confronting her about the nature of her relationship with her new "friend" from work, Lacey.

Not long after meeting Lacey, Nina had come to understand that the unsettling feelings of emptiness and discontent that had dogged her throughout the latter half of her twelve-year marriage to Zack had nothing to do with Zack's success or failure as a husband. The solution wasn't about piecing together something that had come apart. For her, the two pieces hadn't truly fit together from the start.

When she fell in love with Lacey, their relationship felt whole and satisfying, despite its limitations.

Six months in, she began promising Lacey she'd file for divorce, but it would take time. But Lacey grew more impatient with each passing month. Ultimately, she couldn't hang in through all the ups and downs that accompanied loving a married woman who had only recently discovered her true sexual and emotional orientation.

As Nina swirled the toilet brush around the blue water, she again found herself deflecting the question of whether the biggest decision of her life hadn't also been the biggest mistake. She'd broken up her family, taken Noah away from his father, and alienated herself from friendships she'd made during her years with Zack. Served her right, she supposed. She should've paid more attention to her emotional needs instead of spending the last fifteen years focused on her career as a rising corporate executive. Now, in her early forties, her career thrived, but her family and personal lives felt like they were circling the bowl like the foamy water after a flush.

Almost as if she'd summoned his presence, Zack's name appeared on the screen of her vibrating phone. She wanted to let it go to voice mail, but she'd basically done that to him all week.

"Hey," she said, watching the sparkling toilet bowl refill.

"How's Noah doing?"

"Call him and ask him yourself. He's outside on his hover board obsessing over his phone."

"He's gonna break his neck on that thing," he said with a chuckle.

"Too bad you didn't think of that before buying it for him for Christmas."

He groaned into the phone. "Like you did before getting a ten-year-old his own cell phone as a divorce present?"

Nina bit her lip to stop herself from lashing back. "Divorce present? Really, Zack? I need to be in contact with him while he's finishing out his school year in Greenwich."

"Whatever. Look. I didn't call him directly because all I get from him is 'I'm fine.' I want to know how he's really doing in all this."

"He's fine, and I'm not being flippant. I ask him until I'm tired of hearing myself. He's rolling with the changes a lot better than I am."

"We'll see next year when he has to start at a new school."

Nina clenched her jaw. "He's always been resilient. He'll make it work. But you win on passive-aggressive digs. I need to get back to my housecleaning. The movers are coming any minute."

"No cleaning service? I'm sure they have some good golfing in Madison you could be doing on this gorgeous Sunday."

She recognized that as another dig, this time about her and Lacey. That's how they'd struck up the conversation and friendship at work that ultimately led to everything else. She held her tongue on this one, privately acknowledging that Zack had so much to be hurt about and obviously still hadn't worked through it all.

"Zack, please. I'm done going there with you. It's over. Everything is over. If you really want to know how Noah's doing, hang up and call him. He'd love nothing more than to talk to you."

He sighed into the phone and then cleared his throat. "I'm sorry. Honestly, I didn't call you to start something. I want you to be happy, Nina, and not just because it's the right thing to want for my son's mother. I want it for you, too."

She sighed, too. "I know. I want to say I'm sorry, Zack, but I've said it so many times it just comes out sounding trite."

"You had to do what you had to do. I get it."

"I'm not sorry for doing what I had to do." Nina made sure her voice was clear and confident. "I'm sorry it hurt you. But I can't keep harboring guilt. We both need to learn how to move on and be okay where our lives are heading, whether it's what we'd intended or not."

"I'll call Noah now," he said and ended the call.

It saddened her that conversations with Zack always drained her so much. But she was impressed with the conviction in her extemporaneous speech, especially the part about refusing to feel guilty about taking care of her own needs. It was sound advice, and she was more determined than ever to follow it.

After a peek out the window at Noah, she found it fitting to move on to the next toilet.

❖

Daphne loved this time of year. With most towns in New Haven County offering free bulk-trash pickups, people seized the opportunity to clear out old furniture and declutter their cabinets, storage areas, and lives. They did their spring cleaning with a vengeance, and Daphne usually "cleaned up" picking through people's refuse and rescuing forgotten or discarded treasures.

Over the last year or so her acquisitions had been a metaphor for her life. Savannah had wanted to declutter her life, and after she'd disposed of her excess weight, Daphne was the second thing she'd let go. Savannah's sudden marriage to Francesca only confirmed her suspicions that Savannah had had a foot out the door before Daphne even realized they were in trouble.

But enough of that. Sophie was right. It was time to refocus on the positives in her life rather than remain mired in the negative. Yes, her job sucked, and she was alone and lonely in an empty house reeking with memories of her and Savannah, nee Ann Marie, but she still had her dreams.

Since she wasn't able to borrow her coworker Pascale's F150 this morning she was on the hunt for smaller collectibles that would fit in her 4-door sedan: vases, dishware, lamps, etc. She pulled down a street in Madison she'd had luck on last year, an upper-middle-class, manicured cul-de-sac where people tossed out the kind of "junk" that Daphne could use to upgrade her entire house.

She rolled up along the curb of a colonial with a dresser and some end tables stacked up near the driveway. After scanning the pile and seeing only those larger items, she drove on to the next house with a tempting offering of smaller discarded fare.

Before she'd even thrown her car in park, an antique Tiffany-style lamp grabbed her eye. She practically salivated as she walked toward it and recognized it as early twentieth-century slag glass. These people must've been crazy to throw it away just because of a slightly frayed cord. Meh. They probably had five others just like it inside but in perfect condition.

"Come to Mama," she said aloud as she cradled it in her hands. She laid it on the front seat, strapped it in with the seat belt, and gingerly drove away. She could easily sell it to a collector for at least three hundred as is—that is, if she didn't decide to keep it for herself.

She still had several more stops to make that day, but she was surely not going to find anything that would top a treasure like this. Driving away, she glanced in her rearview mirror and noticed a twinkle in her eyes at the rush of excitement in discovering something new and the possibilities it held.

This was going to be a good day.

❖

"Mom, the moving truck was here," Noah said from the bottom of the stairs in the foyer.

Nina wiped the sweat from her forehead after switching the arrangement of dressers in her bedroom. *Wait. Did he just say the truck was here?* She called down to him. "You mean they're here now?"

"No. They dropped everything off. I signed for it, and they left."

Nina bounded down the staircase and stopped at the open front door. "Oh, Noah. You were supposed to let me know when they arrived. My car was blocking the driveway." She met him at the foot of the stairs, upset that she wasn't there to supervise the delivery.

He looked up at her with sad eyes. "I knew you were busy, so I decided to handle it. I thought I was helping."

"Aww, that's okay, honey," she said with a tousle of his hair. "You did help me. C'mon. Let's bring everything in. Your grandpa's baseball cards are in those boxes."

"Okay." He took off and ran down the driveway.

As she approached the heap of boxes at the foot of the driveway, she noted with increasing dread that something was missing.

"Noah, did you take anything inside already?"

"No. I've been out here the whole time."

"Did you watch the men unload the truck?"

"No. I was recording stuff on my phone. I came over to the truck when they called me to sign for it."

Nina sighed and ran a hand through her hair, forcing herself to be patient. "Great-grandma Astrid's antique lamp isn't here. Did they give you a copy of the shipping papers?"

"Yeah." He pulled the crinkled, rolled-up papers from his back pocket.

Nina unrolled them and reviewed the list of individual line items. The lamp was on the list and checked off as delivered. "What the f..." She looked around, baffled.

"What's the matter, Mom?"

"I don't understand. According to the paperwork, they delivered the lamp, so where is it? Damn. I'm gonna have to call them."

After a lengthy discussion with the moving company concerning the whereabouts of her lamp and why the driver would entrust a ten-year-old to oversee the delivery, Nina returned to help Noah cart the remainder of boxes into their garage.

"Honey, you need to go through these boxes and make sure all your stuff is here." She rambled on more to herself than to Noah, who was preoccupied on his phone. "The moving company assured me that they delivered everything correctly and didn't leave any items on the truck. I don't see how they can be so sure. I mean, clearly the lamp never made it here." She sat down on a box, resting her head in her hands. "Of all the things to be lost, it had to be that lamp, my great-grandmother's lamp."

Oblivious to her suffering, he approached her and hovered over her. "Mom, look at this video I took."

"Oh, honey, I'm in the middle of a micro mental breakdown now. Can I watch it after lunch?"

"It'll only take two seconds. It's two squirrels fighting in the front yard. It's epic."

She lifted her head out of her hands and watched as he played the video. He wasn't overhyping it. The two squirrels threw down on the lawn, flipping each other over and then chasing each other until one retreated up a large oak tree on the perimeter of their property. Toward the end of the video, Nina noticed a gray sedan in the background.

"Play that again, from the beginning." She watched the background of the video more closely this time and noticed the gray car seemed to be parked in front of the house for a moment and then drove away toward the end of the clip. "Noah, can you take a few screenshots of that car in background?"

"Yeah. Let me see." He took the phone from her hand.

Maybe it wasn't the movers' faults after all. Maybe a thief was on the loose in their new neighborhood, and her son had caught the culprit on video fleeing the scene of the crime. She couldn't imagine the nerve of someone stealing something out of her yard in broad daylight.

"Like this?" Noah handed her the phone.

She swiped through the series of enlarged screenshots and smiled. "Yes," she exclaimed. "You got part of the license plate, too. Brilliant." She grabbed him and wrapped him in a hug. "I'm contacting the police department. Maybe they've had other reports of thefts in the area. It's worth a shot. Good job, buddy."

His face lit up with pride at saving the day.

She ran inside to get her phone, hopeful the photos would lead to the return of her precious family heirloom.

As Daphne waited for her bowl of clam chowder to heat in the microwave, she stared at her vision board hanging on her kitchen wall. Its title, "Make it Happen," outlined in glitter, always jumped out at her no matter where she stood. She smiled as she perused the images of hearts, various antiques, and a quaint antique shop glued all over it, along with several Carrie Fisher quotes. Her favorite was "Do not let what you think they think of you make you stop and question everything you are." She'd added that one after recalling the last fight she'd had with Savannah during which Savannah accused her of being unmotivated and satisfied to forever subsist on the crumbs of life.

The remark had struck a painful chord but ultimately inspired her to formulate a concrete plan to achieve her dream—which she was absolutely going to do. Eventually. Sooner than later. Yes. She was going to make it happen.

And then the microwave beeped her back to reality. She carried her soup into the living room and sat on the couch in time to catch the end of the six o'clock news. She gazed lovingly at the lamp. It would never make it out of her living room and into her antique shop, when she actually opened one. Despite the frayed cord, it still worked, casting a warm glow over her living room.

"And finally tonight," the anchor said. "A single mom received an unfortunate welcome to her new neighborhood in Madison this weekend when a bandit stole an antique lamp movers had just delivered."

As the anchor spoke, video of an extremely attractive woman with full, glistening lips and brown, wavy hair poking out from a baseball cap streamed across the screen.

"Nina Colombo, a Greenwich native, told us that while she's disappointed in the theft, she doesn't believe her new neighbors are bad people."

Daphne's jaw dropped, and her chowder-laden spoon froze before her mouth in mid-air.

"I just want it back," the woman said, seeming dejected. "Not for the monetary value but for the sentimental one. It's part of my heritage. It originally belonged to my great-grandmother, but my grandmother brought it here when she emigrated from the UK in her youth. She left it to me, knowing how much I loved it growing up."

The camera switched back to the anchor. "Colombo went on to say that her ninety-three-year-old grandmother had recently passed away, and she would pay a reward for the lamp's safe return. Luckily, though, her son, Noah, had been outside recording his new neighborhood and caught a partial view of the vehicle on video as it fled the scene."

Upon Daphne seeing her car skirt away on the TV news, the soup on the spoon that had been suspended in mid-air dribbled down the front of her shirt.

"Fuckety fuck," she said in an exasperated whisper.

The blond co-anchor added, "Mmm. Let's hope someone recognizes this heartless thief's car and notifies Madison police at the number on your screen."

"Heartless thief?" She hit rewind on the remote to see if she could make out her face.

Suddenly, Daphne's phone rang, and Sophie's name and number appeared on her television caller ID.

"Please tell me it's just a coincidence you found the same kind of lamp that's been stolen," Sophie said before Daphne could utter the word hello.

"Of course it isn't a coincidence, Sophie. That's my car." She jumped up and began pacing her living room. "Did you see my face? Can you read my license plate?"

"No, no, honey. Calm down. Just the car, and that's a popular color."

"What am I going to do?" Daphne's stomach felt like it was twisting inside out.

"Call the police department before somebody else does," Sophie said.

"No way," she said, her voice cracking. "They'll arrest me for theft. I was just trash picking. I didn't know it was somebody's actual stuff. It was all piled up at the edge of the driveway, like everyone else's on that street."

"I know it," Sophie said. "Just explain all that to the police."

"What if they don't believe it was an accident? They'll think I took it and that I'm scamming the woman for the reward."

"Don't take the reward, dummy," Sophie said. "It was an honest mistake. The woman isn't out for blood. She just wants her lamp back."

"Ugh. I feel like such a jerk. Maybe I can just drop it off on her porch and go. I really don't want to have to face this person."

"I don't blame you, but still, you better call the police and straighten it out. You don't want them to find you first."

Daphne sighed in dread. "Will you come to the police station with me?"

"Can I collect the reward for turning you in?"

"No, you cannot."

"Then I'm sure I'm busy."

"Sophie, please. This is so embarrassing. I can't do it alone."

"You have to stop saying you can't do things alone, young lady. You're a strong, grown woman." She softened her tone. "But yes, of course I'll go with you. I love looking at men in uniform."

"Thank you. Okay. Let me call the police department and tell them I'll be down with the lamp."

She hung up and sighed again as she looked at the lamp she'd grown to love during the last two days—just not enough to go to jail over it.

CHAPTER FOUR

The next day after work, Daphne picked up the lamp at her house, and Sophie and she headed to the police department, eager to complete her dreaded mission. She pulled into the parking lot and looked over at Sophie in the passenger seat, staring straight ahead with her hands folded in her lap. "You take it in."

Sophie scowled at her as she hugged her handbag close to her chest. "Me? No, sir. You swiped it. You take it in."

"But you said you love looking at men in uniform. The place is crawling with them. Just walk in there, drop it off, get an eyeful, and come back out."

Sophie shook her head. "I'll gladly walk in with you for my eyeful, but I'm not taking the rap for this. Oh, no. They'll think I've lost my marbles, call my son, and he'll lock me in an assisted-living facility."

A wave of panic swept over Daphne. "What do you mean, 'the rap'? You said it was a simple misunderstanding, and I have nothing to worry about."

"That's if they believe your story."

She studied Sophie's exaggerated, worried expression. Was she pulling her leg like she was known to do? "C'mon. You're a cute little old lady who can barely see over the steering wheel. They'd never even question whether you're telling the truth."

Sophie threw her hands up. "All right, already. Jeez, you're a baby, Daphne."

Daphne grinned and then ran around the car to help Sophie out. After carefully taking the lamp from the backseat, she stepped aside for Sophie to go first.

They approached the counter, but Daphne's sneakers squeaked to a stop as the attractive woman from the news story walked toward her, a young boy tagging along at her side. She was even more attractive in person.

"Oh, thank God," the woman said breathily. She extended one hand to shake Daphne's as she took the lamp in the other. "I'm Nina Colombo. Thank you so much for returning this."

"Yeah, of course. I'm sorry I…uh…I mean it was a total accident. I just thought—"

"No need to apologize," Nina said. "I'm just so glad to have it back."

Daphne cringed as she stammered in front of this beautiful woman. "But I really didn't intend to steal it. I thought you'd put it out for the bulk-trash pickup, like the other people on your street do this time of year."

"I can totally see how you thought that," Nina said. "The movers deposited everything at the edge of my driveway because I didn't move my car out of the way for their truck." She smiled, and the little dimple in one corner of her mouth mesmerized Daphne. "So who should I make out the reward check to?"

Sophie elbowed Daphne out of her enchanted stare.

"Oh, uh, my name is Daphne, but I can't accept the reward. It was my mistake. I should've known anybody in their right mind wouldn't have put that out as trash."

"Are you sure?" Nina said. "I'd like to compensate you for taking time out of your busy schedule."

"I'm never that busy." Daphne regretted her words as soon as she heard them. "I'm happy that it's back in the hands of someone who truly loves it."

"Aww, that's really sweet."

"She'll take your telephone number, though," Sophie said, inserting herself between them.

Nina looked as surprised as Daphne felt, although not nearly as mortified.

"What?" Sophie said innocently to Daphne. "You're both obviously interested in antiques. This nice lady is new to the area and maybe wants to make friends so..."

"This is my friend with no filter, Sophie." Daphne glided in front of her to thwart any further embarrassing suggestions.

Nina smiled and tilted her head to look around Daphne. "That's true, Sophie. I am new here and do like antiquing."

Sophie gave Daphne an *I told you so* shrug. "That's all I'm saying."

"Well, I'm what you might call an antique aficionado of sorts." Daphne tried to sound cool but only made herself cringe even more. "Uh, anyway, I'd like it if you wanted to get together sometime to go antiquing." She looked down, anguishing over what was an appropriate length of eye contact to the non-awkward.

"I'd like that, too." Nina wrapped her free arm around Noah's shoulder. "Give me your number, and as soon we get settled into our new house, I'll text you. We can make a plan to meet."

"Sounds good," Daphne said enthusiastically, but inside she was already feeling disappointed. She tugged at Sophie to leave.

"And thanks again for being an awesome, honest person," Nina said as they walked away.

As they headed out the door, Sophie looped her arm through Daphne's. "That was fun. What a cute girl. Perfect for you."

"Too perfect. I'll never hear from her."

"Why not? She seemed excited about having a new friend to antique with."

"She was excited about getting her grandmother's priceless lamp back. Didn't you hear her? She gave me the old 'I'll call you when I'm not busy' brush-off."

"Well, if she's just moving into a new house, I'm sure she's not lying about being busy."

"Then why didn't she offer me her number?"

"Because she took yours. Honestly, Daphne. Stop being so negative. I'm not saying she'll propose marriage, but why wouldn't she want to see about a friendship with you?"

Daphne sighed as she started her car. "You have a point there, Sophie. I am being negative, and that attitude has no place on my vision board. Only good energy. Maybe she'll call when she's free."

Sophie patted her arm. "I'll bet you she will. And if she doesn't, eh, at least you weren't taken into custody today."

Daphne shrugged. "There's that."

❖

As Nina and Noah drove home, she kept glancing at the lamp resting between Noah's feet on the floor of the passenger seat. She hadn't realized how much it had meant to her until she thought someone had stolen it. She'd have to tell Daphne the full story behind it if they ever found the time to go antiquing. At the very least she should invite her out for coffee or a cocktail to thank her for turning in the lamp and refusing the reward money—a paying-kindness-forward kind of deal.

"Honey, if that's bothering you, I can put it in the backseat."

"It's okay," Noah said. "We're almost home."

"Thank you for helping me take good care of it."

"No problem," he said.

She noticed him staring out the window as though taking in everything he could about his new hometown. He seemed a little too calm for the situation. She couldn't seem to relax, waiting for his other Nike to drop and for him to have some horrific emotional collapse during which he'd demand to go back and live with his father in Greenwich. She'd been watching for it like he'd been exposed to a contagious disease.

If not now, she supposed she'd learn how the change had affected him by the end of the school year, when he'd have had to say good-bye to all his friends. Maybe she wouldn't even be able to assess the damage until he started at his new school in September. God, she hoped Zack was wrong.

She sighed out loud after silently scolding herself for stressing over things she had no control over, something she'd promised herself she'd stop doing after leaving therapy.

Noah looked over at her. "Are you going to call that lady?"

"I don't know. What do you think?"

He shrugged. "She was kind of a nerd, but she seemed pretty nice."

"Oh, honey. We don't call people names like that."

"Sorry. She was nice."

Nina chuckled to herself. Daphne was sort of nerdy but also super cute. She had sweet brown eyes that made Nina think of warm, comforting things like puppies and chocolate lava cake. Plus, if she could trust her gaydar, they might have more in common than just a love of vintage collectibles.

None of her close friends were gay, a consequence of life in a heteronormative world where her energies had been directed toward work and raising her son. When Lacey broke up with her, she'd told Nina that remaining friends would be too painful and confusing for both of them, compounding Nina's heartache over losing their intimate relationship. After introducing her to this incredible world from which there would be no return, she'd left Nina to navigate it on her own. How uplifting it would be to have a friendship with a lesbian, uncomplicated by romantic feelings, to rely on and share life's experiences with.

"Okay then," she said. "Since you and I are both going to have to make new friends around here, I might as well start with Daphne."

"Cool." He nodded and then held up his fist for a bump. "We got this."

She smiled at him, realizing the best friend she could ever ask for was sitting beside her. "Yeah. I think we do."

CHAPTER FIVE

Several days went by since meeting Nina, but the memory of her jubilant, Caribbean-water eyes as they flickered between Daphne's and the lamp recurred like a dream she hated to wake up from. She'd checked her phone almost hourly for the arrival of a phantom text that suggested a get-together for that antiques discussion. But when she'd googled Nina just for the hell of it and found her mentioned in a *Forbes Magazine* "Top 20 Female Executives in the US" article, she'd promptly put her phone away and ceased waiting for that unknown-number notification.

On this day, she sat in the break room at work moping as she nibbled her egg-salad sandwich and googled images of Nina. One was from the company website, another from her LinkedIn profile, and a third from some county woman-of-the-year dinner. What an accomplished woman.

The only coworker she bothered with outside of work, Pascale, joined her at the table.

"What's wrong with you today?"

"You work here, too," she said. "Do you really have to ask?"

"What are you looking at on your phone?" He hovered over her as he stood at the microwave heating his lunch leftovers.

"You're awfully nosy today." Suddenly, the smell hit her. "Oh, gross, Pascale. You're really gonna be that guy who microwaves fish in the company lunchroom?"

"I made ahi-tuna tacos last night. They're awesome. I saved you one."

"No, thanks." She fanned the air in front of her nose.

He sat down next to her with his plastic container. "You should talk about stinking up the lunchroom. Your sandwich smells like an old dog farted in here."

She rolled her eyes as she chased a bite of her sandwich with some potato chips.

"Who's that?" he asked, pointing to her screen.

"The lamp lady. She's a bigwig at some health-insurance company."

"Is that so?" He scoffed. "You should ask her if she can explain why our health plan here gets shittier and more expensive every year. Probably so she could buy a new vacation home."

"I spoke to her only that one time. She never texted me to hang out," she added with a frown.

"Of course she didn't. She's too busy pressing the flesh with the other muckety-muck one-percenters at the country club we pay for."

"She didn't come across that way at all," Daphne said. "She seemed down-to-earth, really genuine." She slipped the last bite of her sandwich into her mouth. "Now that I think about it, though, her shoes and purse probably cost more than my car."

"Exactly my point."

"I don't know why I'm so disappointed. It's not like I ever had a chance with someone like her, friend or otherwise. I'm the one you hang out with on the way up and then ditch once you get there."

"Daph," he said, softening his tone. "Don't say that about yourself. You're cool enough for anybody, your narcissistic ex aside. This one's probably straight anyway."

Daphne shrugged. "I thought I picked up a vibe from her. But even if I did get my wires crossed, that has nothing to do with being friends with someone. We bonded over antiques."

Pascale shrugged as he tossed his container into the trash. "What do you need more friends for? You got me and the old lady. Between the two of us, we'll go antiquing with you."

She smirked at him knowingly. "You only go with me when you're single, hoping to meet lonely, divorced MILFs. When you have a girl, you just tell me to borrow your truck."

He gave her a guilty smile.

"As for Sophie, I love her to death, and she's my bestie and all, but let's face it—an eighty-two-year-old isn't exactly wingman material."

"Fair enough," he said. "But I don't think this one is either."

As much as she didn't want it to be true, Daphne had a feeling Pascale was on to something. In truth, she'd dodged a bullet—nothing good ever came out of befriending attractive straight women.

But she would've loved to take her chances with this one.

Daphne pulled into her driveway after work, looking forward to another evening of Netflix streaming and a food-delivery service. What a great time to be alive. So what if that had become more the rule than an exception? Barbecue ribs, cornbread, and an unlimited supply of dramatic series to binge until she fell asleep on her sofa. What else did a woman need? It was Nina's loss. When it came to antiques, Daphne sniffed them out better than anyone.

When she got out of the car, Sophie called her over from her porch.

"Have you heard from her?" Sophie asked, holding open her screen door.

"No, and I'm not going to either, so can we just forget it? You guys asking me about it every day makes her blowing me off even more depressing."

"I have something that'll cheer you up." She opened the door wider and tilted her head for Daphne to come in.

Daphne flapped her hands against her thighs. "Sophie, if you keep trying to fill the emptiness in my life with food, they're going to need a forklift to remove me from my house someday."

"Shut up and follow me." Sophie led her into the kitchen. She opened her refrigerator and took out a small red box. "This came for you today, but the driver couldn't leave it on your porch in this warm weather."

"Aww, Sophie, are you trying to cheer me up sending me chocolate-covered strawberries from a fake secret admirer?"

"I wouldn't know the first thing about how to send something like this."

"Then who did?" Daphne gasped. "You don't think…"

"Read the card and find out, for Pete's sake."

Daphne tore it open and read it aloud. "'Thanks again. Let's go antiquing some time.'" As she looked up, her smile felt like it was about to leap clear off her face. "She gave me her phone number."

"Call her. Now." Sophie picked up the phone on her wall and thrust it at her.

"What? Get out of here," Daphne said, struggling to wrench the receiver from Sophie's hand. "I'm not calling her. Nobody calls, especially from a landline. I'll text her, but not now."

"Why not? She's interested in you, and you're interested in her. You better let her know you feel the same."

"Simmer down, Sophie. She's interested in antiquing, not me. And that's fine. I have to go home and think about what to say before I text her."

"Think? What's to think about? 'The strawberries are delicious' and 'yes' and then press send. Even I can do that."

Daphne bit into a juicy chocolate-covered strawberry and offered the box to Sophie. "I'm too nervous. Let me go home, have a glass of wine, and then I'll do it."

"Okay," Sophie said. "Call me as soon as you talk to her."

After giving Sophie another strawberry, Daphne walked home and tried to settle the butterflies flitting around her stomach with a glass of chardonnay.

She sat on her sofa with her phone resting on the cushion next to her. Before composing the text, she warned herself not to build her hopes too high. Whether Nina was straight or a lesbian, she needed to understand this was about a friendship and nothing more. Now that she'd finally processed her breakup with Savannah (funny how her marrying someone else helped accelerate that process), she needed to widen her social circle beyond her eccentric coworker,

Pascale, and her octogenarian neighbor—not that she didn't love them both and value their friendships.

Since breaking up with Savannah after spending her entire adult life with her, she had been missing the companionship she would have with a woman who was more of a contemporary and shared similar life experiences. And Nina seemed like the ideal person to pursue that type of relationship with.

By the end of the glass of chard, she was ready to compose, read it back a dozen times, and finally press send.

❖

As soon as Nina got home from work and picking up Noah from her mom's, she headed upstairs to her bedroom to change out of her pantsuit into comfy sweats. She turned on the lamp on her nightstand, noting again how she needed to have the frayed cord repaired and smiled at the golden glow coming through the glass. She loved the unique style of the lamp and how the glass appeared cracked, giving it an antique look. She chuckled, picturing her grandmother saying something like, "You bloody well better not lose it again, eh?" She then wondered if Daphne was enjoying her thank-you gift.

Noah came in and dove on her bed. "What's for dinner tonight?"

"I have pulled pork in the slow cooker. Ready to eat?"

"Yes. I'm starving," he said and walked over to examine the lamp.

"Doesn't it look good here next to my bed?"

He nodded. "I'm glad I helped you get it back."

"Me, too." She tickled under his chin. "I sent that nice lady, Daphne, some chocolate-covered strawberries to thank her. What do you think?"

He nodded again. "You should take her for waffles and French toast."

Nina laughed at his cute suggestion. "Oh, yes. That's the proper way to show gratitude to somebody. I guess the strawberries were a fail?"

"No, but I'd like to be thanked with waffles. No, hang on. Cinnamon French toast."

"Then I'm definitely taking you out for it this weekend. Your thank-you is long overdue. Does Saturday morning work for you?"

"Yes," he said with a fist pump.

"Excellent."

"You can ask Daphne to come, too, if you want," Noah said.

She laughed again. "You have the kindest soul. Come on. Let's get some food in you."

As they walked downstairs she thought about Noah's suggestion. Why not invite her to meet for breakfast some time? It would certainly drive home her level of appreciation. Then who knew? Maybe they could check out a garage sale or two after breakfast.

What was the worst that could happen? She'd say no? Nothing ventured…Besides, how else was she supposed to meet new people in this part of the state?

CHAPTER SIX

If Daphne thought preparing and sending a thank-you text to Nina for the strawberries was nerve-wracking, getting ready to meet her for breakfast that Saturday morning nearly sent her cortisol levels orbiting into a previously unknown galaxy. They'd agreed upon the Route One diner for breakfast before embarking on their day of treasure-seeking. Daphne had chosen that one because it also featured a vegan menu. Nina had the healthy glow and fit physique of a grass-eater, so she figured this would cover the bases just in case.

Thanks to her anticipation anxiety, Daphne was always the first one to arrive anywhere. Seated in a booth facing the entrance, she played with sweetener packets as she watched the door. If she'd stuck her leg inside a vat of cream, she would've churned it into butter by now. What was she so nervous about? It wasn't even a date.

Nina breezed in a few minutes later and waved as she headed over to the booth.

"I'm sorry I'm late," she said as she slid into the side opposite Daphne. "I had to put out a fire with the board over an international-client account this morning."

"Oh?" Daphne tried to sound invested but had no clue how to relate in Nina's career world. "I work on Saturdays sometimes, too." That was the best she could offer.

Nina gulped from her tiny diner glass of ice water. "We were about to lose a European hotel chain, so I had to explain to the board that an eighth of a percent loss in profit margin over one year is nothing to panic over, especially if it means locking them into another two-year contract. We'd recoup it and then some in the second year. They're not so easily convinced. How are you?"

"I'm good." Daphne struggled for something more scintillating, but at the moment, the well was dry.

"So what do you do for a living?"

Nina's blue eyes, framed by wavy, golden-brown locks, peered over the menu and momentarily distracted Daphne. After she realized she couldn't possibly make her job sound even remotely as cool as Nina's, she said, "Answer complaints at an airline call center."

"Ooh. That sounds stressful. Which airline?"

Daphne exhaled. Nina's tone and the way she stared at her, as though she was genuinely engaged, helped her relax a little. "Sky-Hi."

"They suck," Nina said excitedly, then toned it down. "I mean at a corporate level, not the service level. I know the front-line employees do the best they can with what little they have to work with. We had to cancel our corporate contract with them."

"Good," Daphne said. "They do suck. They sold out to another major airline, downsized the staff, and now the customers and worker bees have to suffer because they have fewer airlines to choose from—all so a bunch of CEOs can earn fatter compensation packages." Suddenly, she remembered her audience. "You're not a CEO, are you?"

"No. Not exactly," she said with a giggle. "I'm a DEO, Director of Executive Operations, that is. I'm actually one of four in the US for Global Health Insurance, but please don't hold that against me." She embellished her plea with that adorable solo dimpled smile.

"I'm sorry. I didn't mean it like that," Daphne said, furious at her faux pas. "What I meant was…um, so I hear they have a fantastic veggie-and-tofu omelet here."

Nina laughed. "Best non sequitur ever." She opened the menu and browsed it with a demure grin. "I can go for a bacon-and-cheddar omelet."

Daphne smiled. "Make that two."

❖

After breakfast they'd decided to leave Daphne's car in the diner parking lot and take Nina's SUV on their excursion in case one of them found a larger, must-have item. They planned to stop at an estate sale in an affluent neighborhood, scan the area for curbside bulk trash, and then hit a few antique shops along the way.

As they drove the winding country road, Daphne couldn't help sneaking peeks at Nina's profile. Her skin was flawless, probably from regular spa days, overpriced wrinkle creams, and other foo-foo indulgences popular among people with disposable income. She then cautioned herself about making assumptions about others. She'd already mislabeled her as a vegan.

"So tell me about your great-grandmother's lamp. Collectors don't really hunt for Tiffany these days, so there must be a great story behind it."

Nina chuckled. "Well, it's not Jane Austen great, but it's pretty special to me. As I'd said, it belonged to my great-grandmother, whom I met only once when I was around six. She lived in the UK, and my family traveled there to vacation and visit with her. She was ailing and knew she probably wouldn't see anyone again, so she gave the lamp to my grandmother to take back to the US."

"How cool. Kind of like a memento from a matriarchal figure?"

"Mmm, sort of, but actually its sentimental value comes more from my relationship with her daughter, my grandmother. She passed last year and left the lamp specifically for me."

"I'm sorry. So it honors your relationship with her."

Nina chuckled again. "Yeah. Here's where the story gets interesting. You know how it's made out of that funky opaque glass?"

"Yeah, the streaky, pressed glass. It's called malachite, I think."

"Have you ever heard it referred to as 'slag glass'?" Nina asked.

"Now that you mention it, yes, I have."

"Well, when I was like twelve, my grandmother told me that a 'slag' is another name for a slut in the UK."

"No way." Daphne laughed.

"That became a running joke between my grams and me, mainly because I went around calling everyone that name, and my mother was furious with her for teaching me what it meant."

"That's hilarious," Daphne said. She wanted Nina to keep talking because of the way her face illuminated with happiness as she relayed the story. "Your grandmother sounds like a hoot."

"She was a hot ticket," Nina said, her eyes still sparkling with memories. "Loved telling raunchy jokes, and with her British accent it was hysterical to listen to her. It was like hearing Queen Elizabeth talk dirty. She'd told my mother that my great-grandmother had the lamp from her days working in a brothel, and that my mom should be proud that she hails from a hearty line of prostitutes."

After their laughter died down, Daphne said, "That's awesome. Now I see why you would've paid any amount of money to get it back."

Nina nodded. "Every time I look at it sitting there on my nightstand, I hear her voice saying something cheeky to make me laugh. I really miss her."

"I can tell," Daphne said.

Nina turned to her and smiled warmly. "I think we're coming up to the estate sale."

They pulled in front of an enormous Victorian home, the circular driveway lined with furniture and tables filled with various high-end items. As they moved through the small group of treasure-seekers, they stopped at a collection of crystal pieces.

"This is Waterford," Nina said as she gently examined the bowl from top to bottom.

Daphne edged closer to Nina for a look. She smelled so good—a fresh, citrusy lotion or something. Then she actually noticed the bowl. "Oh my God. I love that. It's from the Lismore Essence collection. What do they want for it?"

"Thirty bucks," Nina muttered out the side of her mouth. "Can you believe it? What a steal."

"That's why I love estate sales," Daphne replied, equally clandestine. "Most of the time the family just wants to get rid of their old relative's crap so they can get the manse on the market."

"I'd hardly call this crap," Nina said.

"In some cases, I don't think they have any idea the value of what they're selling. Or care. Who wants to wait around to get everything appraised?"

Nina frowned. "Now I feel guilty, like I'm taking advantage of a grieving family."

Daphne studied her with a cocked eyebrow. "You're really not the typical CEO, are you?"

"We're not all monsters, you know." Nina propped her hands on her hips. "Some of us believe in the companies and the employees we manage."

"That's comforting," Daphne said. "Now you won't have to feel guilty about serving punch from it to the country-club ladies."

Nina giggled and cradled the bowl like a baby. "I don't belong to a country club."

Daphne was getting a charge out of teasing her. "You're just full of surprises today."

"I don't fit in with that lot, never have. I chew too loudly and refuse to vote Republican."

"Well, okay. Just don't use that bowl for a dog dish or anything."

Nina laughed again. "No worries. It won't even be in my house. I'm buying it for you."

"What?" Daphne stopped browsing and whirled around to her. "No. You keep it as a sort of house-warming for yourself."

"I want to give it to you as a thank-you."

"You've already thanked me a million times and sent me strawberries and grabbed the check at breakfast. Honestly, Nina. We're square."

Nina arrested her with the most irresistible expression of mock earnestness. "You've restored my British whorehouse heritage. How could we ever be square?"

Daphne paused to shrug off the twinge of titillation surging through her. "I'm not exactly a heroine for returning something I stole out of your front yard, even if it was by accident."

"Well, you're taking it. I can't keep Waterford crystal in the house with a ten-year-old boy who's begging me for a dog."

"Okay, then. I'll make the punch in it when I have you over to dinner." Daphne heard the words as soon as they came out. Her invitation sounded more like she was asking her on a date than just over for a friendly get-together. She hurried on to the next table, hoping to elude an awkward conversation in case it sounded that way to Nina, too.

After a moment, Nina sidled up to her again. "You know something? I'm glad you swiped my lamp. I'm having a great day."

Nina's smile stole Daphne's breath. "I am, too."

❖

When Nina drove into the diner parking lot early that evening, she didn't want Daphne to go home. They were having such an easy, fun time together all day—alternating between playful banter and deep reflections—that Nina hadn't thought much about all the things that had been stressing her out. She'd checked in with Noah via text throughout the day, but other than that, she'd allowed herself to be absorbed in such rare, elusive, carefree moments.

"I don't live too far from here, if you'd like to come over for dinner," Nina said. "I can throw a steak on the grill and whip up a salad."

"Yeah, sure." Daphne blurted out her acceptance so quickly, she startled them both. "I mean, yeah, that sounds good, if you're not too tired from today."

"I was planning that for dinner anyway. You joining me won't require any more effort."

"Okay. Let me stop for a bottle of wine first."

"I'll text you my address."

Daphne got out of her SUV, and Nina watched her walk to her car, checking out her lanky, boyish frame. After they exchanged what felt like awkward smiles, she texted the address, noting that she felt as enthusiastic about Daphne coming over as she had when she'd begun getting together with Lacey outside of work.

An ugly thought seized her. Now that she was certain she was a lesbian, was she turning into a cliché? Would every attractive woman she met entice her into wanting something more? She really needed a friend like Daphne, a funny, sincere woman with her mental shit together to share life's offerings now that she was in the process of rebuilding hers post-divorce.

She looked in her rearview mirror with a warning. "Don't screw this up," she said aloud, referring to the perils of a romantic involvement with another new friend. She drove away resolved to keep this relationship uncorrupted.

After having dinner inside, seated on bar stools at Nina's kitchen island, they'd moved out onto the patio and sat around a small fire pit in her yard. They shared a second bottle of red, a decision Nina had some reservations about but was relishing their easy, natural connection too much to regret—at this point anyway.

She lit the starter log and propped her feet up on the small stone rim. "This is nice," she said and sipped her wine.

"It's so relaxing." Daphne slumped down into the cushioned patio chair. "Is this how you usually spend your weekends when Noah is with his father?"

"Believe it or not, this is my first weekend without him when I haven't been inundated with stuff to do here at the house."

"Really? How does it feel?"

"Wonderful," Nina said, "but strange. I keep experiencing these little jolts of panic thinking I left him somewhere, and then I remember he's safe with his father."

"That's funny," Daphne said. "It's a good thing I never had kids. I'd probably forget them somewhere or pick up the wrong one from school or something."

Nina laughed. "That fear's stored in the back of your mind, but you wouldn't forget them, especially at Noah's age. They never stop talking. Did you ever want kids?"

Daphne shook her head. "I never thought about it for myself, and my ex certainly didn't want them. But I wouldn't mind if a future partner had them."

"Good answer," Nina said, then added "just kidding" when she saw Daphne's surprised look.

"Oh, yeah, uh," she stammered. "I didn't think you were...um, yeah."

Well, that reaction was a tough one to read, Nina thought. She reminded herself to watch her pithy repartee, especially after several glasses of wine. That was always how it started. "So I've offered you a few details about my past," she said. "What about yours? Who's your ex again?"

"Savannah Locke. She's a weight-loss influencer—flooding social media with all her diet anecdotes. And tears. Lots of tears."

Nina shrugged. "I have a couple of accounts, but I don't spend much time on social media."

"You don't seem like you have any concerns with your weight either, so you're definitely not in her target demographic."

Nina popped a couple of grapes into her mouth. "I've always had a fast metabolism, but since I turned forty it's slowing down."

"Intelligent, beautiful, and a fast metabolism? You hit the woman-winning-at-life trifecta for sure."

She thinks I'm beautiful? Nina looked away in an attack of shyness. "You're much too generous."

"And humble to top it off. How the hell are you single?"

Nina giggled. "I already told you my big, dramatic saga. I didn't ditch my husband fast enough for the woman I had my first lesbian experience ever with."

"That seems kind of unfair. Everyone's coming-out story is different, and yours was especially complicated with a husband and a kid. She should've been more patient."

Nina appreciated her words, feeling a sense of vindication. "I've sort of felt like it was entirely my fault that we broke up. Sometimes at night when I lie in bed in the dark, my mind crucifies me for ruining what I had with Lacey. She was a smart, exciting woman."

"It's usually never all someone's fault. Everyone has her part to play. Besides, it's normal to think you could've done some things to save a relationship—that is as long as you're not a narcissist." Daphne seemed focused on something in the distance as she spoke. "But if a partner isn't meeting your needs or understanding where you're coming from, how much of yourself are you supposed to sacrifice to keep the relationship together?"

"You're so empathetic and insightful," Nina said. "How the heck are *you* still single?"

Daphne sipped her wine as she watched the fire and then turned to Nina. "Savannah outgrew me. When her body shrunk, her ego increased exponentially. Suddenly, our mundane life together wasn't enough for her."

"I'm sorry to hear that. Were you together long?"

"Eighteen years. We met after high school when we worked at a retro-record store."

"Wow. Eighteen years." As Nina's twelve years with Zack flickered through her mind, she felt a sudden kindred connection with Daphne. "Was it a recent breakup?"

"Officially, it's been a little over a year since she moved out and filed for divorce all in the same day, but in hindsight, we started breaking down well before breaking up. The internet notoriety was just the catalyst. And Francesca."

The familiarity of Daphne's story hit Nina with a pang of residual shame and guilt. "There's always a 'Francesca.' But mine was named Lacey. It's weird. Never in my wildest dreams would I think I would have an affair, much less with a woman."

"Not that I'm making an excuse for you, but you didn't just have an affair. You had an epiphany, and it changed who you are as a person."

"Did it ever." Nina shook her head. "Like I said before, you're very generous."

"I'm sure your husband wouldn't agree with me, and I can only speak from my experience, but if it takes an affair for someone to move on from an unfulfilling existence, who is anyone to judge?"

"Someday you must explain how you became so enlightened."

Daphne shrugged. "When you hit rock bottom, you don't have anywhere to go but up."

Nina laughed. "What was yours?"

Daphne shuddered as if recalling a vivid nightmare. "Let's just say it happened after my divorce, and it's as low as I ever hope to drop. I went to a divorce support group a couple of times after that, and it helped me realize I was wasting a lot of mental energy stewing about something that was over and done with—energy I could be channeling somewhere else."

Nina studied her, captivated by her unique, positive outlook. "I can learn a lot from you."

Daphne contorted her face. "Me? My pearls of wisdom occur like real ones—once in a lifetime."

"Be that as it may, you're a beautiful person, Daphne. I hope you see yourself that way."

Daphne recoiled as though uncomfortable with compliments. "I'm not beautiful. It's the firelight and second bottle of wine."

She really had no idea that she was crazy beautiful in an unconventional way. Yes, she had her sandy hair up in a messy bun and hid her upper torso under a hooded sweatshirt, but those cozy brown eyes and that innocent, toothy smile outshone her plain style of dress and minimal makeup. And her unassuming, funny-without-meaning-to-be personality only added to her appeal.

Whoa, Nina thought. That was very specific. If she didn't stop drinking, she might've tried to prove Daphne's beauty to her in other ways.

"Well, I'm not going to sit here and listen to you deny your worth anymore," Nina said facetiously. "Want to come inside before the bugs join the party?"

Daphne got up, too. "I should get going. Thank you for dinner and for today. I had a great time."

"Thank you," Nina said and impulsively enveloped Daphne in a hug. "We'll have to do it again sometime."

"I'd love to," Daphne said warmly and helped Nina take in the empty bottle, glasses, and dessert plates.

Nina walked her to the front door and waved as she backed out of her driveway. When she closed and locked the door, she observed her quiet, empty house, sad that her day with Daphne had finally ended.

Daphne charged through Sophie's back door into the kitchen the next morning for their weekly Sunday breakfast with a container of mixed melon in one hand and a bottle of champagne in the other.

"Oh my God, Sophie. I'm in love."

Sophie was filling the basket with coffee grounds. "With the lamp lady?"

"Yes. And her name is Nina."

"I know her name. You mention it enough. Now sit down." Sophie pushed her into a chair at the table. "Tell me about your date while I scramble the eggs. I want to know everything, even the sex part. I'm not a prude."

Daphne got up to fetch orange juice from the fridge to make mimosas. "That's the last thing I'd accuse you of being, but no. We didn't have sex. It wasn't a date. We just spent the day antiquing, and we had breakfast, lunch, and dinner together. Plus, she bought me a gorgeous Waterford crystal bowl at an estate sale."

Sophie wheeled around with a spatula in her hand and glared at her like she was nuts.

"Okay, I know that sounds a lot like a date, but it wasn't. It was just two new friends with a lot in common taking advantage of a beautiful day, and we both know it's nothing more than that."

"Until you become more than that," Sophie said and resumed tending to the crackling bacon in her skillet.

"No, no, no. That's not what…" Daphne stammered. "That's not how this is gonna go, Sophie. I am not ruining a friendship with an amazing lesbian woman. I need this in my life, a friend I can relate to on multiple levels, and I couldn't ask for a better candidate than Nina."

"You just barged in here and announced you're in love."

"I was being theatrical," Daphne said. "I meant like I'm really into her as a person, you know? She's somebody cool to hang out with who I really vibe with."

"Okay, but if she's so perfect, wouldn't you rather explore the possibility of making her your life partner?"

Daphne scoffed. "Life partner. Sure. It's all champagne and roses until she loses a hundred pounds and dumps you for a bariatric surgeon. No, thank you. If I'm going to get my heart broken again, I'd rather it be by a woman I don't like so much."

Sophie swung around and placed a platter full of bacon on the table. "I don't know what you're saying right now, and neither do you. Are you still drunk from last night?"

"No." Daphne sat down. "I wasn't drunk. I was just buzzed enough to notice how outrageously sexy Nina is and not so much so that I made it embarrassingly obvious that I think she is." She raised her mimosa glass to Sophie. "Here's to friends."

Sophie tapped her glass against Daphne's and took a sip. "I guess when your best friend is eighty-two, you probably do want to line up a few replacements."

Daphne pursed her lips. "Don't say that, Sophie. I could never replace you. You better live forever."

"I'll do what I can, but I make no guarantees."

"Just make the scrambled eggs," Daphne said. "I'll pour the coffee."

Once they sat and started eating, Daphne smiled as she studied Sophie gingerly sipping her steaming coffee.

"What's the matter with you?" Sophie finally said.

"Nothing," Daphne said through a giggle. "You really are my best friend, Soph. I should be grateful to Ann Marie for leaving." She waved a finger between them. "This never would've happened if she hadn't."

Sophie made a face. "I know I'm a barrel of laughs, but I'm sure as hell not worth getting dumped for."

Daphne raised her mimosa flute again. "You're worth that and a whole lot more."

Sophie smiled and raised her glass. "You too, kid. You, too."

CHAPTER SEVEN

Now that summer had nearly arrived and the New England weather was ideal for doing anything outside, Nina had decided to work from home that day. A local contractor had refaced the patio the week before, and the architectural landscaper she'd commissioned had transformed her backyard into a small-scale botanical wonderland. She admired the colorful, fragrant perennials until a pair of feathered summer visitors splashed in the new stone birdbath and further distracted her from her work.

To her surprise, it was only late afternoon when she wrapped up her conference calls and completed her review of the weekly financial reports. Leaning back in her patio chair, she finished the rest of her mango iced tea and closed her eyes to the soothing sound of the new rock water fountain in her yard. After a few breaths, she realized she was alone—truly alone. No more of the brain-rattling chaos of fielding phone calls from work and tending to an energetic ten-year-old, all while trying to be the ideal attentive suburban wife. She should've been grateful to be free of it all. And she was, except for the part about Noah. She missed him.

She picked up her cell phone and called her ex. "Hi, Zack. Are you busy?"

"No. What's up?" His curt manner meant he either really was busy or that was just the tone she now elicited from him.

"I wanted to thank you for taking Noah even though today's not your scheduled day."

"You don't have to thank me for taking care of my own son."

"I know," Nina said. It still felt so awkward having these types of conversations with him, but she was better at gearing up to power through them. "So I ended up finishing work earlier than I expected. I can run down there and get him tonight if you wanted to have—"

"Nina, it's my weekend with him. I'd only have to come there and get him tomorrow."

"Well, no, I'd bring him to you tomorrow after—"

"I promised I'd take him mini-golfing tonight. Look, you can't start shuffling him back and forth whenever it suits you. He needs to know he has a schedule."

Nina did not like that terse, condescending manner. But he was right. "Okay, Zack. Point taken. I just didn't want you to think I was pawning him off on you or anything."

"I don't think that, Nina. If it were my choice, I'd be the custodial parent. But that's not how divorce works for men unless the woman is a degenerate."

Nina rolled her eyes, profoundly regretting making the call. "I said I got your point," she replied calmly. "You don't need to grind your heel into me even more. I feel low enough as it is about separating you two."

"You can't feel too low. You got everything you wanted."

"Yup. Hurting a man I care about and having my own family treat me like I was having a mid-life psychotic episode was all I ever wanted."

"I know you want absolution, but I just don't have any to give you."

Nina sighed, trying to control her growing indignation. "I don't need absolution from you or anyone else. I made my choice, and I don't regret it. Once we've all adjusted to the changes, we'll be happier for it."

"Always the level-headed business executive."

"Have a good time with Noah tonight." She ended the call without waiting for his response. Clearly, Zack still had more healing to do, and she understood that fact. If the truth be told, she had needed absolution, but her lovely new friend, Daphne, had already covered it, reassuring her that self-discovery counted for something.

She texted Noah telling him to have fun at mini-golf tonight, and that she loved and missed him. As she waited for his reply, she thought of Daphne. It was short notice, but maybe she was free and would like to come by for some wine and a light dinner.

❖

To Nina's pleasant surprise, not only was Daphne free, but she'd managed to make it to her house with a bottle of sparkling rosé wine within an hour.

"I'm so glad you texted," Daphne said. "I thought about asking you to get together, but I figured you were probably really busy these days."

Nina spooned some cold couscous, avocado, and bean salad onto her plate, licking the excess that fell from the spoon and landed on her finger. "Believe it or not, I'm not as busy as I used to be. I mean, work still consumes a lot of my time and energy, but now that Zack and I share custody of Noah, I have more 'me time' than I'd anticipated. I guess I still have to find my groove."

"How is all that going?" Daphne said. "I remember you saying it had been difficult with Zack not wanting the divorce."

"It'll be finalized in another month or two. We've done everything we needed to on our end, but he's still struggling." Nina sipped her wine. "He needs to find a girlfriend. Then maybe he won't be so fixated on continually reminding me that I ruined our family."

"But if you've realized you're a lesbian, what did he expect? If you stayed with him, that wouldn't be fair to either of you."

"He didn't think I'm a true lesbian. He said I'm probably bi, and we could deal with that as a couple."

"He really said that?" Daphne grimaced.

Nina smirked. "Mansplaining your wife's sexual awakening for her. That's a new one, huh?"

Daphne shrugged. "Something tells me it's probably not."

They shared a sorority-sister type laugh as they paused their venting session to load pita bread with hummus, cucumbers, and tzatziki sauce. Daphne looked so cute when she took a bite and licked the sauce from the corner of her mouth.

After a few moments of chewing, they resumed their chat. "So he's still trying to make you feel like you ruined the family?"

Nina offered a solemn nod. "That's what upsets me most. I believe in family. I really do." She straightened her back and spoke with passion. "I mean, I agonized over the decision for a long time before filing for divorce. I didn't want that for Noah. But I knew what it was like to grow up in a house where the parents stayed together for the family's sake. It was definitely more convenient for me and my brother when we were young, but it gave us an unhealthy view of marriage. My brother's divorced, too, and no one came out as gay in that marriage."

When Nina finally surfaced for air, she noticed Daphne's awkward expression. "Wow. I've unloaded a lot on you so early into our drinking."

Daphne laughed and refilled their glasses. "To be honest, I'm honored you feel like you can. I like to fancy myself a good listener for friends. But I never feel like I know what to say to make them feel better, so I kind of get this uncomfortable look on my face—at least that's what I've been told."

"Oh, no. Not at all." In an uncharacteristic move, Nina fibbed to spare her feelings. Daphne's empathy touched her so. How could she point out that her facial expression had, indeed, resembled that of a woman receiving a mammogram?

"Well, for what it's worth, I think you did the right thing," Daphne said. "Why should becoming a mother mean you have to completely sacrifice your own happiness? My parents got divorced, and they both went on to have other relationships with nice people. It's not the end of the world."

"My son, for one, would probably agree. He really seems okay with everything." Nina shrugged, and then an anxious thought assailed her. "Unless he's bottling up all his feelings and is going to grow up to be a truck-stop serial killer."

Daphne laughed as she was drinking, and Nina feared the sparkling rosé might spurt from her nose. "I don't mean to laugh," she said. "But Noah is so far from serial-killer material."

Nina smiled at herself. "I know. I'm still worked up from talking to Zack. I should've left well enough alone, but being here by myself made me feel some weird type of way. It's a gorgeous night, and I'm glad you're keeping me company."

"I'm so glad you called me," Daphne said. "You have the best yard for hanging out and enjoying drinks."

"Now to figure out how to expand my social circle so more people can come over and partake of it with us. How do you meet lesbians around here?"

"An excellent question." Daphne sat back in her chair, crossed her legs, and sipped her wine like a philosopher pondering life's great mysteries.

Nina waited, her anticipation mounting. "And the answer is?"

Daphne leaned forward slowly, deliberately, and addressed Nina as if she were about to reveal the Holy Grail. "I don't know."

"You're a goof." Nina laughed and threw a cherry tomato at her for drawing out the suspense. "Seriously, though. How do you meet interesting lesbian friends?"

"Nowadays, you can join lots of online social groups. I belong to this group of local women who like to do outdoorsy things and have met some interesting people."

"How about dating websites? Have you ever met anyone there?"

Daphne shook her head. "I was with Savannah, or Ann Marie, or whatever the hell she's calling herself, for a long time. We had couple-friends, but now that we're not a couple anymore..." She shrugged. "I'm not really outgoing, so I don't meet a lot of new people. Except when I steal from them."

"That worked out for both of us," Nina said. "Oh, well. We'll figure something out. In the meantime, here's to us." She raised her stemless wineglass.

Daphne smiled. "You know something? I used to be so sad that my old friends sided with Ann Marie, but after I got to know my neighbor Sophie much better and I met you, I've realized that even the darkest times can turn into the brightest spots in life. I know that sounds corny but..."

"No, no. I agree. I've had the same realization. If a breakup causes friendships to end, they weren't very solid to begin with. Take out that trash, girl."

"Yes." Daphne gestured with a sweeping hand. "We're decluttering our lives." They both chuckled. "And now that we've decluttered, that leaves us room for more antiques. If you're free this Sunday, there's an indoor flea market in Fairfield. I've found some cool pieces there in the past."

"Flea market? You know, I've never thought of that as a place to hunt antiques. I've always just hit estate sales and actual antique shops. But yes, I am free." Nina felt a smile stretching across her face. What was she so giddy about? A spectacular sparkling rosé, new things on the horizon? Or was it a...no. Please, no. It absolutely wasn't because she was starting to crush on Daphne.

It would certainly help her cause if Daphne would stop flashing that adorable nervous grin when Nina least expected it.

Sunday when Daphne woke up, she followed her usual morning routine of catching up on the news, and then getting sucked down a social-media wormhole for a time. But that morning something was different. After she'd scrolled through her favorite news sites, she put her phone down and got in the shower. While shampooing her hair, she realized she hadn't stalked any of Savannah's sites. No Insta, no Facebook, and no YouTube for her latest Vlog in which she probably espoused, with the utmost vigor, the colon-health and weight-loss benefits of kale smoothies. Again.

Gloriously, indisputably, she simply didn't care what Savannah was up to.

Daphne waited in her driveway for Nina to arrive in her SUV. Was she indifferent to Savannah's postings because she was anticipating the day ahead with Nina, or had she finally turned the corner in mourning the breakup? She hoped it was the latter but didn't want to underestimate Nina's impact on her during their brief acquaintance. Anyway, she'd find out in time.

After they located parking at the crowded flea market, Daphne directed Nina to the area where sellers rented booths for an entire season instead of only a day or a weekend.

"Here's where they sell the good stuff," Daphne said as she playfully dragged Nina by the arm.

"I can see the difference." Nina headed directly to a table featuring vintage platters and service sets. "I love this place already."

"I've had to stay away for a while. I always manage to find such great pieces that I'm running out of room at my house."

"How long have you been a collector?"

Daphne thought back to her childhood but opted for a simple explanation. "Since I was a kid, I guess. I've always loved to save special things. There's something kind of romantic about rifling through an old chest and discovering forgotten keepsakes. Over the last couple of years, the hobby kind of evolved into a way of life."

"I'd love to see your collection sometime," Nina said. "That is, if you ever invite me over." She crinkled her eyebrows. "Are you hiding something there?"

Daphne laughed self-consciously. "What? No."

"Like a wife or a girlfriend," Nina teased her. "Or some priceless stolen artifacts."

Daphne giggled again. "I have no secrets. Just a two-bedroom ranch with no attic and a damp basement, so it's tricky to store anything, priceless or otherwise. At this point, my house could make the ones on *Hoarders* look just a smidge untidy."

"I'm sure it's not that bad," Nina said. "Do you plan to sell things eventually?"

"That's been the plan." Daphne suddenly felt out of her league. How could she talk about her simple business dream with a successful corporate executive? She'd bore her to death. However, during the last couple of months, Nina had more than demonstrated her humility about her own success and her support of female empowerment. "I'll be honest with you," she finally said. "I've wanted to open my own antique business for a long time but have never been able to take the leap. I wouldn't know where to begin."

Nina seemed intrigued. "Hmm. When you say business, what do you mean? A brick-and-mortar place or your own website?"

"Can't I do both?"

"That's the kind of answer I like." Nina nodded in approval as she glanced around at the tables of merchandise. "Do you have enough stock for a booth here?"

"Like a seasonal one?"

"Yes. You can learn almost everything you need to know about running a business here—managing inventory, accounting, overhead, marketing. It would make a perfect little start-up."

Daphne pondered the suggestion. She could barely open the door in her spare bedroom, and in her living room, she had trouble differentiating her own belongings from the ones she'd collected for *inventory*. "Uh, yeah. I could probably fill a small space for a season."

"Perfect." Nina had an almost maniacal look in her eyes. "Before we leave, we'll inquire about renting a space. If you want, I can help with any paperwork for permits. You'll need to name your business, and then we can set you up a website."

"Nina, you keep saying 'we,' but you can't possibly have time to help with all that."

"Don't you worry, sister. I find time for what's important. I started a junior-executive mentoring program at work for teen girls interested in pursuing business degrees after high school. Next year, we'll have our first mentee graduate with an MBA."

"That's amazing." Was there anything this woman couldn't do?

"I don't care much for braggarts," Nina said. "But I'll shamelessly brag about that accomplishment. We have two more young women on pace to earn them."

Daphne sighed with admiration. "When you're free, would you mind also running for president?"

Nina laughed. "It's on my calendar. Anyway, think about a name for your business."

"That's easy. I already have one."

"You do? What is it?"

Daphne closed her eyes, savoring the pleasure of saying it out loud to someone other than Savannah. "Trash to Treasure Antiques and Collectibles."

"I love it."

"Really? You're not just saying that? It's not corny?"

"Not corny at all." Nina's eyes shone with the enthusiasm of a shopping-channel host. "It expertly captures the essence of the business. Not just of the actual product you're selling but the heart and soul behind it. It's very relatable."

"Yes, yes. That's exactly what I was going for but couldn't quite put it into words."

Nina smiled like a proud mother. "You didn't need to. The name says it all."

Daphne basked in Nina's praise and thought back to one of her last arguments with Savannah before their relationship completely fell apart.

Daphne had been complaining about how "Savannah" had taken over Ann Marie, and that their relationship was suffering as a result. Earlier, she'd reluctantly agreed to start calling her Savannah, wanting to support her new enterprise, but Ann Marie had become so tied up in her new identity as a perky, self-purported weight-loss guru, Daphne hardly recognized her.

"Savannah" had not taken Daphne's concerns well when Daphne had approached her "at work" in their den one day.

Daphne stood in the doorway for a moment waiting to be acknowledged. When her mere presence didn't attract Savannah's attention, she coughed slightly. Savannah kept typing away. Daphne then resorted to an abrupt, "Honey?"

"Hmm?" Savannah replied without looking up from the laptop screen.

"Honey, can you take a break from YouTubing and viewing your social-media accounts so we can have a nice dinner out tonight?"

Savannah's head snapped toward her. "How dare you come at me like this?" Her sharp response reminded Daphne of the eighties nighttime soap divas she'd watched with her mother in reruns as a child.

Daphne pleaded. "I just want us to find our way back to how we used to be."

"Those days are gone, Daphne." She rolled away from her computer and stood up. "At long last, overweight, self-loathing Ann Marie is dead. Savannah Locke is the woman I've always dreamed of being, the woman I've always known was buried inside that wretched, carb-obsessed creature I used to be."

"I never thought you were wretched. I love Ann Marie. I mean, I love you. Do you still love me, or is that part of you dead, too?"

Savannah eyed her with obvious suspicion. "Don't play coy with me. You're trying to hold me back in your needy, smothering way."

Daphne was flabbergasted. "What? How could you say—"

"You're clearly jealous—either because I no longer have the time to dote on you every minute of the day like a codependent flake, or because I've achieved the success I've always dreamed about, and you...well, you're still a customer-service rep."

"I'm happy for your success, Ann Marie—"

"Savannah," she snapped. "You promised you'd call me that."

"Look, Savannah. I don't understand why you're lashing out at me when I'm just trying to tell you that I miss you and need—I mean want some of your attention."

"You want all of it, and that's the problem. You know you'll never be as successful as I am."

"Well, no, not in the way you are, but I'll be successful. I'm going to open my own antique business soon."

Savannah cackled. "Do you know how long I've been hearing you say that? I can almost recite the speech along with you."

Daphne looked down, ashamed. Savannah was right. Before Ann Marie ever bit into her first Atkins bar, Daphne had regaled her with musings of self-employment through her passion for treasure-seeking. But something had always stood in her way.

"Face it, Daphne. You don't have the moxie to be a self-made woman."

"I'll do it someday. I'm still in the planning stages," she said, but secretly she feared she'd never have what it took to pull it off.

"Mmm-hmm," Savannah replied. "Meanwhile, you should just sit back, relax, and enjoy riding my wave of success—until your ship comes in."

Savannah smirked. Otherwise, Daphne might've believed she really meant what she said.

Daphne forced the images from her mind. She didn't want to slip back into that shadowy period, especially in the presence of such a bright, positive woman who apparently saw something in her that her own partner never had.

"Want to get some lunch after this?" Nina asked.

Daphne smiled. What a treat to have a friend with no toxic motivations. "I'd love to. I hear there's a great brewery not too far from here."

"Sounds like the optimal location to undertake a new business venture. And by that I mean visiting the market's website and filling out your vendor application."

"If you insist," Daphne said.

"I absolutely do."

At the brewery, Nina and Daphne agreed on a table near an open garage door to maximize the advantages of the gorgeous weather. An early summer breeze played in their hair as they extensively sampled and analyzed each other's beer flights. After they dug into a veggie pizza, a burp escaped from Daphne. Nina tried not to laugh, but she couldn't completely contain a quick snort of amusement. She loved Daphne's simple authenticity. She had no airs about her, measured nothing in monetary value, and seemed to listen solely to hear another person's ideas, not so she could reply with something more profound.

"I'm excited for you," Nina said as she pulled another slice of pizza from the pie. "You're going to be an exceptional business student."

Daphne smiled as she chewed. "This may shock you, but I was the nerd who always sat at the front of the class."

"That doesn't surprise me at all."

"I wasn't an A student or anything. Sitting in front of the teacher just made it harder for the kids to pick on me."

"Oh, no." Nina felt her lips fall into a pout. "They bullied you?"

"Not really bullied," Daphne said. "Nobody ever tried to intimidate me or make me feel unsafe. It was more like good-natured teasing." She looked away and added softly, "A lot of it."

Nina nodded as she envisioned poor, young Daphne with braces and tangled hair sitting alone at lunch doodling gorgons and dragons on her notebook. "Just enough to make going to school every day uncomfortable."

Daphne shrugged, seeming unwilling to admit it.

"I knew the type of girls who did that," Nina said. "The one and only time I was ever disciplined at school was when I shoved a girl into a locker for repeatedly calling this quiet boy gay. Every day coming back from lunch she was on this kid's ass, and I couldn't stand it anymore. I missed the middle-school spring dance as punishment, but I never regretted putting that little jerk in her place."

"I so could've used a friend like you back then."

Nina shrugged. "You have me now, not that I imagine anyone teases you much these days."

"Not since my breakup." Daphne added an awkward grin.

Nina studied her for a moment. Was she kidding? Suddenly, her phone vibrated. "Oh, that must be Noah. Excuse me for a sec." She pulled it from her back pocket and recognized Lacey's number in the missed-call notification. She swallowed hard after a warm wave of surprise and titillation swept up her neck.

"Everything okay?" Daphne asked.

"Oh, uh, yeah. It's a missed call from my ex. That's weird."

"Noah's father?"

"Um, no. Lacey." Nina put the phone down and forced a casual smile.

"Did she leave a voice mail?"

Nina checked the phone and shrugged, but inside she was dying. "Nope. Probably butt-dialed me."

"Call her back and see what she wanted."

"Get out of here."

"What? Aren't you even curious?"

Nina furrowed her brow to downplay any interest. "If she didn't leave a message, it obviously wasn't important. Guaranteed it was accidental."

"I don't think so. She probably felt dumb leaving a voice mail. She's expecting you to return her call."

"I can't imagine what she could possibly want. We had a clean break."

"She wants you back, dummy. She's realized she made a mistake letting you go."

For some reason having that conversation with Daphne made Nina uncomfortable, like she was desecrating the sacred tenet of never speaking about exes on a first date. Except this wasn't the first time they'd been out, and it certainly wasn't a date.

"How did you get all that from one missed call?"

"Why else would she have contacted you? Unless you agreed to stay friends after the breakup."

"No agreement. Definitely not friends."

"Then we're back to my first reason." Daphne picked up Nina's phone and handed it to her. "Call her back and find out what she wants."

"Not now." Nina snatched it out of her hand.

"Why not?"

"We're having quality friend time here. How rude would that be?"

"It's not rude if I'm telling you to. Maybe she's had a change of heart, Nina. You should find out."

"I'm going with being ass-dialed on this one, and that's my final answer. If she calls again, we'll know which of us was right."

Apparently with Daphne, sometimes it was easy to drift off into conversations Nina had successfully avoided with most others.

"Okay. Fair enough," Daphne said. "But I'm willing to wager a round of beer flights at a different brewery that I nailed it. What do you say?"

Nina grinned at the win-win proposition. "You know what, punk? I'm feeling lucky. You got a bet." She reached out to shake Daphne's hand, relieved the conversation had veered away from such pointed inquiry. "Now getting back to your business, the website says there's a waiting list for a permanent booth at the flea market."

Daphne groaned. "I knew it sounded too easy to be true."

"A minor setback. This actually will work to your benefit. It says here you can start out with a weekend setup in early September."

"September?" Daphne looked startled. "That's only two months from now."

"Almost three. But in either case, you'll be ready."

"I will?"

"Yes, of course. I have a friend at work who creates the most innovative graphic arts for websites. We'll get that going for you so you can start advertising, and then you'll just have to select the pieces you want to feature and sell in September."

Optimism was dawning in Daphne's eyes. "This is what I've been missing all along."

"A business manager?"

"A good friend."

Nina tried not to gush as possibility shone on Daphne's face like a brilliant sunrise. It thrilled her as much as the missed call from Lacey.

CHAPTER EIGHT

Although she'd spent a wonderful day with Daphne, on the ride home Nina thought about nothing but Lacey. What if Daphne was right? If not leaving a voice mail was a strategic move to assess Nina's level of interest in speaking to her, then shouldn't Nina at least text her and ask, quite casually, what, if anything, was up? But you know what? Fuck her. Lacey had cut her off despite Nina's pleas and protests, so why should she jump now like she'd been hoping and waiting in quiet desperation to take her back?

Ugh. Breakups. And she'd had to deal with two simultaneously. Although she'd only been in love with one of the partners, she *had* been with Zack at one point in time, and dissolving their twelve-year marriage hadn't been without its complications.

Then, out of nowhere, came the mystery call from Lacey that could've meant either a new beginning or that she'd simply stuffed her phone in her back pocket with the screen unlocked. Nina was nothing if not pragmatic. When she was this conflicted about something, she set it aside before overheating or acting on impulse. She corralled her scattered thoughts toward something less incendiary: laundry. The great mental equalizer. Tackling mountains of dirty clothes like a champ calmed her anxious mind while providing a semblance of purpose.

As she waited for Zack to drop off Noah from their weekend visit, she fluffed, folded, and refused to check her phone for Lacey's number. Instead, she let her mind wander to the night of their final fight.

By that point, the cat had already been out of the bag with Zack, and Nina had been hovering in this bizarre place where her husband had known she'd had an affair with a woman, but rather than jumping into a divorce, he'd implored her to work on repairing their fractured relationship. However, the affair with Lacey hadn't been over. Both of them had still been grappling with their intense emotional connection and explosive sexual chemistry.

Nina climbed the steps to Lacey's front door knowing exactly what she was walking into. Everyone understood what the "We have to talk" preface to any conversation suggested, but she'd heard or read it often enough from Lacey to assume she knew what to expect. She even thought she'd prepared for it.

When Lacey showed her in, she accepted Nina's embrace but didn't linger in it. In fact, she'd practically sprinted across the room and pivoted on her heel like an attorney during closing arguments. "I don't want to belabor the issue any longer than necessary, Nina, but this has to end. You have to stop calling and texting me."

Although Lacey had made this request several times, it eviscerated Nina to hear it this time as much as it had the first. But now Nina knew how to control her response.

She sat on the couch and watched Lacey pace the room. "You're aware how ironic it is for you to ask me to come over to your house to tell me to leave you alone."

Lacey rolled her eyes. "Can we not do that now?"

"Sorry." Nina sat on the couch and rested her elbows on her knees, Lacey's stoicism unconvincing. "I know I have to stop contacting you, Lacey. But you have to stop answering me if I slip up."

Lacey stopped pacing. "You know why I answer you."

"And you know why I text you."

Lacey pushed her hair out of her face in apparent frustration. "Have you filed for divorce yet?"

"I'm working on it," Nina said, her voice small and uncertain. "I told you that."

"Have you even discussed it with him?"

Nina looked to the floor. "Yes."

"It's been a year, Nina. I can't go on like this. I'm in love with you, but I can't stay entangled in this situation. I'm suffocating. It's not healthy."

"I'm just asking for a little more time. All this has happened so fast, Lacey. I'm having trouble managing it."

"I know. So am I."

"You're acting like I'm intentionally trying to drag you down, but that's so not what's happening here. You knew I was married when you started flirting with me. And when I flirted back, I never imagined I'd fall in love with you." Nina's frustration launched her to her feet. "This whole situation is fucked." She contemplated going over to Lacey, taking her in her arms, and silencing the conflict, if only for that evening. But she didn't. She recognized the authenticity of Lacey's angst, felt the desperation in her plea, and it broke her heart even more knowing she was causing it all.

Lacey took a deep breath, as if to reorient herself to her purpose. "I've given you all the time I can, Nina. I don't have anything left to hold on to. Zack hasn't even moved out of the house yet."

Already on the verge of breaking down, Nina dropped into a chair and shielded her face with her hands when she realized her tears were about to burst from her like a broken water main. She hated when she needed to make a point, but the quavering of her voice betrayed her. When Lacey hadn't come to her, she knew this time it really was over.

She picked up her head, sniffed in her snot, and inhaled to catch her breath. "I've been doing the best I can, Lacey. I promise I have."

Lacey remained safely across the room. "You said you never imagined you'd fall for me when we started this. How do you know it's love and not infatuation?"

"Because I've never felt this way before, for anyone...not even Zack on our wedding day. Lacey, you've unlocked a part of me I never knew existed. I can't go back to who I was then. I'm not that woman anymore."

"Then what are you waiting for?" Lacey's voice finally cracked. "If it was me, you wouldn't still be where you are."

"I have a kid, Lacey. My entire life is enmeshed with two other people's. You've been a lesbian since the womb. Can't you cut me a little slack?"

"What do you think I've been doing all these months? Before we hooked up, I liked you, I was attracted to you, and frankly, I thought seducing an unhappily married, curious straight woman was something of a coup, but this…" Lacey began pacing again. "I never expected this. A woman like you is lesbian kryptonite. All us single lezzies know it, but the moment a beautiful straight girl comes along with her flirt game on eleven, we go to pieces. Just like you're having a hard time dealing with all your shit, I am, too—dealing with your shit, that is. I feel like I'm drifting out to sea with you, watching myself grow smaller as the waves carry me farther out."

"I didn't mean to set you adrift." Nina motioned toward Lacey but stopped when she flinched. "It kills me that I've hurt you."

Her arms locked across her chest, Lacey nodded and wiped the corner of her eyes. "I know."

Nina sighed with a mirthless chuckle. "Well, this is certainly a new experience for me—being a hot mess." She studied Lacey from across the room, searching for something in her eyes that alluded to another chance, some day when the timing was appropriate, but Lacey didn't seem able to even look at her. "You're right, baby," she said softly. "I still have a lot to sort out. I shouldn't drag everyone I know and care about down with me. I'm sorry."

She walked to the door and looked back at Lacey once more before leaving. Lacey's lips parted as though a leftover poignant sentiment or two was rattling around her brain.

When Nina's ears felt like they'd pop from the pressurized silence, she opened the door and left.

Nina snapped back to reality. Was she over Lacey or not? She'd better figure it out before another phone call came in.

Monday morning, Daphne slithered into work with even less enthusiasm than usual, greeting whomever she passed on her way to her cubicle with merely a chin jut. Pascale dared approach her a few minutes later, offering a cup of black coffee.

He sat on the corner of her desk. "Bad weekend?"

She accepted the coffee with gratitude and answered him only after her first sip. "No. Literally the best weekend ever. That's what makes Mondays suck so much more ferociously than they normally do."

"Yeah? What did you do? Finally get laid?"

"Pascale, why is it every time someone mentions a good time, men have to presume it's sex-related?"

"I wasn't being presumptive. I was being optimistic. How long has it been for you anyway?"

"Way too long." She took another sip and savored the taste as it blanketed her throat in warmth.

"That also explains this mood. We have to get you a date. How about dating sites? Ready to give one a try yet?"

"Not even remotely," she said as she scanned her personal email on her work desktop. "Oh. The Outdoor Lesbian Club is having a kayak outing next weekend," she announced more to herself than him. "I should ask Nina if she'd like to go."

He scowled. "Don't take a straight woman to a lesbian thing. She'll twat-block you. The single women will think you're taken."

She looked up at him, confused. "Why are you still on me finding a date? I told you that's a hard pass for now."

"You said that for dating sites. You're going kayaking, for God's sake. Finding a woman to date there is as easy as finding ants at a picnic."

"Pascale, first of all, that's a terrible analogy, likening women to an invasive species. And secondly, I've already told you Nina is a lesbian, a full-on, card-carrying member. She left her husband for a woman. Well, she left him but didn't end up with the woman she left him for, but she may be getting back with her after all, so who knows?"

Pascale's arms flailed like an inflatable tube man. "Daphne, if Nina's a lesbian, my God, what are you waiting for? She's so hot."

She wrinkled her forehead. "We're just friends, Pascale. Boy, you love your gay stereotypes, don't you?" She shook her head.

"Lesbians often have friendships without ever hooking up with each other. Nina is good people, and I wouldn't want to jeopardize our healthy, platonic relationship."

"You guys put too much thought into this type of thing." His eyes widened as though the mere act of thinking was irrational. "Oh, wait. Is that a stereotype, too?"

"Completely. But nonetheless true."

He winked and sipped his coffee. "Besides, isn't she the one who's still into her ex-girlfriend?"

"And there's that."

For some reason, Pascale found that funny, and after a moment, Daphne did, too. When the hilarity died down, he glimpsed over his shoulder for a supervisor check as their eight a.m. start loomed.

"Keep hope alive, Daphne. You're a great catch." He turned around to leave and then spun back. "Someone's bound to realize it sooner or later."

Daphne nodded in appreciation as she adjusted her headset and prepared to face another shift in paradise.

During her lunch break she texted Nina to see if she was available for a chat. Within a couple of minutes, Nina called her on FaceTime.

"Happy Monday." Nina beamed from her office, her face backlit from the sun streaming in through the large window behind her desk.

Daphne's soul soared as her day suddenly became a thousand percent better. "Hey, you. So did you hear from Lacey again?" *Subtle, Daphne, so subtle.* She shook her fists at herself below her phone's screen.

"No. And I'm glad I suppressed my urge to text her, especially now that it really seems it was accidental."

Daphne felt a twinge of what she could only identify as… jealousy? Was she reading into things, or had Nina sounded a tad disappointed?

"Are you okay with that?" Daphne asked.

"Oh God, yes. That's the last thing I need."

"Exes." Daphne slapped her palm against her forehead. What the hell was happening? She was acting like a dork in the FaceTime chat but couldn't reel herself in. "So if you like kayaking, there's a lesbian meet-up this Saturday morning."

"I love kayaking, but this is my weekend with Noah. We're spending the day in my mother's pool."

"Bummer. I'll wait so you can come, too. Now that summer's here, someone will arrange another one soon."

"No, Daph. Go," Nina said as she seemed to study her computer monitor. "It'll be fun. The weather's supposed to be nice."

Although it didn't make any sense, Daphne wanted Nina not to want her to go on the outing without her. Actually, she wished Nina had invited her to join them for their pool day at Nina's mother's house, and not just because Nina would be in a bathing suit. *Ewww, Daphne. Why are you being so weird?*

"Oh. Oh, yeah," she stammered. "I'm gonna go. I know a few people who RSVPed that they would. It'll be fun. You and I can go some other time."

"For sure. Listen. I have to get ready for a conference call in a few. I found a great place for happy hour this week. Are we on for Wednesday?"

"Do you really have to ask?"

Nina chuckled. "I'm glad I don't. I've come to rely on our outings each week. They may not help my liver, but my psyche feels ever so refreshed."

"Me, too. For some reason, Wednesday seems like the day all the impatient travelers pick to call and yell at me."

"Jeez, I hope it wasn't you I went off on when my flight was canceled during my last business trip." Nina's playful expression was too adorable.

Daphne teased her back. "Your voice does sound kind of familiar. Now you go have the best conference call ever." She framed her silly grin with two thumbs up.

"We usually refer to those as 'cancelled ones.'"

"Fingers crossed." Daphne ended the call and again found her disposition much bubblier than it had been before their chat. She packed the remnants of her lunch into her lunch bag and tossed out the trash. As she headed back to her cubicle, she'd hoped she hadn't come across as a spaz. They'd been friends for a while now. What was it about Nina that still made Daphne so angsty about making an impression?

Brilliant, successful, and sophisticated. Oh, yeah. That was it.

After she hung up with Daphne, Nina headed down the hall toward the conference room for the call between her staff and the northern California division. She sighed. After nearly twenty years in the health-insurance business, she was struggling to keep her enthusiasm level high enough. No matter what aspect of the company she'd involved herself in over the years, it all inevitably led to the same outcome: how to avoid paying claims.

She silently thanked the universe for tossing Daphne into her life, even in the most unorthodox way imaginable. Nina had quickly become accustomed to her almost daily lunch phone call from Daphne, even on days she was too inundated with work to answer. Something about Daphne's innocent motivations and uncomplicated ways always made her feel lighter after they spoke, like maybe the weight of the corporate world didn't always have to rest on Nina's shoulders.

And Daphne herself was somewhat of an anomaly—plainly beautiful and funny yet virtually unaware of how attractive she was to others. An endearing touch of goofiness mixed with a wholesome simplicity, yet she could engage in an array of multi-faceted conversations. Her duality appealed to Nina.

CHAPTER NINE

D aphne showed up at the boat launch at the appointed time Saturday morning, her kayak strapped to the roof of her Subaru. When she got out, she inhaled the delicious aroma of salty summer air, the perfect potion after a long week of customer-service drudgery. She adjusted her sunglasses and glanced around for a familiar face. When her gaze landed on Max, an older acquaintance who frequented outdoor events on the local lesbian scene, she waved, not only because she was the only one in the group she'd felt comfortable talking to, but also for help getting her kayak down without impaling someone.

"Daphne." Max shrieked as she rushed over to her. "It's been so long. We thought you might've gotten back with Savannah."

"Hi, Max," she said as she slid out of her boa-constrictor hug that usually included a slip of the hand below the appropriate lower-back boundary line. Max was pushing seventy but seemed hornier than most women half her age. "You look great," Daphne said once she'd broken free.

"Oh, you're just saying that." Max lightly pinched her cheek with appreciation.

"Honestly, I'm not. Your new haircut is so flattering." She'd meant the compliment. Daphne hadn't minded that Max groped her during nearly every greeting because she was quite attractive, but their thirty-plus-year age gap made a relationship impractical.

"Well, thanks, honey," Max replied. "I try to keep everything where it's supposed to be, but you know…gravity." She adjusted her boobs inside her bra. "Here. Let me help you get your boat down."

Daphne looked around and sighed. If only Nina were with her. Yes, she'd been acquainted with most of the six other women paddling to the island but not like she was with Nina. After only a few months, she truly felt like she'd known her forever. Their casual conversation flowed like an estuary into boundless emotional waters with little to no effort. Small talk, chitchat, and all-around general socializing had always drained Daphne, but with a confident, outgoing friend like Nina by her side, she would've been more relaxed as they navigated the various interactions together.

When she and Max reached the edge of the water, they laid her boat next to Max's, its front half in the water. Preparing for the launch, Daphne straddled the boat, snapped her oar together, and fastened her life jacket. Max returned after gathering her waterproof essentials bag and invaded Daphne's personal space once more.

"There's a woman I want you to meet," she said, her lips grazing Daphne's ear. "Her name is Brynne, and she's gorgeous. You two will hit it off famously."

As Daphne tried to lean back, she lost her balance and fell ass-backward into her kayak, her feet dangling in the air.

"My goodness," Max said.

"I'm okay." Daphne casually checked to see if anyone else witnessed her clumsiness. "I got this. No worries."

As she tried to work herself upright, Max straddled the boat in front of her and helped yank her to her feet by the forearms. The force of her pull and the sloped angle on which they were standing propelled Max backward. Still clinging to Daphne, she stumbled back and fell into the shallow water, pulling Daphne down on top of her. The spectacle had drawn a small crowd around them, some obviously concerned for their safety, others laughing at their inadvertent display of slapstick.

As they both made it to their feet, Daphne noticed the expression on one really cute woman standing closest to them—an amalgam of genuine concern and suppressed hysterics.

"Daphne, this is Brynne," Max said.

"Brynne? Of course it is," Daphne said in a sardonic drawl as she shook the woman's extended hand.

"You're quite the acrobat." Brynne was biting her lip in a clear attempt not to laugh.

"Go ahead. Let it out," Daphne said. "It can't be healthy holding anything in that hard."

Brynne let out a chuckle. "I'm sorry. I'm not laughing that you fell. I mean, obviously, you both could've gotten hurt. It's just that it was so perfectly choreographed."

Daphne smiled awkwardly and fixed her visor lower on her forehead, hoping the blush stinging her cheeks would be interpreted as sunburn.

"I'm new to the group," Brynne said. "If you don't hate me for laughing at your tumble, maybe you wouldn't mind shepherding me along today."

Daphne relaxed in the warmth of Brynne's demeanor. "If you want to hang out with me after witnessing that, how could I not say yes?"

After she and Brynne and Max secured each other's boats fully into the water and paddled away from the dock, Daphne reflected on this latest development. Usually invisible to attractive women, in only the last three months, she'd won the interest of not one but two alluring ladies, one by stealing from her and the other by falling out of a kayak…while on land. A how-to dating handbook was clearly in her future.

About an hour of paddling across the Sound, and the group reached their destination, an uninhabited dot of an island. They dragged their kayaks onto shore and assembled on the sand for a picnic lunch. While the others pulled out such delicacies as sushi rolls, tofu and kale salad, and micro-charcuterie plates from their cooler bags, Daphne hunched over and furtively unwrapped a peanut-butter-and-jelly Uncrustable.

She wanted to sit next to Brynne after discovering how outgoing and talkative she was. That way she could just nod, laugh, and offer periodic "Oh, wows" whenever Brynne or someone else offered an insightful observation on politics, religion, or tiny winter dog sweaters. The introvert's dream social scenario.

After the group completed their expedition late in the afternoon, they went for drinks and apps at the marina restaurant. By this point, Daphne had stopped pining for her missing bestie, Nina, and become aware of Brynne. This woman absolutely checked all the same boxes as Nina: intelligent, fun personality, and sexy. And as a bonus box, they hadn't polluted the dating waters by becoming friends first.

Max, seated on the other side of Daphne, leaned toward her. "So what do you think of Brynne?"

"She's great. But could anyone really have a different answer for that question? She has more than a few admirers in the group."

"Are you among them?"

Daphne bristled in defense. "Why are you asking me that?"

"She asked me about you earlier. Since you're here today, I'm assuming you're still single."

"Oh, I'm still single." Daphne finished her beer.

"You should ask her out," Max said. "Or at least get her number."

The suggestion weakened her spine. "Max, do you know anything at all about me?"

"You're a little shy," she said with a shrug. "This I know, but wouldn't this be the perfect opportunity to work on overcoming that trait?"

"No." Daphne shook her head. "No. Shy suits me just fine, thank you very much." Daphne shook off the idea by turning back to the other conversation she'd been half following as though she'd never left it. When her phone vibrated, she checked it. It had to be a text from Nina.

The phrase *"Lacey texted me"* appeared under Nina's name in the text bar.

Daphne's stomach plummeted as her thumbs feverishly replied. *"What did she say?"* She watched the three undulating dots with a growing sense of foreboding as Nina responded.

At first it was just a "how's it going'" type of thing. Then she finally asked if we could meet for a drink and talk.

The conversations and restaurant din faded into white noise in the background as Daphne's brain processed the implications.

What did you tell her?

I haven't replied. I just left her hanging.

Daphne released her breath. Leaving Lacey hanging was a good sign.

What are you going to tell her?

I don't know, I mean about meeting her. Probably that I need time to think about it.

Daphne frowned. Nina sounded so wish-washy, something completely antithetical to her personality. What had it portended? Closure? Reconciliation? The latter would likely have an unfavorable impact on their friendship. If she reconciled with Lacey, she probably wouldn't have the same interest in their friendship or the extra time for it. After a moment of tailspinning, she reassured herself that whatever Nina decided, she would fully support her friend.

Well, what do you want to tell her? Do you want to see her? Daphne hit send, fearing the answer she was about to get.

Tbh, I'm curious to know what she wants but not sure how I feel about seeing her again.

Hmm. You should probably go with needing time to think first, especially if you're not sure.

I kind of would like to see her again… Nina typed the wide-eyed emoji.

Brynne tapped her arm. "Everything okay?" Translation: stop being a rude asshole on your phone.

"Oh, yes," Daphne stammered. "I was just, uh…issue resolved so I'll just…yeah." She locked her phone and stuffed it into the pocket of her athletic shorts. Resting her chin on her knuckles, she pretended to be enthralled in the real-time conversation again, but inside she was dying to leave and call Nina on her way home.

"We were just talking about why," Brynne said, "even within the lesbian community, there's still such a stigma surrounding dating rejection."

"Because rejection sucks?" Daphne offered.

Brynne led the outbreak of laughter at Daphne's unintentional quip. "Not untrue," she said. "But as women supporting women and lesbians trying to make meaningful connections, we should free ourselves from that fear."

"Preach, sister," Max said. As she leaned in to toast with everyone, her boob landed on Daphne's upper arm.

Brynne grinned. "I'm going to shatter that ceiling now…" She looked around the table and took a hearty sip of her drink "…by asking Daphne out for coffee, knowing full well she may reject my offer, as is her prerogative."

Suddenly, every set of eyes at the table trained on Daphne.

Daphne's face was aflame with self-consciousness. "Oh. That's an actual question?"

"Mmm-hmm," Brynne muttered, still grinning.

From the other side of her, Max kicked the outer part of her calf, eliciting a strangled groan that sounded like "sure." The ladies at the table applauded, and Brynne smiled as she squeezed Daphne's hand playfully.

Daphne should've been ecstatic. Who knew she wouldn't be? But the thought of being with Nina pulled at her. Were things about to change between her and her new best friend?

She wanted to be positive, to stay in the moment, but her mind was a kayak taking on water as she contemplated losing their time together to Lacey.

❖

Nina lay stretched out on a lounge chair around her mother's in-ground pool, an umbrella shading her from the July sun. After a slew of texts from Daphne and the anticipation Lacey had stirred in her, Nina needed this afternoon of simple summer bliss to recharge. She'd tossed her phone between her feet as though it were a live grenade and finally settled her hyperactive brain. With eyes closed, she smiled to herself, listening to Noah splash around in the pool as he voiced a variety of characters in his imaginary aquatic world.

Perched on the edge of the diving board, he shouted, "Mom, watch this."

Her eyes popped open at the dread that phrase usually inspired in mothers of boys. "Be careful, honey," she said. "Whatever you're planning to do, make sure your head clears the board."

"Are you watching?"

"Yes, I am."

He began bouncing on the edge of the board, several times to catch air, then vaulted himself out over the pool, doing some kind of twisting maneuver before he hit the water.

"Jesus," she muttered to herself as she waited for her daredevil to resurface.

"How was that?" He blew the dripping water away from his mouth as he swam toward her.

She pretended to hold up a score card. "That was a solid nine point five."

"Wait," he said, climbing out of the pool. "Let me try for a perfect ten."

"No, baby. That's okay. Remember how we agreed no emergency room this summer? Why don't you practice your laps instead."

"Okay." He jumped back into the pool. "I'm hungry."

"Gram's making lunch now. We're gonna eat in a few. Come out and have something to drink."

He climbed the ladder, grabbed a juice pouch from a cooler, and sprawled out with his phone on a lounge chair next to hers.

Nina followed his cue and reached for her phone, hoping one quick glance would calm her mind as it raced again.

Another text from Lacey. The latest one had a cricket GIF and basically said if Nina didn't want to meet her, she understood and had no hard feelings. Lacey was clearly doing recon work. Daphne had called it. She must've wanted to get back together. Nina assumed so, anyway. Why else would she want to talk in person?

With a deep breath, she opened the text and limbered her thumbs as she plotted her reply.

Hey, sorry, Nina typed. *I just got these,* she lied. *We can meet sometime if you want.*

She impressed herself with the stellar level of indifference she'd managed.

Lacey's instant reply surprised her. *Cool. When are you free?*

Wow. Okay. This was really happening.

Whenever.

That had to grind Lacey's gears. Who knew passive-aggression toward the woman who broke her heart could feel so uplifting?

Could you narrow it down a tad?

Mission accomplished. She then admonished herself to tone it down.

"Mom," Noah said, drawing her out of her head. "Can Cody and I sleep over at Gram's tonight?"

"Wait, what?" She looked over at him, but he was still staring down at his phone. "Does Gram know anything about this?"

"She'll say yes if you say yes."

"How is Cody getting here?"

"His mom will drop him off."

"Okay. If Gram doesn't mind, it's fine with me."

"Thank you," he said and ran inside to work his magic on Nina's mother.

Nina returned to her phone.

Does tonight at eight at Sweet Life wine bar narrow it down enough?

Lol. To the finest of points. Looking forward to it.

Me, too.

Nina immediately thought of Daphne. She wanted to call her with this latest development, but she was probably still out with her kayaking friends. She sighed. She'd have to settle for a text imploring her to call the moment she was free.

After a cool shower, Daphne slipped into fresh shorts and a T-shirt and collapsed on the sofa to reflect on her intriguing day. As she rubbed aloe gel on her burnt arms, her thoughts ricocheted between Brynne and her call with Nina on the way home. Nina was practically hyperventilating as she regaled her about her texts with Lacey and the fairy-tale possibilities in their upcoming date. She'd never heard her so wound up about anything before. Lacey's spell still clearly had her in its clutches.

She then thought about how Brynne, a woman who performed flirtation like it was an art. She'd walked Daphne to her car and kept the conversation going even though it seemed it had run its natural course.

"It was so nice to meet you." She gently lifted Daphne's hand into hers and held it as she stared into her eyes.

"Yes, you, too." The sting of shyness averted Daphne's eyes. She knew she was supposed to say something more, but she froze with awkwardness.

Brynne's eyes lingered on her as she let Daphne's hand slip from hers. Her lips parted as though she were about to speak, but she only licked her bottom lip provocatively.

"Your freckles came out in the sun," Daphne said and immediately regretted her words

Really, Daphne? She screamed at herself in her mind as she flicked through the remote, looking for reruns of TV shows she hadn't watched during the regular season. *You have this sexy woman standing at your car flirting with you, and you respond by mentioning her freckles?*

Daphne shook the cringe-worthy memory from her head, then thought of Nina. Nina would've known how to respond. She seemed born to stare down any situation of monumental social awkwardness like Clint Eastwood in one of his old westerns. She would've instructed Daphne on exactly how to play it. It would be a miracle if Brynne asked her out, but if she did, Daphne should propose a Cyrano de Bergerac thing where Nina fed her responses through an earpiece.

That is, if Nina hadn't reconnected with Lacey and still had time.

❖

When Nina arrived at the wine bar, Lacey sat at a high-top table, a bottle chilling in a bucket. No doubt a pricey chardonnay, a beverage they'd shared an affinity for since they first met. Lacey stood in anticipation as Nina arrived at the table and wrapped her in a warm hug. After she finally released Nina, she slid her arms across her back and down her arms so sensually, the act could've qualified as foreplay.

"I hope you don't mind that I also ordered some apps for us to pick on while we chat." Lacey pulled the bottle from the bucket and filled Nina's glass.

Nina smiled. "As long as you included something with tuna, rare, on it."

"I couldn't show my face around you if I didn't.'"

Lacey's eyebrows lurched seductively, like she'd cornered her prey and would enjoy toying with it before moving in for the kill. She was the only person who could pull that alpha-woman crap on Nina and get away with it. Nina hated that she knew it, too.

"Do you like the wine?"

"You know it's my favorite." Nina smirked before taking another sip. She actually found playing along seductive.

"It's nice to realize some things haven't changed—although I have to say you've never looked more beautiful."

Nina couldn't suppress an eye roll.

"What? I'm not just saying that," Lacey protested. "You're radiant."

"Sometimes a change does do us good."

"Knowing you as I do, I wouldn't expect anything less."

Lacey brought her A-game tonight. Nice. Nina vanquished her glass of wine before the first app arrived. "So how did you find out I'm divorced?"

Lacey smirked. "Is that why you think I texted you?"

"Isn't it?"

"Are we going to keep talking like we're in a film noir?"

Nina laughed as she looked down into her glass. So many feelings, and they were all slamming into her at once.

"I saw you on the news," Lacey finally confessed. "I wanted to call you that night, but it seemed like you had your hands full with the transition."

"Ah, yes—the infamous human-interest piece on the beleaguered and victimized single mom." She shook her head with an ironic smile. "I can't tell you how many friend requests I got from single men after that piece aired."

"I don't doubt that. You looked so lovely, irresistible, in fact, in a damsel-in-distress sort of way." Lacey flashed that smoldering half smile that could make any woman want to work for her attention.

"Thank you, but you know I'm the furthest thing from a distressed damsel."

The server arrived with several plates of apps, just in time to dilute their simmering flirtation.

"I do know that," Lacey said. "It's one of the many things that attracted me to you."

Now she was using her smoldering screen-siren eyes to knock Nina off her guard. For as adept at seduction as Lacey was, she was forgetting Nina knew all her tricks.

"So how's the new job going?" Nina asked.

"It's actually going great—another good thing that came out of our ill-fated romance."

Nina chuckled as she swirled a piece of pita bread in hummus dip. "You must enlighten me on the list of good things that resulted from our affair."

Lacey flicked her auburn curls off her shoulder. "Aww. It makes me sad that you need be enlightened."

Nina shrugged. "While it certainly had its charms, I wasn't fond of the way I felt when you left me." She sipped her wine and pretended to observe the crowded bar, creating some distance between herself and the memory.

"It killed me, Nina. I wish I could find a way to prove it to you." Lacey reached for her hand, but Nina rolled it back before their skin touched.

Nina straightened her posture. "Not that I want to play one-up or anything, but I was in a slightly more vulnerable position than you were. I take full responsibility for my actions, but you kind of lured me out into the wild then just left me there."

Lacey nodded. "Looking back with what I know now, I definitely could've done things differently. But you were my first married woman."

Nina sighed. "We're not here to replay that awful time, are we?"

Lacey shook her head and topped off their glasses. "Not at all. Nina, I want to try again, now that you're actually free. It can be completely different this time."

Nina swallowed the wine she'd been holding in her mouth since she'd heard "try again" spill from Lacey's lips. The feel of those silky lips and that powerful tongue, the touch of the eager hand she'd just rejected. Those were some of the good things that had come out of their union—good and torturous in so many ways. She shifted in her chair as the tingle between her legs made her squirm.

"You're speechless," Lacey said. "Something else I'm not used to from you."

"Oh, I could say several things. I'm just not sure in which direction I want to steer this conversation."

Lacey's eyes bored into her. "Do you miss me?"

Nina sucked at her teeth. "That's such a douchie question to ask the person you dumped."

Lacey frowned. "I wish you'd stop saying it like I just tired of you and moved on to my next conquest."

"What do you want me to say, Lace? I was in love with you. It hasn't even been a year since we broke up. I mean I've healed from the heartbreak, but yes, I have moments when I do miss you."

"Thank you for being honest." Lacey caught hold of Nina's hand before she could retract it. "I still love you, Nina. I never stopped. I think you may have been more successful moving on than I have. But then success seems to be written in your DNA."

Nina was caving; she felt it. The wine, Lacey's eyes, her on-point verbal repertoire were all slowly undressing her stoic reserve. If she'd arrived at the wine bar thinking she had everything under control, the sexual tension simmering between them was about to make a fool of her.

"We've gone through a lot, Lacey—life changes, personal growth, hopefully some healthy introspection. Do you honestly think we can pick up where we left off?"

Lacey slid a seasoned olive in her mouth and licked the oil from her two fingers. "How about a fresh start? As two single women who are attracted to each other's minds and bodies. The canvas is totally blank, Nina. We can paint whatever vision we want for us."

Nina blinked at the glare of optimism coming off Lacey's face. She emptied the bottle into her glass despite already having a heavy wine buzz. "Lacey, we should revisit this conversation with sober heads. I have to get going." She slipped off the tall bar seat and grabbed the edge of the table for support.

"Where are you going? You just poured the last of the wine."

Nina's attention drifted between the glass and Lacey. "And I know better than to drink it."

"Are you okay to drive?"

"Yes. I'm just down the street a few miles."

"Can I see your new house?"

"You want to see my new house?" Nina had to make sure she'd heard her correctly.

"You shouldn't drive, Nina, even a few miles."

Nina unlocked her phone. "Fine. I'll Uber it then."

Lacey slipped the phone from her hands. "Please. Let me drive you."

Nina licked her lips and dangled her keys in Lacey's face. "I do not need to be walked inside."

Moments later, the precise scenario Nina had not wanted to transpire began transpiring when Lacey trailed her into the kitchen from her garage and corralled her against the chef's island in the middle of her stainless-steel oasis. Although she was only pleasantly wine-buzzed, Nina's complete absence of inhibition rivaled that of a sailor during Fleet Week. Had a wet T-shirt contest broken out in her kitchen, she would've been the first to sign up.

Lacey's strong hands held her face steady as she slowly traced her bottom lip with her thumb. Nina writhed. The moment their lips touched, warm wetness flowered between her legs. She grabbed Lacey's rear end with both hands and pushed her hips toward her, grinding against her to alleviate the ache.

"Take me upstairs," Lacey whispered as she licked behind Nina's ear.

Nina's head fell back as the natural ecstasy swept her away from reality. "I want your tongue so bad, Lacey."

Lacey tore into the button and zipper on Nina's pants and plunged fingers into Nina's panties. It had been so long since she'd felt the bliss of determined fingers swirling around her. Nobody had ever got her wet like this before, but then she'd only ever been with one woman.

Lacey dropped to her knees and rolled Nina's pants down with her. Too far gone for patience, Nina shoved Lacey's head into her and pumped against her warm, thick tongue, gasping in the sheer pleasure. They eventually made it upstairs, but not before Lacey brought her to a prompt, explosive orgasm there against the counter.

After they completed their animalistic, half-I-hate-you, half-I-miss-you lovemaking marathon, Nina lay in her bed next to Lacey with her eyes wide open in the dark. While she felt thoroughly satisfied physically, she wasn't so sure where the experience had left her head. Lacey threw her arm across Nina's stomach as she settled into a deeper sleep. Nina hugged her closer, not so much for the "and they lived happily ever after" moment their actions might have suggested but for the comfort of feeling the closeness of a familiar body against hers.

She couldn't wait to discuss the implications with Daphne, who was a master at listening. Even if she didn't have the answer Nina was seeking, Daphne's effusive empathy calmed almost any unsettling situation.

She smiled in the dark thinking about Daphne's sweet, unobtrusive, and often unintentional hilariousness. No matter what they were discussing, their conversations always brimmed with laughter and good vibes. Yes, she would talk to her about this first thing in the morning, and together they'd craft this into a narrative that Nina would feel better about.

Lacey twitched and made a snoring noise.

Hmmm. Does Daphne snore? Is she one of those people who have night terrors or need to sleep with a white-noise app blasting? How did she make out today kayaking? Maybe she met someone. I don't know why she hasn't yet. She's just adorable and quirky and funny. She has such nice lips, too.

As the volume of Lacey's snoring escalated, Nina picked up her arm and gently rolled her onto her other side to quiet her.

Yes, Daphne actually has perfect lips. Never dry but never greasy with gloss either. They seem soft, like really soft, like pink pillows that probably taste like the tropical-fruit Blistex she's always applying. People with nice lips are usually good kissers, too. Is Daphne a good kisser? Soft lips, tropical-fruit flavor, warm, tantalizing...

Nina suddenly sprang up in bed and looked at the lump of covers beside her. What was wrong with her? How the hell could she go from having wild, gratifying sex with Lacey to fantasizing about making out with Daphne? She laughed inside her mixed-up head. She'd heard of fucking your brains out, but she'd always thought the phrase was hyperbole.

She lay back down, rolled over, away from Lacey, and fell into a blissful sleep.

The next morning at Sophie's, Daphne sat back down at the table after Sophie yelled at her again for trying to help. She should've known better. Making the mimosas and Bellinis was the only job Sophie allowed her to do. Nina shot Daphne a covert look, and they smiled like parochial schoolgirls after the mother superior had reprimanded them.

"It was so nice of you to invite me for brunch, Sophie," Nina said.

"I'm glad you could come, and I finally got to meet you," she replied. "If I waited for this one to introduce us..." She bobbed her head toward Daphne.

Daphne turned to Nina. "She's a slick operator, isn't she?"

"Are you sure I can't help with anything?" Nina asked.

"You can help me eat all these goddamn pancakes." Sophie flipped the first batch. "I made too much batter. My mind's been going mushy on me lately."

"Are you feeling okay?" Daphne asked.

"Oh, yeah. I've just felt a little more tired than usual. Bette Davis wasn't joking when she said 'old age ain't no place for sissies.'"

Daphne had never heard Sophie talk like that before. To her, age was only a number, and she'd referred to it only out of convenience to avoid things she hadn't wanted to do. "Soph, let me know if you need any help around here. I'm right next door. I'll come over any time."

"I know you will, honey. Anyway, I'd like to hear about this new lady you met yesterday, Daphne."

Nina's head whipped toward her. "Yes, Daphne. I'd also like to."

Daphne's shoulders tensed in embarrassment. "I don't really have much to tell. Brynne is her name, she's an engineer, and she asked if I'd like to go for coffee with her sometime."

"When? Where?" Nina said.

"I don't know. I'm waiting for her to text me. And that's if she was being sincere."

"Why are you waiting for her?" Sophie said with attitude. "You should text her. How does that work with two women, anyway?"

Daphne laughed. "I already explained it to you. Whoever suggests the idea is responsible for making the arrangements."

Nina looked at her. "Where'd you hear that?"

"It's in the handbook," Daphne replied.

"There's a handbook?" Sophie asked.

"She's messing with us." Nina gave Daphne an admonishing glare.

"There should be," Daphne said. "I'd buy it."

"For real," Nina replied. "With a chapter or five on dealing with exes."

Daphne rested her chin in her palms. "Hmm. Speaking of that, how did it go with Lacey last night?"

"Uh…" Nina's convulsing eyebrows seemed to note Sophie's close proximity. "That's actually why I texted you this morning."

Daphne leaned closer as Nina's cheeks reddened. "Nina. What happened last night?"

Sophie brought a platter of pancakes to the table and sat down with them. "Something happened last night?"

As Nina's gaze darted between Daphne and Sophie, Daphne knew exactly what had occurred. Still, she blurted, "You slept with her?"

Nina's face deflated like a beach ball. "Daphne, why don't we discuss this later, hmm?"

Sophie glared at her. "You think I don't know women can have sex with each other? I get quite an education from her." She flicked her thumb toward Daphne.

"No, I just..." Nina stammered. "I just didn't want to be indelicate over Sunday brunch."

Sophie spread butter over her small stack of pancakes. "Well, I don't need a slide-show presentation, but we can have some girl talk, can't we?"

"I'm sorry. I didn't mean for it come out like that," Daphne said in response to Nina's glare.

After Nina had explained the entire situation in detail, concluding with her having to usher Lacey out of her house this morning, Daphne was speechless. She hadn't been sure what would come of Lacey's urgent series of texts, but a night of soft-core porn hadn't even made the list.

Nina looked at her, and they both stared at Sophie, whose mouth was still hanging open.

"You're offended, aren't you? I'm sorry." Nina's eyes were glossy with remorse.

"I'm not offended," Sophie said. "I'm jealous."

Daphne burst into laughter and raised her hand to Sophie for a high five. "Me, too. The only offer I got was for coffee."

When the laughter died down, Nina's face grew somber. "When Lacey finally left, I leaned against my door and wondered why I'd done it."

"Did you talk about getting back together?"

"She did, but I didn't answer her one way or the other. When she broke up with me, for months all I'd dreamed about was that she'd come back. Now that it's happened, practically out of nowhere, I don't know if that's what I want."

"How did you leave things?"

"She said she'd call me."

"Okay, well…" Daphne wasn't sure what else to say. Hearing the details made her jealous, too, but to be honest, it wasn't just about who was getting laid and who wasn't. She didn't like the idea of someone else being added to their equation. She shook off what seemed like possessiveness. Something warned her against feeling that way about a friend.

"And this is the woman you left your husband for?" Sophie asked.

"She's the woman who made me realize I wasn't happy with my husband anymore," Nina replied, clearly still defensive about the semantics.

"And you don't know if you want her back now?"

Nina shook her head. "A big part of me says, yes, we should absolutely give it another try. We only stopped seeing each other because I wasn't available. But then I flash back to when Lacey broke up with me for the last time, the look in her eyes. It was so cold, so definitive, like her love for me was dead and nothing I said or did would've brought her back to me." Nina paused. "It terrified me."

"I remember what that felt like, too," Daphne said. "I didn't think I'd ever get over it."

"How did you?" Nina said. "Just give it time?"

"She showed up at her ex's wedding," Sophie blurted out.

Nina shot her an incredulous look. "Savannah's? You never told me that."

"It must've slipped my mind," Daphne said, glaring at Sophie. "In retrospect, yes, it was a grossly ill-conceived plan, but it sure pushed me over that final hurdle."

"That's funny," Sophie said. "I would've said that happened when you began your friendship with Nina."

Daphne's stomach tightened as she anticipated Nina's reaction. "It was a combination of things. But yes, friendship is the best medicine for heartbreak."

Nina melted into the sweetest smile as she squeezed Daphne's hand. "Aww, that's so poignant, Daph."

"I agree," Sophie added. "I lost Willie three years ago, but since Daphne and I became close, it hasn't been so hard."

"Aww, Sophie." Daphne mimicked Nina's exact inflection and gestures.

The three of them held hands around the table and shared a hearty laugh.

"So are you excited about meeting this new woman?" Nina said.

Daphne shrugged. "It's just coffee, and who knows if I'll even hear from her. She may have had second thoughts once she sobered up."

"Stop it." Nina gave her arm a playful shove. "If she passes up a coffee date with someone as great as you, then you don't need a fool like that in your life."

Sophie smiled as she sipped her coffee. "Listen to her. She knows what she's talking about."

Daphne smiled, appreciating both their efforts.

"I don't know why you two just don't go out together," Sophie said as she nibbled a slice of bacon.

Daphne exchanged an awkward grin with Nina. "No. That's not how this...no, Sophie. Friends don't go there unless they're interested in making things super uncomfortable."

Sophie shrugged. "Like I said, I don't know how you ladies do things, but I think you'd make a beautiful couple."

Nina opened her mouth to speak, but Daphne cut her off.

"Thank you, but she's practically back together with Lacey, and who knows where it might go with Brynne. If she ever contacts me."

"Okay. Fine," Sophie said and began clearing the breakfast dishes. "So what do you girls have on your agendas today?"

"I have to pick my son up from my mom's," Nina said. "But that's not till later. Daph, if you want to take a ride with me, we can review some graphics options for your new website."

"Yes. I'd love to." Daphne looked over at Sophie. "I'm finally getting my business going—with Nina's help."

"It's about time. I've been hearing about it every week for a year now. You know how many times she's dragged that vision board over here?"

Daphne demurred like a proud daughter. "I had to, Sophie. At one time, you were the only person who believed in me."

"I'm glad you have someone to show you the ropes now."

Nina nodded. "If I can just convince you, then you'll have three people who believe in you, and that's all you need to officially launch your own business."

"I may be the toughest sell in the room," Daphne said. "But I'm sure you wouldn't waste your time if it wasn't worth a shot."

She looked at Sophie and Nina and smiled. All her life, she'd measured her value by the quality of her relationship with Ann Marie. Now that she had two such strong, diverse women in her life, she realized the immeasurable value of unconditional support from friends.

CHAPTER TEN

Nina and Daphne sat on the same side of the shaded picnic table in the park near Nina's mother's house as they studied the iPad screen. Nina had two unanswered texts from Lacey waiting for her, but at the moment, she challenged herself with the task of simultaneously pumping Daphne up about her new business venture and calming her down.

"What if I do all this, and the business fails anyway?" Daphne said as a breeze blew through her hair.

"Then you'll be like nearly every person who's ever gone into business for themselves. It's not uncommon for the first incarnation of a small business to falter, if not fail altogether. But since yours is small, with little to no overhead, it's relatively low risk, so why don't we focus on the what-is instead of all the what-ifs?"

"The what-is?"

Nina nodded. "You can't embark on something this important if you succumb to the early temptations of self-sabotage. Here's what *is* today. We're getting your website up and ordering you a set of business cards. You already have the stock at your house, so you're basically ready to go when your flea-market booth becomes available in a few weeks."

"I am?"

Nina giggled, finding Daphne's newbie vulnerability endearing. "Yes, you are. I wish you'd stop acting like I'm air-dropping you into a war zone without weapons. You know antiques. All you have to do is sell them to people."

"It's the people part." Daphne grimaced. "Flea markets are so peoply."

"An astute observation," Nina said dryly. "I'm trying to understand your aversion to engaging with customers. You're quite personable with me and other people I've seen you interact with."

Daphne sighed, visibly anxious. "I'm okay once I know someone, but initially meeting them makes me feel inside like a dentist's drill sounds. You don't remember how awkward I was when we met?"

Nina recalled Noah's assessment of her being a nerd. "I was so relieved to get my lamp back I wasn't paying attention to anything else. If it makes you feel any better, you weren't so awkward that that was my first impression of you."

"It does a little." Daphne groaned as she examined the layout of her website prototype.

Nina watched her study the screen. "Daph, do you really want to do this?"

"Yes. I do." She sat straight up, seeming determined. "I swear."

"Maybe the people part isn't the true issue." She turned her gaze from the iPad back to Daphne. "Maybe you're afraid of success."

"Wait. Did you say success?"

Nina nodded. "Sometimes people hesitate to move on big ideas or dreams because deep down, they know their lives won't be the same anymore once they've achieved that next level. You can't fall back on the same old excuses you're used to."

Daphne looked at her in surprise. "That really happens to people?"

Nina nodded again. "For my MBA, I took a business-psychology class that explored the correlation among success, failure, and the human psyche. We can self-destruct in many ways, and fear of success is one of them."

"Hmm. Savannah sure as hell never had that fear. She eats success like a dozen Krispy Kreme donuts."

"It all depends on your definition of success. If you're just looking for ego validation, then yeah, fear of success won't be an obstacle. But that's not you."

"That's so accurate. I just want to be fulfilled in the way I earn a living. What better way than to infuse your personal passions with your livelihood?"

"That's the very foundation of the American dream." She studied Daphne for a moment, proud of her progress. She wanted to grab her in a hug and reassure her that she was on the right course, but wouldn't that have seemed kind of weird? Anyway… "I wish I was like you—that I felt passionate enough about something to turn it into a career. I mean, besides Noah."

Daphne's mouth twisted in the cutest way. "If he's your passion, you're doing a great job fostering it. Think about it. You provide security for him and his future through your career, even if you're not exactly doing the kind of work that personally interests you."

"Thanks." Nina smiled, genuinely touched. "I take raising a small human seriously. We have more than enough dicks in this world, and I don't intend to add another one to the mix."

Daphne laughed and nodded. "I can't express how much I appreciate what you're doing for me. You've really helped me sharpen my focus on what's important."

"No thanks necessary. It's not even like I'm helping you. I'm having fun with all this stuff."

"Well, I'm glad." Daphne fixed her with an earnest gaze. "Even if this never turns into a profitable business, I already feel good. Just seeing the website with my business name on it is a dream come true."

"And I'll be there for your first sale at the flea market."

Daphne threw her arms around her and squeezed, whispering "Thank you, thank you." Without saying a word, Nina closed her eyes and leaned into her. Maybe a celebratory hug between friends wasn't so weird after all.

Suddenly, as though Siri was watching and had tipped off Lacey, another text chimed on Nina's phone.

"It's Lacey again. I have to answer her."

"Sure," Daphne said.

Nina smiled as she read the series of texts. Lacey had an amazing time last night, couldn't stop thinking about her, and hoped they could do dinner this week.

"Must be something good," Daphne said with a grin.

"Yeah. Dinner again this week."

"Looks like we're both getting what we want."

Daphne held up her hand for a high five. Nina swiftly slapped her palm as she powered off her iPad, and they left the park to pick up Noah.

On the car ride home, Daphne remained silent lest she say something dumb and be called out for it by a ten-year-old who hadn't yet missed a chance to share his insight. It didn't matter anyway. She was reveling in the banter between Nina and Noah, who seemed to have such a tight relationship. Nina's ability to relate so comfortably to anyone she talked with, regardless of age, awed Daphne into silence. At one point during brunch that morning, she thought Nina and Sophie would exchange phone numbers and start hanging out together without her. Every woman should have someone like Nina as a friend.

"You must be excited about dinner Wednesday," Daphne said, softly enough for Noah not to hear.

"I am." Nina raised the volume on the radio. "I wish I hadn't slept with her last night, though. It muddied the waters on something I should be approaching with a clear head."

"Meh. It's not like you just met and did it. You guys have a complicated history with some unresolved stuff."

"That's true." Nina gripped the steering wheel tighter. "Still, I'd like to be able think things through logically, without the influence of hormones."

"Good luck with that. You're still in love with her. The hormones would take over even if you hadn't acted on them. They'll probably do the same thing Wednesday night."

Nina's brow wrinkled. "Now that I think about it, I should probably change our dinner date to a night when Noah will be home."

"Don't be a wuss. You can handle this. Besides, what do you still need to think about with Lacey? She wants to come back."

"I don't know. I guess I'm locked in self-protect mode. I mean, should it bother me that she didn't stand by me through my divorce?"

"What do you mean?"

"Well, I was going through an excruciatingly painful time, faced with making critical decisions that would change other people's lives. And she just...she just bailed. I didn't adhere to her strict timeline, so she just leaves me. Is that what you call true love?"

"Ugh. I hadn't thought about it that way."

"How had you thought about it?"

"That she was on the outside looking in. I read an article once that said most people who have affairs don't leave their spouses. The affair fills a temporary need, and the person doing the cheating compartmentalizes the other person while they continue to live in their primary worlds."

"That's fucking deep," Nina said. "But that's not what I was doing. Lacey wasn't just a fling. She'd led me down a brand-new path, one that finally felt comfortable under my feet. Once I started, I didn't intend to turn back."

Daphne shrugged. "It must've been hard for her to see that. Sometimes people will tell you what you want to hear just so they can get what they want from you. I lived it long enough to know. Savannah was stringing me along until she was certain things were solid with her stomach surgeon, Francesca. Once Francesca released Savannah from her care and was free from a medical-ethics violation, she told Savannah she was in love with her, and then it was adios, Daphne."

Nina was staring at her, aghast. "That's awful."

"It's all good now, honest. I'm so much happier now than I've ever been. It truly was for the best."

"I suppose it would make more sense to talk to Lacey about it instead of spiraling down a rabbit hole of speculation."

"'A rabbit hole of speculation.'" Daphne giggled as she repeated the phrase. "I spend so much time there I should buy a vacation home."

Nina laughed, too. "We need to make a pact. From now on, we'll make sure we both keep our feet planted on the firm ground of reality. No spiraling anywhere."

"This will be a game-changer," Daphne said with a resolute nod. She then chirped in surprise when she felt a vibration on her butt, having left her phone in her back pocket.

"What's the matter?" Nina looked concerned as she drove down the exit ramp.

"Oh, my God. It's a text from Brynne." Daphne looked over at her and smiled. "She wants to meet for cocktails on Thursday."

"She upgraded you from coffee to cocktails already. You must've made a lovely impression." Nina held up her hand for a high five.

Daphne slapped her palm and added a squeeze of Nina's fingers. "There really is a first time for everything."

Nina gave Daphne a playful shove. "You're a goof. This is so exciting. Let's meet up Friday night at my place and compare notes on our dates."

"Is it wise to plan that far ahead? You could be moving Lacey in by then."

"Lacey's moving in with us?" Noah asked from the backseat.

"How long have you been eavesdropping on us?"

"Not long," he said. "You have the radio so loud."

Nina shot Daphne a knowing grin. "Mom tricks." She then looked into her rearview mirror again. "No, honey. Nobody's moving in with us. Daphne was just joking."

"Okay," he said. "I wouldn't mind too much if she did."

Now Daphne shot the first look.

Nina smirked. "What did we just say about spiraling?"

"Right. And I'm pretending that I'm not spiraling about meeting Brynne for drinks this week. I'm totally cool about it. It's whatever."

"Did you reply to her yet?"

"Oh. Yeah. I should probably do that, huh?"

Nina nodded, and they remained quiet for the rest of the ride to drop Daphne off at her house.

Nina had decided to keep her dinner date with Lacey on the night originally planned. It seemed ridiculous to have to procure a sitter for Noah when he already spent Wednesdays with his dad. Besides, Nina didn't have to rely on safety nets and escape hatches. She fancied herself evolved enough not to do things she hadn't wanted to and to accept responsibility for the things she'd chosen to. Sleeping with Lacey last weekend after she'd appeared out of nowhere hadn't been the smartest idea, but Daphne had correctly observed that they'd left a lot of loose ends.

"We didn't have to take two cars tonight," Lacey said during a lull in the conversation. "If you hadn't wanted me to move so fast last Saturday, you could've said so."

The statement pulled Nina's gaze away from the sun setting over the harbor. "Did my behavior that night indicate I didn't want it to happen?"

Lacey smiled and moved a wisp of her shiny auburn hair off her face before sipping her Manhattan. "To be honest, I had no idea what to expect, from myself or you. I was more than pleasantly surprised."

"The power of unfinished business," Nina said.

Lacey smiled in agreement. "It was more than that. I mean it was for me. It felt so good to make love with you again, Nina. And without the shadow of a third party lurking in the room, it was like a brand-new experience."

"We've come a long way since we first made love two years ago," Nina said pensively. "I'm different now, stronger, I think."

"You've always been strong. That's one of the many things I find attractive about you."

"Strength is relative. We're only as strong as the hardest situation that's tested us. I'd never been thrown a significant curveball before in my life. But you, though." Nina smiled ironically as she braved the memory of Lacey's first seduction. "The more involved we became, the more I felt I was losing myself. Some days I didn't know how I'd get out of bed and function in my daily life. Most days I didn't want to. I just wanted to run to you, climb into your bed, and never leave."

Lacey wrapped her fingers around Nina's. "I would've gladly let you, baby."

Nina picked at her scallop-and-bacon app, trying to deconstruct her conflicted feelings about Lacey. She'd wanted this a year ago; she'd practically begged Lacey to hold on for it. She'd also mourned losing it like a widow. Then through a series of misadventures involving that damn lamp, she'd revived the fantasy she'd clung to for survival during her loneliest hours. Now it was real and tangible, yet something was holding her back.

"I'm surprised you didn't meet anyone in the past year," Nina said, trying to redirect the mood of the conversation.

Lacey grew sullen. "I went on a few dates," she said, "but nobody could compete with your memory. It was still so alive within me. That's why I began dating so soon, trying to replace you…well, the pain of losing you."

Nina was growing annoyed that Lacey's talent for making her swoon threatened to chip away at her guard. "You didn't lose me, Lacey. You walked away from me."

What was happening? This was supposed to be a romantic, reconciliatory dinner, but Nina's cynical musings about Lacey were spilling out all over the table, seemingly of their own volition.

Suddenly, the glow of possibility faded from Lacey's face. She remained patient. "Nina, I've already told you how sorry I was for hurting you, and I meant it with all my heart. How many more times will you need to hear it?"

Nina sighed. "I'm not searching for an apology. I just want to understand how you could've trashed what we had without looking back. I mean, I know you couldn't keep seeing me while I was married, but you never even texted to see how I was doing. You shut me out of your life like I hadn't meant a thing to you."

Lacey's pooling eyes sparkled in the candlelight. She looked as though she wanted to speak but couldn't push the words past her emotions. Nina's heart sank. Was that what she'd been looking for from Lacey? The petty victory that comes from drawing the first tear? She clutched Lacey's forearm and faced the window to give her a moment.

"It's not what I wanted," Lacey finally said. "My therapist recommended no contact whatsoever. She'd told me I'd never be able to grieve and then move on if I was still connected to you emotionally."

Nina shrugged. "I suppose if you're paying that much for advice, it would be pretty dumb not to take it."

"Nina?" Lacey said gently. "What are we doing here?"

Nina continued to stare absently at the names on the stern side of the leisure boats docked in the harbor.

"Have I made a mistake contacting you after all this time?" Lacey said after a moment. "Do you not love me anymore?"

She looked into Lacey's eyes. Despite her reservations about Lacey returning to her life in what felt like a poof of magician's smoke, the answer to that question was easy. "I still love you, Lacey. I learned to live without you, but I never stopped loving you."

"That's exactly how I feel, baby. When I saw you on TV and realized my eyes weren't playing tricks on me, I knew that if I didn't at least try, I'd regret it for the rest of my life."

The warmth radiating from Nina's heart started making its way to her face.

"It's so good to see you smile," Lacey said. "I've missed that so much."

Nina suddenly felt shy. "I want to try, Lacey. If we don't, we'll both regret it."

Even though the restaurant they'd chosen was known for its array of house-made fruit and ricotta tarts, Nina and Lacey decided to pass on dessert. What was waiting for them at Nina's house was far more enticing.

❖

Arriving early to the café for happy hour, Daphne sat in her car fidgeting as she waited for Brynne's Range Rover to pull in. Daphne's lunchtime conversation with Nina about her dinner with Lacey last night still had her rattled, increasing her usual degree of nervous anticipation on a first date. Nina was so excited for this second chance with Lacey, and while Daphne expressed equal enthusiasm over the phone, she was disappointed in herself for not truly feeling that way.

She hadn't wanted Nina to get back with Lacey. How selfish. Nina would make time for her and continue to help her get her business up and running, even with a significant other. Unless Lacey was possessive and set so many boundaries that it eventually became too annoying to maintain the same level of friendship.

Daphne sighed, chiding herself for her lack of faith in Nina. Now who wasn't behaving like a true friend?

Suddenly, a tap on her window startled her. Brynne stood outside her car waving.

"Oh, I'm sorry," Daphne said, getting out. "Have you been waiting long?"

"No. I just got here. How are you?" Brynne wrapped her in a light hug, and they walked inside the café.

As Brynne ate her gazpacho and regaled her about herself in the usual first-date fashion, Daphne studied her face and mannerisms, tuning in and out at times. She was quite attractive, petite with a cute button nose. She was also intelligent and didn't go overboard selling herself. She seemed as self-assured and personable now as in the group setting the prior weekend. In those ways she was like Nina.

Something had to be wrong with her, some glaring imperfection. Daphne had been out of the dating loop so long, she could have missed even the most vivid red flags. But if she kept studying her, she'd find what was lacking.

"So, besides kayaking, what do you like to do for fun?" Brynne asked her.

"Well…" Daphne said, then paused. How was she supposed to make TV binge-watching, getting drunk with an eighty-year-old woman, and picking through people's trash sound as appealing as

Brynne's litany of pastime endeavors? She couldn't possibly match Brynne's extensive volunteer work with LGBTQ youth, the annual women's film festival, and a recreation program for the elderly in her community.

"I'm involved in antiques." She sipped her cocktail with pride at the quality of her response.

"How interesting. You're a collector or dealer?"

Daphne crossed her legs and feigned the air of a sophisticate. "Collector at present, but I'll soon be branching out into dealing… or being a dealer…of antiques."

"That's exciting. I don't know much about antiques. I've always leaned toward a modern, art-deco mix, but I suppose it would be fun to learn about them, especially from a woman as attractive as you."

Suddenly, Brynne's matter-of-fact engineer demeanor melted into sensuality as her gaze scaled down into the cleavage Daphne's loose shirt inadvertently presented. She shifted forward in her seat and adjusted the back of the shirt she kicked herself for not ironing before going out.

"Sure," Daphne said. "I'll let you know when my booth is up at the flea market next month."

Brynne arched an eyebrow at her. "Okay…"

Daphne smiled as she picked at her nachos.

"Actually, I was hoping I could see you again before next month."

"You were?"

Brynne nodded and reached over to pull a string of cheddar cheese off Daphne's chin.

"Oh, God." Mortified, Daphne grabbed her napkin and blotted her chin. "Thank you. I should've ordered something less messy for a first date. In case it isn't obvious, I haven't dated in like forever."

Brynne giggled. "I don't know if dating gets easier with practice. But it's good that you're out there again after your breakup last year. Eighteen years with someone is a long time, so kudos to you."

"Thank you for jump-starting my return to the dating world," Daphne said. "Aside from the cheese thing, I'm enjoying myself."

Brynne beamed and brushed her leg against Daphne's. Was it intentional? Wasn't the first date too soon for calculated leg rubsies? Whatever. Good thing she'd remembered to shave, or she would've notched up two strikes already.

When their server came over and asked if they wanted anything else, they agreed on one more round of drinks. Thankfully, Brynne was talkative, which helped keep Daphne's nerves in the neutral zone. At that point, Daphne wished so hard that Savannah and her doctor wife would stroll into the café and see her sitting there with an attractive woman who seemed enthralled with her. What a glorious vindication it would be for the wedding-crash debacle.

She was excited about calling Nina the moment she got home to report on her date. Hopefully, she wasn't out with Lacey. Or home doing it with her. She absently grimaced.

"Are you okay?" Brynne asked.

"Oh, yes, just a leg cramp." Daphne felt stupid again.

Brynne nodded knowingly. "It's hard to stay hydrated in this heat. Want me to get our server for more water?"

"No. No, thank you. I'm fine." Daphne smiled at her thoughtfulness. She still hadn't detected any flaws in this woman. What the hell?

Before Daphne knew it, Brynne had grabbed the check folder, placed her credit card in it, and signaled for the server. "I'd love to keep this date going since it's still early, but I have to visit my mother at rehab."

"Jeez, I'm sorry. Well, one day at a time, as they say." She added a thumbs-up in a show of support.

"She had a double knee replacement."

"Oh. Oh!" Daphne said, wincing once she realized her miscue. "I wish her a speedy recovery. And please, let me give you half for the check." She reached into her pocket and pulled out a wad of wrinkled bills.

"Next time," Brynne said with a smile as she stood. "Gives me an excuse to see you again…if you'd like."

"You don't need an excuse, Brynne. You're great," Daphne said, basking in the glow of flattery. Then her feet tangled in the chair legs as she stood.

"You're pretty great yourself," Brynne said as she extended an arm. Once Daphne was upright and steady, she gave her a tender kiss on the cheek before heading out of the restaurant.

Daphne found herself smiling again as she watched Brynne leave. But where were the butterflies in her stomach? Where was the longing to see her again the second she was out of her sight? Had being emotionally dormant for so many years stunted that part of her heart?

Evidently, she'd have to discuss those questions with Nina.

CHAPTER ELEVEN

After Daphne left the café, she had to make a tough decision. Should she go home and have manhattans with Sophie or see if Nina was around to split a bottle of wine? Both women would give her excellent feedback on her date with Brynne but from decidedly unique viewpoints.

Since it was after eight o'clock, heading home and stopping in on Sophie was the more convenient option. So she asked Siri to call her first to let her know she was on her way home. No answer, so the call went to voice mail. Odd, but she'd probably settled into an old film on TCM, as she was wont to do, then fell asleep. So she sent off a text to her, saying she was thinking about her, and called Nina.

Once she arrived at Nina's they hadn't wasted any time opening a bottle of rosé and plopping down at the angle of Nina's sectional in her comfortably air-conditioned family room.

"Are you sure it's not too late?" Daphne asked. "It wouldn't have offended me if you'd said don't come over."

"It's eight thirty. I run on five hours of sleep and can never get Noah to bed before eleven in the summer anyway."

Daphne smiled at Nina, who looked so cute and comfy curled up next to her in basketball shorts and a V-neck tee, her hair pulled back in a bun and headband. "Where is Noah, anyway?"

"Upstairs in his room allegedly making slime. I told him to come down and say hi when you got here, but the mad scientist is probably wrapped up in his project."

"That's okay. Don't interrupt his research."

Nina consulted the clock on the TV stand. "He'll be down for a snack soon anyway. The kid's never gotten over his infant feeding schedule of every two hours."

As they shared a laugh, Daphne again noted the dimple in Nina's left cheek that never failed to catch her eye. She also noted, while sipping her wine, the butterflies in her own stomach as she studied the nuances of Nina's countenance. The butterflies. Where were they two hours ago when Brynne had been regaling her with witty banter and tasteful flirtation?

And suddenly it hit her. *Oh no…*

"Daph," Nina said. "Are you drunk already? I asked you how it went with Brynne."

"Oh, sorry. I just spaced out."

"How did it go? And why was it over so soon?"

"She had to visit her mother in the hospital."

"Oh…" Nina contorted her mouth in pity.

"What? Her mother had a double knee replacement." Despite her conviction, she wasn't getting Nina to buy it. "Was that just an exit strategy?" She frowned, feeling like a fool. "How did I not see that? I'm such an idiot."

"No, no, no," Nina said, patting Daphne's knee. "Don't listen to me. I'm jaded. It's entirely possible that it's true. I'm sorry."

"Don't be sorry. It does have kind of a 'my dog ate my homework' ring to it."

"Stop it. I'm sorry I projected onto you." Nina rubbed Daphne's forearm. "Aside from that, how did it go otherwise? How was the conversation? The chemistry?"

"The conversation was great, especially since she did most of the talking. But the timing of my 'uh-huhs' and 'oh reallys' was spot on."

"How about the physical part?"

"What about it?"

"Any incidental touching? Accidental caressing? Boob brushing?"

"Boob brushing?"

"My goodness, Daphne. You weren't kidding when you said you were out of practice."

Daphne retreated into herself. "I'm going to be honest with you." She hesitated, pushing through her embarrassment. "I'm not really out of it. You have to have had practice at some point to be out of it. Ann Marie, or Savannah, was my first and only girlfriend, and we met when we were eighteen."

Nina seemed to recoil, not as if Daphne had announced she had the stomach flu, but more like she'd just admitted she'd descended into Area 51 from an alien spacecraft.

Daphne sighed. "I probably shouldn't expect to hear from her again, huh?"

Nina sipped her wine and scratched at her head through her bun. "Well, how did you leave it?"

"She said she wants to see me again and sooner than a month."

"Okay. That's good. We clearly let our speculation get away from us. I knew there was no way she wouldn't like you."

"Really?"

"Oh, my God, Daph." Nina shook her head and sipped more wine. "Yes. Really. So how was it for you? Did you like her as much one-on-one as you did in the group?"

"Yeah. She was great." *But she wasn't you.* The abrupt thought made her bobble her wineglass. Luckily, the small amount of rosé in it didn't spill on Nina's expensive-looking white sectional. Just on her leg.

Nina smirked and poked her in the thigh with her naked foot. "What's the matter with you? Talking about Brynne getting you all hot and bothered?"

No, but your constant touching me is about to.

"Aww, cut me some slack." Daphne leaned back against the sofa cushions. "I had a few at happy hour earlier."

"Once we polish this off, you may have to sleep over."

Daphne grabbed the bottle from the bucket and refilled their glasses. "Come on. It's your turn. What happened last night with Lacey?"

Nina's face lit up. "It was perfection, like a scene out of a Hallmark movie, if they made gay ones. She took me to Wave for dinner and drinks, and then we ended up back here for a very romantic night."

"On this couch?" Daphne jerked forward, pretending to be grossed out. However, the thought of Nina and Lacey having sex was making her feel some type of way…

"No, you idiot," Nina said, laughing. "We were able to control ourselves until we got up to my bedroom."

"So are you guys like officially back together?"

Nina took a slow sip and seemed to ponder the question before swallowing her wine. "Yeah." A blush began to bloom across her face. "I guess we are. I mean we didn't say it in so many words, but given the reasons it ended, it just seems like the natural next step."

Daphne made sure her smile was long and sincere enough to mask the disappointment stirring inside. "You seem very happy, Nina. I'm happy for you."

Nina clutched Daphne's hand. "Thank you. After the year I've had, it's pretty remarkable where I've ended up. And I actually owe it all to you."

"Me?"

"Yes. You set off the chain of events by taking my lamp. Lacey found out I was single because of the news story. You're stealing junk and changing lives, my friend."

Daphne leaned back and willed her face to exude joy. Only in her world would she single-handedly chart a course that would steer the most amazing woman she'd ever met into the arms of someone else.

"We're simpatico," Daphne said. "I'm helping your love life, and you're helping my career. It's frickin' awesome."

"It's not just my love life. I want you to know how much your friendship means to me. You stormed into my world at a time when I needed a friend the most. I've so appreciated having you to talk and hang out with over the last several months. You didn't just steal my lamp. You stole my heart, too."

Daphne offered her best deadpan. "That is the gayest thing you've ever said."

Nina guffawed and sprayed a modest sip of wine over Daphne's arm. Then they laughed even harder at that.

"I'm serious, Daph," Nina said, wiping laughter tears from the corners of her eyes. "With all the changes and growth I've experienced over the last couple of years, I've come to understand the importance of true friendship with an honest, empathetic woman. And one who makes me laugh all the time, too? That's the golden ticket."

"Did you have that with Lacey, too, before you fell in love?"

"Pretty much. And then we had sex and everything changed. Beware the woman who tells you sex won't screw up a friendship, especially if it's the best you've ever had."

"She's still your friend, though. Your best friend?"

Nina nodded. "But it isn't the same. The friendship is only as solid as the relationship, and if that falls apart, the friendship usually follows."

"Some couples stay friends after the relationship. I couldn't."

"I couldn't either, but Lacey and I were in a much different place than you and Savannah." Nina shrugged. "When you think about it, you and I are in the best possible place. We have promising relationships with great women and friendship with each other, no matter what the future may hold with Lacey and Brynne."

Daphne relaxed in the warmth and safety of Nina's reassuring words. Having Nina as a confidant and partner in wine was more valuable than any relationship. She'd never want to do anything to compromise that.

Suddenly, her text chimed. "That must be Sophie." She reached for her phone. "I called her earlier." She looked down and was surprised. "It's Brynne."

"Yes." Nina hissed as she gave Daphne a fist bump. "What did she say?"

"That she's still thinking of my timid yet alluring eyes and can't wait to see them again in person."

"Get out. That's what she wrote?"

Daphne nodded in excitement.

"Damn. That woman's seduction game is on point." Nina emptied the bottle into their glasses. "What did you say she does for a living?"

"Engineer."

"Talk about duality. The mind of a scientist and the soul of a poet. And you have her under your spell."

Daphne demurred. "Well, I don't know about having the pizazz for casting spells or anything…"

Nina pointed at her with a grave expression. "You need to stop selling yourself short. I know it can be nerve-wracking starting with someone new, but try to resist the temptation for negative self-talk."

"I'm just glad I didn't sneeze and blow a glob of snot out, like I did on one of my early dates with Ann Marie."

Nina stared at her. "Do not say that to Brynne. Not now. Not ever. Should we open another bottle?"

"I should get going. I want to check on Sophie when I get home." She stood and stretched. "She probably fell asleep, but she always responds to my texts. She was so proud that she taught herself to text when her son gave her a phone."

"Call her now and see," Nina said, also standing.

"It's late," Daphne said. "I don't want to wake her. I can peep into her windows when I get home and see that she's okay."

"Sophie and I are both lucky to have you."

Nina wrapped her in a tight, full-body hug and held on. Daphne wasn't sure if it was an expression of gratitude or that Nina was too buzzed to stand by herself. Whatever the reason, Daphne didn't care. She closed her eyes and stood there holding Nina, waiting for her to pull away first.

When Daphne pulled into her driveway, Sophie's house was completely dark, and since Sophie hadn't returned Daphne's voice mail or text, she now decided it was appropriate to panic. She trotted across the yard and knocked on her door and rang her bell. Nothing.

She kicked herself for never taking down her son's phone number. It was after eleven, so she called the hospital before resorting to smashing in her back window.

Sure enough, that's where Sophie was. While she couldn't find out why she'd been admitted, once she started crying, someone at the nurses' desk told her she was okay and would likely be released the next day. It was enough to allow her to eventually fall asleep.

❖

After Daphne left, Nina cleared the wine bottles from the table and went upstairs to check on Noah.

"Hey, buddy," she said after a light tap on his door.

He lay sprawled sideways across his bed with the TV on, his nightstand cluttered with several days' worth of snack wrappers and empty bowls.

"This kid didn't brush his teeth," she muttered. "I know it."

After tidying up and turning off the TV, she walked into her master bath to get ready for bed. She thought about Daphne and her puzzling lack of confidence as she brushed her teeth. With her lovely features and such a disarmingly sweet and funny way about her, how could she be so insecure? Whoever this Brynne woman was, she'd be a fool not to explore the possibilities with Daphne.

If she wasn't in love with Lacey, she would go for Daphne. Probably. But now that they'd become good friends, the threshold for that type of relationship had closed. Being romantically involved would feel weird. Wouldn't it?

Anyway, why speculate on "what ifs" when the "what is" was so promising? She was getting back with Lacey, Daphne was embarking on new romantic adventures, and they had each other as friends. It was all good.

"Uh, oh," she said out loud as she remembered actual Lacey. She grabbed her phone and saw three texts from her over the last two hours. She texted back and confessed that time had slipped away from her as she and Daphne discussed her date over a bottle and a half of rosé.

That's awesome." Lacey wrote. *I hope it's only the beginning for them. I just wanted you to know I was missing you.*

I miss you, too.

Did I mention that I LOVE having you all to myself now?

Yes, I think you have. Nina added a heart and a smiley face. *It's wonderful for me, too.*

Can I steal you away this weekend? My sister's having people up to the place she's renting on the Vineyard.

I have Noah this weekend...

It took a couple of minutes for Lacey to reply. *Any chance you can switch weekends with Zack?*

Nina sighed. Here we go, she thought. *Not at eleven fifteen on a Thursday night. I'd need more notice.*

I know. It was a spontaneous thing my sister threw together. He's welcome, too. Think about it. Good night, my love.

Lacey signed off with heart and kiss emojis, but did the hasty ending to the chat mean she was disappointed or frustrated or worse? Not an auspicious way to begin their new, legitimate relationship, but what was she supposed to do? Her son was her priority, and Lacey had known that from the start.

She was about to change into her sleep T-shirt when she caught the trace scent of Daphne's perfume from their earlier hug still on the T-shirt she was wearing. She pulled it up to her nose for a closer sniff, smiled, and decided to sleep in it instead.

❖

The next day, Daphne visited Sophie in the hospital as soon as she left work. As she zipped down the hall to her room, she tried to mentally prepare for the sight of Sophie lying inert and full of tubes, half out of it. The woman was in her early eighties, but she was so young at heart, Daphne never viewed her as elderly. This development certainly put things in perspective.

She quietly entered her room and walked past the aged roommate balled up asleep only to find Sophie sitting up, looking spry as ever as she watched *Judge Judy*.

"You scared the bejesus out of me, Soph." Daphne bent down to give her a kiss and a small bouquet of flowers in a vase.

"I hope you didn't buy these in the gift shop," Sophie said as she inspected them. "They're a rip-off down there."

Daphne took the vase from her and made a place for it on the nightstand. "I didn't have a lot of options. I raced here from work."

"You didn't have to come at all, let alone race. When you called me this morning, I told you I was fine."

"You're clearly not fine if you're in the hospital," Daphne said as she sat at the foot of the bed.

"I feel like I can leave now, but the doctor wanted me here one more day because I hit my head."

"Oh, my God. You probably have a concussion. You're lucky you didn't crack your skull open. You need one of those Life Alert necklaces."

Sophie waved her off. "Stop being such a nervous Nelly. I never lost consciousness. I just got a little dizzy and lost my balance."

Daphne shook from her mind disturbing images of how much worse her fall could've been. "At your age, you have to take this stuff seriously, Soph. What if you had lost consciousness?" She took out her phone. "Please give me your son's cell-phone number."

"What do you need that for?"

"So I can keep in touch with him about you."

"I don't know it off the top of my head. I'll give it to you tomorrow after I get home. Now what happened on your date? Was this with the one who came over for breakfast?"

Daphne gave her a stern glare. "No. That's Nina, my friend."

JEAN COPELAND

"She's a beautiful girl, Daphne. She's the one you should be dating."

Daphne sighed and sprawled out across the foot of the bed. "Yes, you've already said that, but that's not how these things work."

Sophie rolled her eyes. "Oh, right. All these lesbian rules you keep telling me about."

"They're not rules. It's not like we have by-laws or anything. They're just common-sense social parameters."

Sophie seemed to puzzle it out in her head. "So some women you go to lunch with and some you sleep with."

Daphne propped herself up on her elbow. "It's more like some women you can do both with, but some you can only go to lunch with."

"I see. So Nina, you only have lunch with. But this other one—"

"Brynne."

"This Brynne you can also sleep with?"

"Maybe. We've only had one date, so I'll have to see how things go."

"How many dates does it take before the sex happens?"

Daphne laughed. "I don't know. It's different for everyone. Let me guess. You and Willie waited till your wedding night."

"Yes, we did," Sophie said with a smile. "I was nineteen when we married, mind you, so it wasn't such a big deal to wait—not like you kids today who can't be bothered with marriage."

"Hey," Daphne said, lightly offended by the generalization. "Ann Marie and I did get married when it became legal, but a lot of good that did me. She fell in love with her stomach doctor, and next thing you know, I'm served with divorce papers so they could march down the aisle."

"I thought you were over her," Sophie said.

"I am over her, but sometimes I think about how I felt when she left me for pretty, successful Francesca. After all those years together, she tossed me to the curb like trash. I'm still processing that part."

"Fair enough. I imagine that would be devastating. But just remember, she may have made you feel like trash, but you have two new ladies in your life who certainly don't see you that way."

Daphne smiled and gave one of Sophie's feet a playful rub. "How do you always know what to say to make me feel better?"

"Not bad for a woman who never had a daughter or a granddaughter of her own." Sophie pretended to polish her nails on her hospital gown, then looked up at her in earnest. "You're nobody's trash, Daphne. Don't ever let anyone make you feel like that again."

"Thanks, Sophie. I won't. I've come a long way in knowing my worth. At least that's how all the Instagram memes say I should feel anyway." She chuckled at her own quip.

"That's good. I'd hate to see you wind up on a *Dr. Phil* episode about middle-aged women who get taken to the cleaners by someone they met online."

Daphne laughed too loudly for a hospital room, then stopped abruptly when she remembered her online dalliance before Savannah left her. If she hadn't accidentally left her browser open to her messenger, Savannah might never have discovered the conversations. Who knew what Daphne could've agreed to during that period of weakness?

Sophie shook her head in apparent reflection. "Life was so much less complicated when we all married at nineteen."

"You didn't have the internet then," Daphne said. "What else were you supposed do?" Her jovial tone belied the fact that she was a tad jealous of Sophie's decades of marriage to the love of her life. It was a dream she'd watched sift through her own fingers.

CHAPTER TWELVE

As the summer waned, Daphne's flea-market debut had finally arrived, and Nina seemed more excited than she was. She and Noah had picked Daphne up early in the morning, and they stopped for breakfast before driving to the flea market and helping her set up in her booth for the day.

As nine a.m. rolled around, Nina stood beside Daphne trying to calm her. For some reason she was twitching with the same level of angst as a theater actress on opening night—who'd forgotten to memorize her lines.

"Daph, are you truly this nervous about sitting in an antique booth, or are you just over-caffeinated?"

"What if I mess up?" she said, rubbing her thumbs and forefingers in circles. "What if I'm overcharging people, and then I'm blackballed from ever doing business here again?"

Nina shook her head as though Daphne had set it spinning. "What have I said about all the *what ifs* in business? Nothing ventured, nothing gained, remember?" She touched her arm in another effort to calm her. "Besides, we spent a lot of time in August researching the value of your pieces. Your prices are exactly where they should be."

"Okay. You're right," she said, shaking out her hands at her sides. "And you'll be here if anything goes wrong, so it's all good."

"I just have to drop Noah off at my mom's, and I'll come back for the rest of the day."

Daphne's eyes went wide and glassy. "You're leaving me?"

Nina tried not to laugh, but Daphne's irrational panic was so cute. She wanted to wrap her in a big bear hug. "My mother lives twenty minutes from here. I'll be back before you even realize I'm gone."

"I'm going to realize you're gone the moment you walk away. Can you wait like an hour, just so I can get used to the idea?"

Nina felt sorry for her. Sometimes she seemed afraid of everything. It was no wonder her vision board was yellowing at the corners.

"Noah, should we hang out here a while with Daphne before I take you to Gram's?"

He nodded. "Can I go over there and look at the comic books?"

She looked in the direction he was pointing and saw the booth was in her line of vision. "Sure, but do not leave that booth without telling me first. You hear me? It'll take all of two minutes for you to get lost and kidnapped."

After another nod, he made his way to the comic-book booth. Nina surveyed the crowd slowly starting to fill in the market, then joined Daphne in the other chair behind her table.

"Where's Brynne today?"

"Kayaking with friends," Daphne said ambivalently.

"Is she coming down later?"

"She might. I told her to stay out and seize the day. Who wouldn't want to be out on the water?"

Nina tried to keep her face neutral, not wanting to pass any judgments. If she were Daphne's girlfriend, she'd be here with her from start till finish. Actually, she would be, with the exception of dropping off Noah.

"You're such a good girlfriend," she said. "Most women would expect their significant others to be by their side for something like this."

Daphne shrugged. "I'm not sure how significant we are."

"What do you mean? I haven't asked because I didn't want to pry, but how's the sex?"

Daphne looked at her, seeming embarrassed.

"You don't have to tell me if you're uncomfortable talking about it."

"We haven't done it yet," Daphne whispered.

"Are you kidding? You've been together a month."

"Almost a month and a half."

Nina was trying to wrap her head around this new information. "What the hell? Is it you or her?"

"I think it's me. I just haven't felt ready. I want to get to know her better."

"Good for you. I admire your self-restraint. But does Brynne find it admirable, too?"

Daphne's mouth twisted in concern. "I'm messing it up with her, aren't I?"

"I don't know," Nina said, thinking, yes, quite possibly. "Look, every relationship is different, and if you both agree on abstaining, then that's cool. Do you want something more meaningful with her?"

"I think so. I really like her, and we have fun when we spend time together."

Lacey's incoming call interrupted Nina's response. After noting Noah's whereabouts, she walked away to answer.

"I miss my sweet babe," Lacey said in a sultry morning voice.

Nina smiled into her phone. "Hi, honey. What's going on?"

"After last night, I'm having Nina withdrawals. How about dinner later this afternoon?"

"I'd love to," Nina said. "But I'll be with Daphne at the flea market till around four. Then I have to pick up Noah at my mom's and catch up on some work at home. How about Tuesday or Wednesday?"

Nina stuck her finger in her other ear to hear through the crowd noise. Lacey hadn't answered.

"Are you there, honey?" Nina said.

"Yeah. I'm here." Lacey's tone was a bit more rigid. "Do you have to stay with her all day?"

"I told her I would. It's her first time running her booth, and she feels a lot better having me here while she gets used to the routine."

Lacey exhaled into the phone. "You can't see me tomorrow either?"

"Lace, you know Mondays are bad. I have a bunch of meetings tomorrow and won't get to leave by five, more like six or seven."

"Do you need me to pick up Noah if you run late?"

"Daphne said she would. She lives closer to my office than all of us."

"Jeez, it's starting to seem like you spend more time with her than you do me." Lacey said it with a chuckle, but Nina clearly heard the tinge of resentment in the quip.

"That's not true, honey. It just feels like that this weekend."

"How about you just cut out of there early? She'll be fine after a few hours of you babysitting her."

Nina bristled. She didn't feel like she was babysitting her at all. Was her friendship with Daphne starting to be a problem for Lacey? She breathed in slowly as she chose her words.

"Lace, I made a plan and a promise with Daphne, and I'd like for you to understand and be okay with it."

There. That sounded mature and reasonable.

"Okay. Fine. I understand. No big deal. Have fun."

"You don't sound like you're fine with it."

"It is what it is, Nina. I know how important your commitments are to you."

Wait. What? Was that a shot at the fact that she'd cheated on Zack with her? Or maybe she was suggesting that she'd strung her along because of her commitment to Zack? Or was she just being hypersensitive? She couldn't deal with this now.

"I have to take Noah to my mother's. I'll call you tonight." She hit the end button and waved Noah back to her.

After he'd signaled one more minute with his finger in the air, Nina turned toward the table in time to see Daphne bright-eyed and talking with an old couple. The woman held a set of vintage candle lanterns as the man paid Daphne cash. She hung back and waited for them to complete the transaction before returning.

"Did you just make your first sale?" Nina indicated the old couple walking away as she approached the table.

Daphne was jumping up and down and nodding, as excited as a kid who'd hit a game-winning homerun in Little League. Nina rushed at her behind the table and attacked her with the bear hug she'd thought of earlier.

"I'm so proud of you," Nina said, still embracing her. "And you did it on your own."

"I was so nervous at first when the wife started asking me questions, but then I just answered her, and we started talking. They were both so sweet."

"You're officially a businesswoman."

Daphne beamed. "I am, aren't I?"

"You know what this means, don't you?"

"I have to activate my website now," Daphne said with a cautious grin. She took out her phone and clicked on the app.

"Would you like a drum roll?"

"Done." Daphne looked up, and exhilaration simmered in her eyes.

"How does it feel to know you've made your biggest vision come to fruition?"

Daphne closed her eyes as though breathing in success. "Wonderful. I don't know how to thank you for all your technical and emotional support. I couldn't have done it without you." She hugged Nina so tight their bodies came together from head to toe, like a hand sliding into a supple leather glove.

As Nina held onto her, inhaling the light scent of perfume mingled with sweat on her neck, a burst of excitement raced through her—but not the traditional kind for a friend's success. When she realized Daphne's hug was arousing her, she withdrew.

"You give me too much credit, Daph," she said casually. "All you needed was a little push in the right direction."

"Nina, you designed my whole website for me and basically held my hand every step of the way. I'm definitely not giving you too much credit."

Nina laughed at Daphne's dramatic gestures as she spoke. She'd loved helping Daphne through every phase of her new venture. It had filled her with joy watching a woman clueless to her potential slowly but surely starting to realize it.

"I think you have other customers." Nina jutted her chin toward two young women browsing the table. "I'm gonna run Noah over to my mom's, and I'll be back."

"No rush. I got this," Daphne said with a playful smirk.

"That's my girl," Nina replied, instantly chastising herself as she walked away with Noah. *That's my girl*? What the hell was that all about? She'd come off sounding like a condescending daddy. Or, worse, her lover.

While heading to the car, Noah told her all about the vintage Spiderman comic he was able to procure for a discounted price, but she couldn't concentrate on anything except the way Daphne's hug had made her feel.

While Nina was gone Daphne had sold another item, an early twentieth-century mantel clock that still kept perfect time and chimed as daintily as it likely had when it was a practical item a hundred years earlier. She'd bought it for a hundred, added a little antique polish, replaced the glass over the face, and sold it for two-fifty. She could get used to this.

She checked her phone again to see if Brynne had replied to the text she'd sent after her first sale two hours earlier. Nothing. In Brynne's defense, it was probably hard to respond to anything while paddling down a river. She'd try again later.

After about an hour, Nina returned with sandwich wraps and flavored waters from a gourmet deli near her mother's house. She was so thoughtful. She could've eaten lunch at her mother's by the pool, but instead she came back to have it with her. Lacey was a lucky woman. Good thing she'd come to her senses and grabbed Nina before someone else realized how amazing she was.

"Any big plans with Brynne this week?" Nina sat with her feet up on the edge of the table as she ate, her long, tanned legs stretched out before Daphne.

Daphne shrugged. "I'm sure we'll get together, but now that the website's up, I feel like I should take a ride treasure hunting. I still have stuff at home, but what if my stock runs low and I can't fill orders? What do you think?"

"Ah, the beautiful dilemma of every entrepreneur," Nina said as she licked honey mustard from the corner of her mouth. "If you're asking my opinion, I'd say see how you do today and this week on your site before you start panicking about inventory. Zack has Noah next weekend, so I can sneak off with you if you want."

"Sneak off?" Daphne smirked. "You have to hide from your girlfriend already?"

"It was just an expression," Nina replied, seeming slightly defensive.

"I'm only kidding." Daphne reeled in damage control. "I didn't mean anything bad against Lacey."

"I know you didn't. I must still be a little sensitive about the idea of sneaking around."

Nice play, Shakespeare. Daphne stiffened at her uncanny ability to offend people even in the most laid-back situations.

Thankfully, as if on cue, Lacey's name appeared as an incoming call on Nina's phone. "Hey, babe." Nina shifted away from Daphne as she talked. "About four thirty...Yeah, but she may need help packing the items that don't sell."

Daphne strained to continue eavesdropping as Nina's voice started growing softer.

"I know, but it's just this one time...All right. Let me call you later, okay?" She looked back at Daphne self-consciously and mimed that she'd be off the phone in a minute. "Yeah, okay. I'll text you when I'm on my way home." She seemed a bit exasperated as she ended the call and turned back to her.

"Nina, you don't have to stay till the end. I've got the hang of this now. Call Lacey back if she wants to get together."

"That's not really the point, Daph. I made arrangements to help you today, and she should respect my plans with my friends, not give me a hard time about them."

Daphne tried not to let disappointment flower on her face. It was starting already. "It's fine, though," she said. "It won't be a problem loading the rest of the stuff myself. I'd feel terrible if I caused the first rift in your new and improved relationship."

"Ha." Nina leaned back, sipping her water. "If the relationship really is new and improved, something like this shouldn't cause a rift."

"How are you always so logical?" Daphne asked. "I'm dreadful at confrontation, even if I have a valid point." She glanced at her dormant phone on the table. "It's kind of nice that she wants to see you so badly."

"It's a fine line between being eager to see someone and being demanding. I used to cave to pressure from Zack and change things to accommodate him even if it wasn't convenient. I've since dropped that bad habit. And besides, Lacey and I spent Friday and last night together, so it's not like I'm neglecting her."

"Okay. As long as you don't feel obligated to stay here with me…"

Nina smiled. "It's a gorgeous day. I'm hanging out with my bestie. Where's the obligation?"

Daphne smiled back, secretly stoked that she was Nina's choice. For now, anyway. Would Lacey start demanding more of her time as they grew closer or try to narrow her social circle? If things kept moving along the way they were, they'd probably move in together eventually. Then what would happen to her friendship with Nina? No way they could remain as close as they were now. She hadn't realized her expression had faded into gloom.

"What's wrong? Still haven't heard from Brynne?"

Daphne shook her head solemnly, more about Lacey than about Brynne.

"You might want to think about having sex with her," Nina said. "I mean, if you like her enough to want to foster something more meaningful, now's probably the time to show her."

Daphne studied her hands in her lap.

"Do you?" Nina said.

"What? Like her enough or want to foster something meaningful?"

"Both. They kinda go hand in hand."

"I suppose they do." Daphne was pensive. She didn't like how she couldn't answer Nina's question with any degree of certainty. "I'm going to decide on the way home before I call her tonight."

Nina stared at her like she'd begun shape-shifting before her eyes. "Uh, yeah. Do that."

Daphne laughed at Nina's playful sarcasm. "Cut me some slack. I'm not as experienced in relationships as you."

"Did you just call me a whore in euphemism?"

At that they broke up into pure silliness, bumping each other as they laughed, snorting or gasping until they caught their breath.

"Can I be honest without you making fun of me?" Daphne asked.

Nina gave her a stern glare. "Do you really have to ask?"

She knew she could tell Nina anything, but the verbal reassurance made her feel better. "Okay. Here it goes…Savannah is the only relationship I've ever had, not just the first woman."

"Ever? Not even in high school?"

Daphne shook her head. "I was chubby, awkward, and wore a scoliosis brace. And I also never liked boys."

"I think the latter accounted for the lack of boyfriends more than anything else," Nina said. "And so what if you've had only one relationship? Lots of people married their high school sweethearts and stay married forever."

"You really don't think it's weird that I'm thirty-eight years old and only ever had one girlfriend?"

"Not at all. But it looks like you're well on your way to your second one, if you can just relax and go with the flow."

"I'm working on it," Daphne replied.

They sat there smiling at each other so intently that her next customer had to clear his throat to get Daphne's attention.

"Oh, I'm sorry, sir," Daphne said, standing abruptly. "How can I help you?"

"I'm sorry to interrupt," the well-dressed older man said. "You two are adorable." His grin insinuated a whole backstory for them.

Daphne smiled bashfully. "Thanks. We're just friends."

Nina threw her arms around Daphne from the side of her in dramatic fashion. "Oh, darling, don't deny our secret passion. The whole world can see it."

"We're just friends," Daphne repeated as the man laughed with Nina.

"Well, you'd make a gorgeous couple if you were," he said. "Are these dessert plates part of a set?"

"I'm sure they were at some point," she replied. "But that's all I have."

"Very well. I'll take them."

After she swiped his card through her credit-card app and packaged his dishes, she turned to Nina. "That was cute."

"What was?" Nina asked, playing coy.

"You must really be bored sitting here."

Nina leaned back in the small folding chair and laced her fingers behind her head. "Actually, I'm having a great time."

"Me, too." For Daphne, there literally was no place she'd rather be.

CHAPTER THIRTEEN

Nina and Noah lugged boxes of Halloween decorations out of the garage and piled them on the lawn in front of the porch. As she separated the items into two groups, hers and Noah's, she watched for Daphne's car.

She'd texted earlier and asked if she could stop by in the afternoon to discuss an update between her and Brynne. No details, just a cryptic sense of urgency. What could it be? Daphne wasn't prone to theatrical entrances, so she must have big news.

Her musings were cut short as she noticed her son winding himself up in a knotted set of lights. "Noah, can you take those headstones and skeleton parts and arrange them over there? I'll string the lights on the bushes." She mused at how gaudy the place would look after they finished adorning it with all the spooky tchotchke Noah had begged her to buy at the hobby store. Some battles warranted an early surrender, for sanity's sake.

"I can put them anywhere I want?" he asked.

"Sure. And keep an eye out for Daphne's car."

"I thought Lacey was coming."

"She is, for dinner."

"How come you get to have all your friends over tonight, but I can't have Justin and Tyler sleep over?"

"My friends require much less supervision than yours," she replied, then muttered under her breath, "and my friends bring alcohol."

"Next weekend it's my turn to have my friends over."

"Sounds good to me. It's your father's weekend," she said with a giggle.

A little while later, Daphne's car came rolling up the driveway. Nina finished layering a bush beside the porch with orange pumpkin lights and wiped the sweat from the early October sun from her forehead. "Afternoon. Did you want to meet in person so you could casually wave an engagement-ring-clad hand around as you talk?" She acted out her suggestion as she approached the car.

But Daphne didn't laugh. She shut off the ignition and sat behind the wheel frowning.

"Oh, no." Nina knew what had happened. "There's no engagement ring, is there?"

Daphne shook her head, still frowning. "I'm two for two."

"Oh, honey. Come out of there and talk to me," Nina said, feeling empathy ooze from her pores.

Daphne trudged to the porch and plopped down on the top step. "I've been dumped again."

Joining her on the step, Nina rubbed her forearm, then squeezed her hand. "I'm sorry. It's such an awful feeling. Are you okay?"

Apparently unable to answer without an accompanying deluge of tears, Daphne shrugged and gazed up at the autumn palette of leaves on the surrounding trees.

Nina tensed at Daphne's painful silence. She hated the fact that she always felt compelled to solve everyone's problems—a byproduct of her years as a corporate executive. But in matters of the heart, sometimes there were no solutions. Just a friend who'll sit beside you while you try to hold yourself together.

"Wouldn't it be nice if we could stop viewing it as being dumped?" she finally said. "If a relationship isn't working for one or both people, somebody has to make the move. It doesn't mean something's wrong with the other person."

"Is that how you looked at it when Lacey broke up with you?"

"No. Not at first. But after a really inspirational episode of *Ted Talks*, I realized that if I changed my perspective, I might be able to change or even lessen my grief over it."

Daphne's lips formed a smirk. "When we met six months ago, you were still pretty salty about it."

"I didn't say it was an instant fix. It's just healthier for your self-worth and overall mindset if you find a positive spin to everything that sucks in life. Besides, didn't you tell me that hindsight's given you the clarity to see that your life is better now that you and Savannah aren't together anymore?"

"Yes, it is. But this really sucks. I had fun with Brynne, and I think I could've caught feelings for her with a little more time."

Nina pondered that remark. Daphne *thought* she *could've* caught feelings for Brynne? It had been over two months, but she still wasn't sure? She was clearly bummed out, but Nina began to contemplate whether it was actually over losing Brynne or that she'd experienced rejection again.

"I'm sorry, Daph." Nina playfully butted her shoulder against Daphne's. "If you need a shoulder to cry on, I have two. You pick. Cryer's choice."

"Thanks." Daphne let her head fall gently against Nina's left one.

"Did Brynne say why? How did she do it? She didn't ghost you, did she?"

"No. She was gracious enough. She came by my house and said she just wasn't feeling from me what she wanted, and that if we spent any more time together, it would only impede us from meeting a more compatible mate."

"She literally used those words? *Impede* and *compatible mate*? Ick."

Daphne laughed through her nose and bopped her head against the side of Nina's.

Nina got up and headed back to the bin of decorations. "Wanna help me get the rest of these lights up? Then I'll feed you some dinner. Lacey's coming over at six."

"I'll help you decorate, but then I'll get out of here. Nobody wants a third wheel on their romantic dinner date."

"We already have a third wheel," Nina replied with a nod in Noah's direction. "You can make it a foursome."

"If you're sure she won't mind."

"She won't, and Noah would love it. He gets a kick out of you."

"Great. I appeal to ten-year-olds," Daphne said, twisting her mouth. "Take that, Brynne."

Nina giggled despite not wanting to encourage Daphne's self-deprecation. "Besides, I want my girlfriend and best friend to get to know each other better. Tonight's the perfect opportunity."

Daphne nodded in appreciation, and all three of them completed decorating the yard with time left over to put up their feet on the veranda with two pumpkin beers and a cold glass of apple cider.

When Lacey pulled up, she seemed to take in the scene before putting on her "happy to be here" face. This did not go unnoticed by Nina.

Had she committed a faux pas not texting Lacey a heads-up about the added dinner guest?

Thankfully, the displeasure Nina had interpreted on Lacey's face had resulted from her own eagerness to please. She had a second chance with Lacey, and she wanted to make her feel like a priority, something she couldn't do while she was still married to Zack.

They'd had a lovely dinner, the four of them engaging in various conversations aimed at revealing and discovering. Nina was delighted that even Noah seemed to be having fun, despite his earlier crankiness at not having his friends over, too. Daphne's interest in his favorite phone games definitely won his favor.

Daphne was the ideal dinner guest in that she'd excused herself shortly after dessert, avoiding the possibility of awkward looks between Nina and Lacey as the clock ticked.

After Nina had gotten Noah ready for bed and settled up in his room, she and Lacey relaxed on the sofa in front of whatever TV channel had been on previously. She thought she'd detected notes of impatience buzzing around Lacey throughout the evening, but Lacey dispelled those thoughts when she slid her arm across her shoulders and drew her closer.

"Dinner was delicious, babe," she said.

"Thank you for bringing dessert." Nina patted her thigh in gratitude.

Lacey kissed her tenderly, staring into Nina's eyes with the same incendiary passion that had swept her into this new world two years earlier. She'd had a way about her then that had Nina under her spell, commanding and sensual and a little dangerous. When Lacey looked at her that way, Nina felt like the most desired woman in the world.

"The tart was delicious," Lacey said. "But you're my favorite dessert, hands down." She eased Nina down on the couch and began kissing her neck.

Nina moaned softly as Lacey's lips grazed her skin up to her ear. She became sensitive to Lacey's thigh between her legs as the heat of arousal spread throughout her. Apparently sensing the effect she was having on her, Lacey reached under Nina's shirt, pushed her bra over her breasts, and began working her nipple. Nina arched up toward Lacey as her mouth watered with desire.

"Do you think Noah's asleep?" Lacey now had both of Nina's nipples between her fingers.

"I'm sure he's not," she whispered. "We better stop."

"Can't we go up to your room and close the door?"

"I'm not comfortable with that yet. He's only known you as a friend."

Lacey sat up and straightened her shirt. "When are you going to tell him we're much more than friends?"

"Soon," Nina said as she adjusted her clothing. "I'm working on the appropriate time and place."

Lacey leaned back in apparent frustration. "I hope it's not going to take as long as it did with Zack."

The burn of passion inside Nina faded into embers of indignation. "Are you gonna leave me again if I don't adhere to your timeline?"

"That's not fair." Lacey's eyes flared with hurt.

Nina leaned forward, resting her elbows on her thighs. It was a very fair question, given that Lacey had known about Nina's delicate circumstances since day one. She wanted to lace into her about her profound lack of patience, but something in her said no, not again. Lacey had a point, too. The hardest part was over. Nina should be able to just tell Noah what was going on and be done with it. But she wasn't about to apologize to anyone for taking her time in ensuring her son's emotional well-being.

"I shouldn't have gotten snarky with you," Nina said. "I'm sorry. But it's only been three months. It's not an unreasonable request that you hang in there just a little longer until I feel my son's ready for the conversation. If you can't, just say it now."

Lacey took her hand and kissed it. "I can, and I will. I really didn't know what I was losing when I walked away from you before."

"Thanks for understanding. I love you for it."

Lacey leaned toward her and kissed her sweetly, and the heat between them reignited. The heat. It's what Nina always felt first with Lacey.

"I have an idea," Lacey said. "Why don't we go up to your room, and if Noah wakes up, I'll jump out the window."

Nina giggled. "Let me go see what he's doing."

On her way to Noah's room, she grabbed her phone and checked to make sure Daphne had gotten home okay. She smiled at the text and replied with a good night and a heart. Poor Daphne. She must've been feeling so down about Brynne, going home to her small, empty house. She would call her first thing in the morning to remind her that she wasn't alone in her grief.

When she reached Noah's room, his door was open a crack, and as was his recent habit, he'd fallen asleep with the TV and every light in his room on. She turned off the lights but left the TV on in case he woke up.

"Is he asleep?" Lacey asked in a whisper.

Nina nodded and took her by the hand. Instead of heading back upstairs, she led her to the laundry room on the other side of the house.

"What are you doing?"

"Taking you where I can devour you without interruption."

Once in the laundry room, Nina swung around, locked the door, and shoved Lacey up against the washing machine.

The issue with Noah might not have been fully settled, but it was for the moment.

❖

The next morning, Daphne woke after an unsatisfying night's sleep. She needed coffee. It was a half hour before Sophie expected her for breakfast, but she couldn't wait. She decided to head over early and help her prepare whatever she had on the menu.

After she shot Sophie a text warning her she was coming over early, she brushed her teeth and traipsed across the yard in sweats with her hair bunched up in a scrunchie.

The front door wasn't unlocked like it usually was in anticipation of her arrival. That was weird. She checked her phone to see if Sophie had read her text. She hadn't. Maybe she'd just overslept. Should she knock on the door and risk startling her out of a sound sleep? Calling would probably be better. She let the phone ring several times but no answer. *What the hell?*

Daphne walked around the back so she could look through the window in the kitchen door. Peeking inside as she turned the knob, she pushed the door open.

"Soph, it's me," she called out. "Where are you? Are you awake?" She rounded the corner near the refrigerator and found Sophie lying on the floor in the hallway. "Oh, Jesus. Sophie." She bent down and checked for a pulse. Thankfully, she felt a faint one in her neck. "Hang on, Sophie." She reached for her cell and dialed 911.

After the commotion of the EMT crew checking Sophie's vitals and securing her onto the stretcher, they loaded her into the back of the ambulance. Daphne climbed in after them without thinking, not wanting Sophie to wake up alone, wondering what was happening to her. The EMTs placed an oxygen mask on her and hooked her up to an IV line but couldn't answer any of Daphne's questions, not even if she was going to be okay.

When they arrived at the emergency room, Sophie was whisked into triage, and Daphne retreated to the waiting room. She'd called Sophie's son on the way, but he'd gone to Vermont for the weekend with his wife, so it would be a few hours before he'd get to the hospital.

She wished they would come out and tell her what was going on. She also wished she'd thought of telling them she was Sophie's daughter, so they'd keep her informed. What had happened to her? Had she regained consciousness yet? Was she wondering if she was all alone there? Daphne had been texting Nina back and forth, but told her it wasn't necessary for her to come down to the hospital and sit with her.

Later, a tap on her shoulder from Sophie's son woke Daphne from her uncomfortable position in the waiting room.

"Daphne," he said gently.

"Hi, Will." She shook herself awake and stood up.

"Mom's had a stroke," he said. "She hasn't woken up yet, and frankly, they're not certain she will. It's kind of wait-and-see at the moment."

Daphne stood frozen before him processing his words, hoping in her loopy state that she was having a bad dream.

"I can't tell you how much I appreciate you being there for her as much as you are. I don't know what would've happened if you hadn't gone to check on her."

"She's my friend, Will. We have breakfast together every Sunday."

"I know," he said with a smile. "She's mentioned it more than once." He looked around and ran a hand through his thinning gray hair. "There's no point in you hanging around here. Why don't you head home, and I'll keep you posted on how she's doing."

"Can I say good-bye to her before I go?"

"She's still unconscious."

"I know." Her face must've reflected the sadness in her heart, for he'd agreed with a pat on her arm like a kindly uncle.

When she walked into the room, she started at the pallid, frail-looking old woman in the bed. This wasn't Sophie, certainly not the

Sophie she knew. Yes, she was eighty-two, but when Daphne was in her bubbly presence, it was easy to forget she was an octogenarian.

"Hiya, Soph." She caressed Sophie's arm, already black and blue from the IV insertion. "If you didn't feel like cooking breakfast this week, you could've just said so." She wrinkled her nose as it tingled with the emotion she was holding down. "Listen. Rest up, and breakfast is on me when you're ready. I'm taking you out for an omelet at that expensive café downtown I told you about. And I don't want to hear your speech about how you can buy an entire dozen eggs for ninety-nine cents."

She smiled at Sophie's son and his wife and headed out.

Although she'd told Nina she'd grab an Uber home, Nina flatly rejected the idea and said she was on her way to pick her up. Nina pulled up at the curb, and when Daphne got in the car, the sound of Nina's voice and the touch of her hand made all the sadness she'd bottled up come spilling out.

"Oh, honey. Don't cry," Nina said. "She'll be okay. She's in really good hands now, thanks to you. You might've saved her life."

Daphne loved her for trying so hard to comfort her. But at Sophie's age, nobody could say for sure if she'd be okay. First she had to wake up from the stroke. Then the doctors would have to assess the level of damage it had done, which Daphne prayed would be minimal.

When they got home to Daphne's, Nina followed her inside with the gourmet cheese platter she'd insisted on buying after they left the hospital—that and a chilled bottle of a fruity white wine to go with it.

"You really didn't have to do all this," Daphne said, but in reality, she was thrilled that Nina wanted to stay and hang out with her.

"I know I didn't have to," Nina said. "I wanted to. I've always wanted to try this orchard wine, and what better time than on a gorgeous autumn day with a friend who could use a drink."

"I could definitely use a drink," Daphne said. "But first I should put some food in my belly." She grabbed a bowl of green grapes from her fridge, and they assembled around her small kitchen table.

"You've had quite the weekend of misadventure," Nina said as she filled their stemless glasses. "Sit down and relax."

"Yes, quite," Daphne said as she plopped down in the chair. "I wonder what the Fates have in store for an encore."

"Don't ask that," Nina said, teasing her. "They say bad things usually happen in threes."

"Fantastic. I'll just keep drinking until the weekend's over."

"That's not a bad idea, but since I can't stay and drink with you all day, I'll have to advise against it." Nina released her low, rumbling laugh that Daphne found so sexy.

"Well, as I was just reminded this morning, we have only this moment, so let's make the most of it." Daphne raised her glass toward Nina and imbibed a long, refreshing sip.

"I need to remind myself of that more often," Nina said. "My life's been all about checking my calendar for upcoming meetings, plans, and appointments for what seems like forever. I don't get to experience nearly enough impromptu afternoons like this." She nibbled a slice of Gruyère cheese. "Why do we always wait until something bad happens and forces us to slow down to reassess how we're living our lives?"

Daphne shrugged as she plucked a few grapes off the stem. "Existential crap, like 'that which does not kill us makes us stronger' yada yada."

"Some days I feel like I'm so deeply entrenched in my rut I wouldn't know how to get out if I tried."

"You? Don't tell me that," Daphne said, feeling a corner of her mouth rise in a wry smile. "If you can't claw your way out of the trenches, what hope do the rest of us mortals have?"

"I'm being serious. Yes, I'm what you'd call a successful corporate exec with a Type-A personality, and I can run circles around my male colleagues, but I feel stifled. I'm sick of the health-insurance racket. At times I feel like the president's press secretary, having to push an agenda I don't personally support, but it's what pays the big bucks."

"Is it just the company you work for or the whole industry?"

"Pretty much the entire industry. When profits are at stake, the ones we're supposed to serve are always the last ones we consider."

"Isn't that true in most of corporate America? Sky-Hi Airlines talks a good game, but when they bought out that other airline last year, they sure didn't do it for the consumer's sake."

When Nina smiled, Daphne caught what seemed like admiration twinkling in her eyes. Impossible.

"What?" Daphne asked, a little self-conscious.

"I'm witnessing your evolution."

Daphne was a little slow on the uptake. "Because I'm bitching about my job?"

"No. It's evident you've outgrown your safe position tucked away in your call-center cubby. Intellectually, you're ready to spread your wings."

"How poetic. You should become a motivational speaker." But Daphne wasn't entirely joking. Nina had a natural way with words and an attentiveness that made Daphne feel like she was one of the most important humans in the world. She made pumping her full of self-confidence, albeit temporary, seem effortless. Nobody had ever made her feel that way.

Nina clearly hadn't taken her remark to heart. "That market is flooded with upwardly mobile semi-middle-aged women with great hair and lots of overcoming-adversity stories. I'm afraid I'd have nothing new to offer."

"Well, you do have great hair."

Nina playfully puffed it with her hand. "I pay enough for it." She checked the time on her phone. "I should be heading out."

Daphne nodded, and they started clearing the table. Nina helped wrap up the remnants of the cheese platter and then grabbed the sponge off the sink.

"I got this. Don't bother," Daphne said. "I'm gonna run the dishwasher."

Nina leaned against the counter and seemed to be studying Daphne as she dried her hands on the dishtowel. Daphne found her scrutiny a bit unnerving, as though Nina was having a private conversation about her in her head. When she slipped into one of her pensive moments, Daphne found it difficult not to stare back. What was the social protocol in these cases—leave her to her thoughts or jolt her out of them? But she was fixed on Daphne, not just some random object.

"What are you staring at?" she finally asked.

"Nothing," Nina said defensively. "I'm just tired."

"Oh," Daphne said, feeling like a jerk. "I thought I had a giant spider in my hair or something."

Nina chuckled. "You're such a goof. I better get home. Lacey's watching Noah, and I have a strong suspicion he hasn't even started his homework for tomorrow."

Daphne nodded. "I have to check the website. An order may have come in this afternoon."

"They're arriving kind of regularly now, huh?"

Daphne shrugged with a modest smile. "Three or four a week, sometimes five or six."

"That's fantastic. You might be ready to start scoping out a permanent space for Trash to Treasure Antiques and Collectibles."

"I have one now at the flea market."

"That's not your own place, Daph. Don't you want to see your catchy business name on a sign above the door of a cute little shop?"

"I'd love that, but I'm not ready for it. Not yet."

"Not ready? Are you kidding?" Nina grabbed her hand and pulled her down the hall into the spare antique room. "Look at how much you've sold already. I'm not saying do it tomorrow or next week, but we should definitely start looking around for space."

Daphne loved that Nina threw that "we" in there. While she needed Nina's business savvy to help her navigate this new venture, she truly loved her emotional support and enthusiasm. Nina was the absolute best cheerleader. "Okay. I promise I'll do that."

Nina's warm smile sent a shiver through her. The orchard wine must've been tinkering with her perception.

"Thank you for everything," Daphne said and moved in for a hug.

Nina's arms enveloped her and pulled her tightly against her. "Oh, you're welcome. I'm so glad I was around today, so you didn't have to go through Sophie's emergency all alone." While she spoke in her soft, comforting tone she'd held onto Daphne. "I wish I could stay longer."

Daphne drew back to reply but kept her arms locked around Nina. "I wish you could, too."

Their eyes fastened on each other. Daphne licked her lips as Nina looked down at them and then into her eyes again. Although it would've taken a photo finish to call, Daphne would have to accept blame for the initiation as their mouths slowly drifted together. They allowed the kiss to happen seemingly of its own will. Tenderly, Nina brushed her lips across Daphne's. Their lips parted and delicately grazed each other's with tantalizingly small, warm kisses.

Daphne forgot to breathe through the surprise of the kisses and the ecstasy that swept through her. She finally exhaled lightly through her nose, fearing she might pass out. Nina slid her hands onto Daphne's face and drew her closer, her breath quickening as she kissed her harder, flicking her tongue around hers.

After a soft moan escaped from Daphne's throat, Nina suddenly set her free and avoided looking her directly in the eye.

"Well. I guess that was bound to happen once, right?" Nina said, looking painfully uptight. "Hashtag lesbian friends."

"That's what lesbian friends do?" Nina's response made Daphne even more unsure of how to interpret the situation.

"I don't know," Nina said. "I don't have that much experience with them."

"Neither do I, but with the few I've had, that's never happened before."

"Hmm." Nina ran her hand through her hair. "Then it was my bad. I'm sorry about that."

"You don't have to apologize."

"Uh, yeah, I do. I have a girlfriend. That was a major boundary breech to her and you."

Daphne's self-consciousness quickly dissolved into sadness as she watched Nina try to explain away their kiss as anything but what she'd felt it was.

That kiss burned inside her unlike anything she'd ever felt. Now she was supposed to stand here and listen to Nina dismiss it as something all lesbian friends do? Forget that.

"Don't worry about it. It was nothing." She walked out of the room and toward the front door to escort Nina out.

"Are you okay?" Nina asked at the door.

"Yes, I'm fine." But Daphne's terse reply betrayed her effort to sound convincing.

"Okay." Nina opened the door and stopped before stepping out onto the porch. "Text me the minute you get an update on Sophie."

Daphne nodded, almost dismissively. "Careful driving home."

After watching Nina's car drive away, she closed the door and leaned against it, finally exhaling all the breath she could've possibly stored in her lungs. What was happening to her? She'd naturally felt lingering awkwardness, but something else prickled her as she replayed their moment. It was an empty, bottomless feeling, like one of those scenes in old war movies when a young soldier boards the train, and his windswept sweetheart in her flowery dress chases the train down the platform sobbing until the distance swallows her.

In those movies, the girl was hopelessly in love with the soldier. But Daphne wasn't in love with Nina. Falling in love with her best friend would be the absolute dumbest thing she could do, especially when said friend already had a girlfriend.

Daphne shook her head in an effort to expel those crazy, hypersensitive thoughts. But then came an even crazier notion.

What if falling in love with Nina was the Fates' third and final act?

CHAPTER FOURTEEN

A few nights later, Nina invited Lacey out to dinner at an elegant and pricy Italian restaurant. Since she'd kissed Daphne, or Daphne kissed her, or they both kissed each other, guilt gnawed at her relentlessly. She'd tried her best to frame it in a way that made it seem less nefarious, playing all kinds of games with words to justify her actions: it was an emotional time for Daphne; she needed support; it's not like they'd had sex—not even close. She'd even tried to pass the entire blame onto Daphne, reasoning that the poor woman had lost her wits in her grief over Sophie. But that flimsy storyline lasted only a minute or two. Regardless of who initiated it, Nina was culpable for her part and had to own it.

"What do you think, babe?" Lacey said as she read the wine list.

Lacey's voice rescued her from the stark recesses of her head. "What's that?"

She looked up with a mildly impatient glare. "I asked if we should get a bottle or go with individual glasses."

"Let's have a bottle. You pick."

Lacey returned to the menu. "Merlot or a blend?"

"Surprise me," Nina said, toning down the smile she felt was a little over the top.

"You're quite agreeable tonight." Lacey leaned back and seemed to relax. "I think I'll try to use that mood to my advantage later."

Nina loved Lacey's expert flirtatious banter. She had no doubt Lacey could charm a Supreme Court justice out of her robe if that were ever her goal. Lord knows she'd had little difficulty charming a married, former straight woman out of her conservative world and her pants, on numerous occasions. Indeed, Lacey was a passionate woman with a killer allure.

"Your place or mine?" Nina said, laying on her A-game.

"I'll take you anywhere." Lacey sucked at her teeth as her bare toes started crawling up Nina's thigh. "We can run over to the ladies' room if you can't wait."

Nina's juices were flowing, but the anticipation was half the fun. "How about we just enjoy dinner but skip dessert, so we'll have more time?"

Before Lacey could answer, the server's approach cooled the table...for the moment.

"This cabernet comes highly recommended," he said, displaying the bottle against his forearm.

Lacey checked Nina with a glance, then nodded her approval. As he filled their glasses Lacey ordered a raw-oyster app, not that they needed the aid of an aphrodisiac.

After they gave him their entree order, Lacey leaned to her over the table. "Do you know what I can't wait for?"

"Does it have anything to do with me being naked?"

"In a way," Lacey said as she fingered the rim of her wineglass. "I can't wait for the day when we don't have to ask your place or mine."

Suddenly the playful air was siphoned out of the room. Nina drummed her fingers on the tablecloth as she crafted her reply. "That will be nice someday."

"Have you explained our relationship to Noah yet?"

"Not yet." Nina smiled as she omitted the usual follow-up of "but I will." That line no longer reassured Lacey as much as it irritated her.

"He and I have always gotten along well. How about we sit down together with him and tell him?"

"I think one-on-one is the better approach for this situation at first. But when we discuss moving in together, we can and should include him in the conversation."

Lacey's eyes lit up, and not because they'd caught the light of the flickering candle. That was the one thing Lacey wanted more than anything, but in her heart, Nina simply wasn't ready to make the leap. She was just beginning to settle into her new life as single mom and the head of their household.

"Let's talk timeline here," Lacey said, practical determination dousing their naughty flirtation. "I'm assuming it would be easier for everyone if I moved in with you and Noah. I could sell my place in a month or two, and we could use the proceeds for a vacation home somewhere. How does that sound?"

Nina held her wineglass in front of her mouth, hoping to conceal the terror rising in the back of her throat. What was her problem? She loved Lacey, of that she had no misgivings. But to be honest, and now would be a good time to be, she'd have to admit that the full-court-press aspect of Lacey's personality unnerved her a bit. Nina was not an all-or-nothing person. She carefully considered all the nuances of a crucial situation before committing to a decision.

"That sounds like a great idea, Lacey, but maybe we could pump the brakes a bit on the timeline."

"Nina, in a couple of months, you and I will have been together for a year and a half."

"Well, that's sort of—"

"I would think, given our history and our ages, that's enough time for you to be sure, no?"

"You've made that point before, Lacey, but don't forget that we had a solid year in between of no contact at all. I just want to relax and enjoy the fun of dating you. Do you know what I mean? Our first year together was intoxicating, life-altering, and I fell head over heels for you, but it was also full of guilt, worry, and close calls. I'm just trying to catch my breath."

After appearing to listen intently, Lacey sipped her wine and glanced around the room, seemingly searching for the appropriate response. "I get where you're coming from, Nina," she finally said.

She took Nina's hand. "I guess I'm just looking for the promise that we have a future, that this isn't just the second act of a play that'll be closing soon."

"Lacey, I love you. I have for over two years now. Our time apart didn't change that. But now that we're free to be open about our relationship, we don't have to dive into something so big, so soon. Let's let it evolve organically."

Lacey nodded. "It's been a long two years for me, but if I have to wait a while longer, I'm okay with that. At least I won't be sharing you with someone else while I wait."

Nina caught her breath at a fresh stab of guilt. Should she tell Lacey about the kiss? The one that didn't go any further and resulted only from acute emotional vulnerability and would most certainly cause way more trouble than it was worth if it was revealed?

"Thank you for understanding, baby," Nina said. "Here's to a future full of dreams coming true."

Lacey raised her glass. "And to the immediate future when we go back to your place after dinner and create more smokin' hot memories together."

"I can never have too many of those." They both leaned over the table and exchanged a sweet peck on the lips.

As she watched Lacey talk and chew and dip her bread in olive oil, Daphne's face kept swaying in and out of her mind. She had to stop this. People made mistakes, but to keep crucifying herself over it was mentally draining.

And Lacey looked so sexy. Nina was heavily drawn to her intensity and Type-A Ultra personality that allowed standard Type-A Nina to luxuriate in the experience of someone else being in charge.

She smiled as she dove into the oyster app, relieved that Lacey seemed to agree with the idea of letting things flow naturally for the time being.

After work Daphne drove to the hospital to see Sophie. It had been several days since Sophie suffered the stroke, but that morning her son had texted to let her know she'd regained consciousness and that she could visit her if she'd wanted. *If* she wanted? Apparently, he hadn't realized that, despite their more than forty-year age gap, his mother was her best friend.

As she hurried from the parking garage into the hospital, she wondered what she would see this time when she walked into her room. Her son had been brief in his text and never responded when she'd asked how she was. Maybe that was a good sign.

She entered Sophie's room with another bouquet of overpriced flowers Sophie would surely scold her for buying. She'd risk the lecture if it meant Sophie had something nice to look at while she recuperated.

"Hello," she said. Sophie's daughter-in-law, Marley, sat knitting in the corner of the room.

"Hi, Daphne, right?"

She nodded and turned to Sophie. Although she was awake and sitting up in bed, something was definitely off. "Hey, Soph. How ya feeling?"

Sophie looked at her with only a hint of recognition, her face drooping on the left side.

"She hasn't been able to speak since she woke up," Marley said. She joined Daphne at the bedside. "She also has partial paralysis on her left side."

The whole scene had shaken Daphne. "How long will she be like this?" She was speaking to Marley but couldn't take her eyes off Sophie sitting almost catatonic and appearing bewildered as she watched them converse.

"They don't know yet," Marley said.

"She's not going to be like this permanently, is she?"

Marley shrugged. "They ran another brain scan earlier but haven't told me anything. Will's on his way, so I'm hoping the doctor will have more information for him when he gets here."

Daphne sighed and tried to ignore all the scary potential outcomes bombarding her brain. Instead, she forced a smile and held the flower bouquet in front of Sophie. "These are for you. But don't yell at me for buying them at the gift shop. It was either overpay there or buy you a bunch of carnations in a bucket from the tweaked-out guy outside on the street."

"They're so pretty, aren't they, Sophie?" Marley said.

Sophie's eyes shifted back and forth between them, but her mouth didn't move.

"Can you stay for a moment?" Marley asked. "I'd like to run to the ladies' room."

"Sure." Daphne dragged a chair next to Sophie's bed and sat. "I've been dying to tell you what happened with Nina the other day. Do you remember Nina?"

Another glint of familiarity but nothing more. God, this sucks so bad, Daphne thought. Sophie was such a good, caring, generous woman. Why would something like this have to happen to her? Daphne took Sophie's hand and sheltered it between hers, rubbing the top of it, hoping the contact brought Sophie a sense of comfort.

"So Nina and I kissed on Sunday. Can you believe it? I know. I still can't believe it either. But you know what's weird? We've only spoken once in a text in the last three days, and neither of us mentioned the kiss." Daphne reclined as best she could in the uncomfortable chair and stretched her feet out onto the frame of the bed. "Maybe it's better we don't. I mean, maybe we need a few days to get over the awkwardness so we can return to friendship as usual. What do you think?"

Daphne jumped when Sophie cleared her throat. She sighed when she realized that was all it was. "Do you recognize me, Soph? Can you squeeze my hand if you understand me?"

Sophie's fingers tightened ever so slightly around Daphne's. Exhaling in relief, Daphne rested her forehead on top of Sophie's hand for a minute. "I knew you were still in there. It's gonna be okay, Soph."

When Marley returned with her husband, Daphne got up, greeted Will, and reiterated that she'd be happy to help with Sophie in any way. He thanked her and assured her that he'd keep that in mind, as that was what Sophie would want, too, if she were able to voice her opinion.

On the ride home, Daphne reflected on the swift turns her life had taken, none of which were pleasant—except for the kiss. That was pure euphoria, but even that had consequences Daphne still hadn't been able to fully assess.

One of her best friends had suffered a massive stroke, but she couldn't talk about her feelings to her other best friend because she'd kissed her a few days earlier, and now they were both clearly feeling weird about it. And she'd kissed one best friend and made things all weird, but she couldn't talk about it with her other best friend because she was currently catatonic. What a mess.

She always had her other friend, coworker, Pascale, but he was hit-or-miss in the comfort and compassion department, depending on whether he was in love and getting laid. Last she knew he was, so tomorrow she'd run her problems by him during lunch and hope for the best.

❖

After the customer with the missing suitcase sufficiently purged his rage into Daphne's ear, she ripped off her headset and placed her phone on DO NOT DISTURB ten minutes ahead of her lunch break. Slowly dragging her hands from her jawline up to her hair, she muttered, "I hate my life," loudly enough for Pascale to hear her declaration as he was approaching her cubicle.

"Come with me," he said, indicating the pizza box in his hands. "You can tell me why this week over lunch. Bacon makes everything better."

Despite the chilly temperature outside, they sat in Pascale's car eating pizza out of the box.

"What did you kiss her for?" he asked. "Everyone knows you don't shit where you eat."

Daphne grimaced at his analogy as she chewed on a slice of bacon-and-onion heaven. "I may have leaned closer first, but it was pretty darn close to a tie in who kissed who first."

"Well, that was dumb."

"You think I don't already know that? But I was really upset over Sophie at the time, so…"

"What does Nina think about it?"

"She basically laughed it off after it happened, which kind of irked me at the time, but it's been days since we talked. I hope I haven't ruined everything."

"Why don't you just call her and ask if you're cool?"

Daphne huffed. "If I do that, then I have to acknowledge what happened between us. She has a girlfriend, Pascale. Maybe she doesn't want to talk about it."

"Then don't. Can't you guys just slip back into your friendship with the unspoken agreement that you both fucked up, and it won't happen again? Women have to make things so complicated." He shook his head as he nearly devoured a whole slice in one bite.

Daphne sipped a spiked seltzer nestled in a koozie as she identified the source of his venom. "Let me guess. Natalie Ann broke up with you."

"You can sense that without even the tiniest suggestion, yet you can't figure out kissing your best friend's a bad call?"

"You must've really liked this one," Daphne said, teasingly.

"I wouldn't have kicked her out of the sack."

"Pascale, are you ready for a meaningful relationship?" Now she really laid on the teasing. "My little boy is finally growing up."

"I don't get it," he said, licking pizza grease off his fingers. "Women always want to talk. All the time, about everything. They're always asking questions, never thinking if they really want the answers. Apparently, I have to delete all my social-media accounts if I want a relationship. I mean, am I supposed to like pics only from dudes? Then she'd probably get suspicious about that, too."

"That's not a woman thing. That's a maturity thing."

"I can't help that I'm attracted to younger women, and they're all immature."

"They're not. You are. They're behaving like they should for their age. You're the one who never gives women your own age a chance. Try it sometime. You might find it refreshing."

"Oh yeah? You might find it refreshing not kissing women who have girlfriends."

Daphne bit back her initial impulse to react and chose to go high instead. "On second thought, maybe you're dating right in the appropriate age range."

They both reached for the last two slices and ate them in silence. Who knew Pascale had such depth? She actually felt sorry for him but stopped short of inviting him over to watch a Diane Keaton movie that night.

He wiped his mouth and tossed the crumpled napkin in the empty box. "Sorry I was all anti-woman. I'm a dick. But I did really like her."

Daphne nodded. "I figured." She paused then added, "Sounds like it's worth another conversation with her. You should give it a shot."

Staring straight ahead, he nodded. "Maybe I will."

"Cool." She nodded, too, then motioned toward the building. "Ready to get back in there?"

"Not at all," he said, getting out of the car.

"Great. Me either," she replied, and they slowly marched into the lobby as if to the beat of a funeral dirge only they could hear.

CHAPTER FIFTEEN

It had been a week since the now-infamous kiss, and Nina was finally feeling better about how she'd chosen to handle it: a hearty regime of silent, torturous penitence. Things were going well with Lacey, and Noah was enjoying having her around again, but she was missing her daily communications with Daphne. Early on, they'd fallen into a routine of pithy texts and funny memes and lunchtime FaceTime that Nina hadn't realized had become a welcome respite from the mental rigors of her day as an executive and mom. It didn't make sense to allow that one little glitch between them to taint an otherwise healthy friendship.

Sitting in front of her work laptop in her home office, she kept glancing at her phone in anticipation of Daphne's call. She'd texted her that morning, telling her to call when she was on her lunch break. Nina wanted to hear her voice and tone, not just pass typed words between them.

"Hey, stranger," Nina said when the call finally came in. "How's it going? Sophie home yet?"

"She's in a rehab facility trying to learn how to talk again." Daphne's voice sounded laden with sadness.

"What? Why didn't you tell me that?" Her skin prickled with the feeling of being slighted.

"I don't know," Daphne said after a lengthy pause. "I wasn't sure what to do. Things have felt a little weird since…you know."

Nina wavered between agreeing with her and feeling furious that she hadn't shared such a critical update with her. "Can we just file that in the past now? It happened. And yes, it was awkward and surprising, but it really wasn't that big of a deal in the grand scheme of things."

"Valid. I hated not talking to you about what's happening with Sophie. Whatever's going on, you always manage to make me feel better about it."

"Yeah, well, I can do that only if you let me know what's going on."

Daphne sighed. "I'm glad we straightened this out, Nina. I've missed you."

"I've missed you, too." Nina paused, noticing that they both sounded a little like long-distance lovers yearning for a reunion. Or was that just her imagination? Whatever. "Listen. I texted because I heard about a small commercial space available in North Haven. Wanna take a look at it with me?"

"Uh, when did you have in mind?"

"Whatever day or night works for you, but it should be this week. It's in a great location and probably won't be available long."

After a long silence, Daphne said, "I don't know if I'm ready for that step."

"How come? Because of Sophie?"

"No. Because of me. I'm feeling sort of overwhelmed."

"With what?"

"The website traffic. I've been so busy filling all the orders and watching my inventory level. I don't even know how I'm getting so many all of a sudden."

"I've been promoting your site for you, in antique-collector forums on social media. I'm so glad it's working."

"It sure is."

"Daph, is something wrong, other than Sophie? You don't seem like yourself."

A pit of dead silence, then finally, "To be honest, I'm feeling too much like my old self, neurotic and insecure."

"Okay, well, I certainly don't want you to feel that way, especially about something that's supposed to make you happy. We can pass on the retail space for now. There's no rush."

"Are you horribly disappointed in me?"

"What? No. Why would I be?"

"C'mon, Nina. You're this hugely successful businesswoman who's practically set me up in my own business with everything from the website, to the promotion of it, and now to finding me retail-space. And here I am doing everything I can to sabotage it. Classic Daphne being Daphne."

"Whoa. What's with this defeatist attitude? That's not classic you, not the you I know."

"My 'fake it till you make it' strategy must be failing."

"You need to come over for dinner tonight so I can slap some sense into you. And don't tell me you have plans."

Daphne chuckled. "I could tell you I do, but you wouldn't believe me. What time and what should I bring?"

"Seven o'clock. Just bring yourself. Lacey's marinating shrimp and chicken for a taco bar."

"What's the alcohol you put in margaritas?"

"Tequila?"

"I'll bring that."

"Perfect." Nina ended the call, and despite securing Daphne as a dinner guest that night, she felt a lingering sadness at the way she'd sounded on the phone. Had that kiss taken them beyond the point of no return? Maybe it was a mistake calling her. Whatever. If it was, she'd be able to assess how big of one it was later that night.

After Nina ended the call, Daphne's appetite deserted her. She returned to the break room only to clean up and toss out the soggy salad she'd left unattended. For once, a conversation with Nina hadn't lifted her spirits. Waiting each day for a positive word on Sophie was wearing her down. She looked forward to taking the edge off later with a margarita or two. But something else was bugging her—the way Nina just casually threw in at the end of the call that Lacey was joining them.

"Why'd you rush out of the break room? Lunch wasn't even over yet," Pascale said from the edge of her cubicle.

She pulled off her headset. "I don't know what's wrong with me. Everything's terrible."

"What's going on? Have you worked it out with Nina yet?"

Daphne nodded. "She insisted I come for dinner tonight for tacos."

"If that doesn't solve everything, you may need professional help."

"Her girlfriend's going to be there, too."

"So what? Doesn't she have a kid, too?"

"The one has nothing to do with the other."

He folded his arms across his chest. "From my experience, a kid is a way bigger cock block than the friend that hangs around. At least you can get rid of her."

"Pascale, what in the hell are you saying? I'm the friend, not Lacey. If there was a cock-block issue, it's me. I'm the cock block."

"Oh. Well, if you weren't hoping to get laid, then chill out. It doesn't matter who's there."

Daphne dropped her forehead into her palm, then looked up at him. "Then you wonder why I say I can only talk to my female friends about adult things. You're a complete ass."

"I just like to keep things simple, Daph. You're constantly with Nina…"

"Not constantly."

"You made out."

"Kissed, not made out."

"And now you're jealous the girlfriend's coming to dinner because you're catching feelings for her."

"Not catching—" Daphne narrowed her eyes at him. "What do you mean, catching feelings? I don't have feelings for her. I just want to spend some quality time with my friend without having to watch her Alpha female girlfriend make googly eyes at her the whole time."

He stared at her for a moment. "Why do women always do that?"

"Do what?"

"You try to have an honest conversation with them, and all the while they're denying their feelings until months later, when they're finally hit over the head with them like a meteor. Life would be so much easier if you could just acknowledge what others see from the start."

Daphne jumped up from her chair. "First of all, your sweeping generalizations about women are offensive." She pushed him out of her cubicle and down the hall toward his. "Second, if I had anything like that to admit to you, I would, because everyone knows men listen only about thirty percent of the time you're actually talking to them anyway." She then shoved him down into his office chair. "Third, I'll thank you to spend your afternoon coffee break anywhere but in my cubicle."

As she marched back to her desk, she laughed when she heard Pascale apologizing from the edge of his cubicle. "I forgive you, but you're still banished," she replied over her shoulder.

Although she loved him, he irked her with his simplistic philosophies and observations about life. If anyone would know she was catching feelings for Nina, it would be Daphne. Nina was extremely attractive and compassionate. Anyone could have a weak moment around her. It didn't mean they were falling in love.

After work Daphne stopped in at the rehab facility to visit Sophie. She walked in as Sophie was eating dinner with the help of an occupational therapist.

"Hi, Sophie," she said, then looked at the therapist. "Should I come back?"

"No, no," he said. "She's almost done. I'm Scott, her OT." He extended his hand. "Besides, I'm sure she'd like the company. She had lots of therapy today, didn't you, Soph?"

Sophie looked at him and nodded. She then looked at Daphne with a glint of recognition in her eyes.

Daphne dragged a chair next to her bed. "Do you remember who I am? I'm Daphne, your neighbor and bestie."

"Daphne," Sophie muttered. "Neighbor."

"Oh, my God." Daphne looked at the therapist. "She's talking. That's awesome."

"Only single words, but it's a big step."

"She's responding to therapy then?"

He nodded with just enough optimism to encourage her. "She has physical therapy for the partial paralysis, speech therapy, and occupational therapy with yours truly." He pointed to himself. "She's still got fight in her, don't you, Big Mama?"

Daphne thought she detected the side of Sophie's mouth rise in a smile.

"She likes it when I call her that," he said.

Daphne clutched her wrists gently. "You absolutely are a fighter, Soph. And when you get home, we're going to toast to your speedy recovery, okay?"

Sophie looked as though she was formulating something to say, but all she managed was a barely perceptible nod. Daphne didn't want her disappointment to show, so she smiled and shook her hand. "And it's a good thing you're a lefty, so your pouring hand wasn't affected."

The therapist got up and grabbed Sophie's dinner tray. "She's all set with therapy for the day, so feel free to sit and chat with her."

Daphne shook his hand. "Thank you for taking good care of her. I can't wait till she's ready to go home."

He looked as though he was about to say something, but smiled and patted Sophie's shoulder. "You're working really hard at getting better. I'm proud of your effort."

Daphne sighed when he walked out. That was not the response she'd hoped for. She needed to be realistic, given that Sophie was in her early eighties and a full recovery from a stroke was a lot to expect. But what the hell. If any elderly person was capable of a full recovery, it was that old bird sitting next to her.

"So listen, Soph. Since you're not too talkative these days, you won't mind listening to me for bit, will you?"

"Daphne. My neighbor," Sophie said out of nowhere.

"Yes, that's me. I'm your BFF, too. Don't forget that. Can you say BFF?"

Slowly Sophie repeated the initials, and Daphne clapped.

"You're going to be back to your old self, dragging me about my lifestyle choices in no time. I can tell." She slipped her hand under Sophie's. "Speaking of which, listen to this. You know my coworker, Pascale? Do you know what he had the nerve to say to me?"

Daphne grabbed a napkin and blotted the corner of Sophie's mouth still experiencing paralysis.

"He accused me of having feelings for Nina. Remember Nina, my friend who likes antiques, too? He said that I'm jealous that Nina's girlfriend, Lacey, is going to be at her house tonight when I go over there for tacos. That isn't even remotely true. What do you think?"

Sophie nodded.

Daphne was confused. "What's that? You're nodding. Who are you agreeing with, Pascale or me?"

Sophie looked like she was trying to formulate a "P" sound with her lips.

"Pascale? You're agreeing with him? He's an idiot. He doesn't know what he's talking about." She sat back in her chair and folded her arms. "Is that what you're doing, agreeing with Pascale that I have feelings for Nina?"

Sophie nodded once.

"I can't believe this. You suffered a stroke and can barely communicate your basic needs, but somehow you've managed to call me out on my alleged feelings for Nina—which, by the way, I do not have."

Sophie's eyes flickered with a smile, although she appeared to be growing weary, periodically closing them for several seconds.

"I'm not denying that I love Nina. Of course I do, but only as a friend. I love you, too, as a friend, but I wouldn't get all bent out of shape if you got a boyfriend or something."

"Willie," Sophie whispered.

Daphne turned around, expecting to see Sophie's son, Will, walking into the room, but nobody was there. "You want your son? Has he been to see you recently?"

Sophie shook her head and repeated, "Willie."

Daphne felt bad, wondering if her son had basically dumped her here from the hospital and hadn't bothered with her. "I'm sure he'll be here to visit you soon." She thought about texting the jerk and letting him know his mother was asking for him but didn't.

A nurse walked in pushing a computer cart. "Good evening, Sophie. Can I get a blood-pressure check?"

"Hello," Daphne said. "Do you know if her son has been to visit her?"

"Um, I'm not sure if it was earlier today or yesterday. She gets a visit every day, whether it's her son or daughter-in-law."

"Oh. Okay." Daphne felt quietly ashamed for assuming the worst about her son, especially since in Sophie's condition, she might not always be aware of all of the visitors coming and going.

"So anyway, I was telling you about Pascale accusing me of being in love with Nina…"

"Willie," Sophie repeated, and the expression in her eyes when she said it this time suggested she wasn't calling for her son.

The look nearly brought Daphne to tears. "Are you talking about your husband, Willie?"

When Sophie raised her hand to her heart, Daphne panicked. *Oh, my God. Does she think her husband is still alive and she's calling for him, or is she just missing him?* A third option occurred to her, and she whipped her head around to see if she'd glimpse the ghost of Mr. Gorski floating into the room.

She was asking for her husband. How incredibly, romantically gut-wrenching.

She remembered hearing that you're not supposed to keep reminding Alzheimer's patients that their loved ones are dead. Did that apply to stroke victims, too?

She decided to play it safe, and instead of saying anything, she just squeezed Sophie's hand and nodded.

As it neared the time of Daphne's arrival, Nina wished she'd picked a night when Lacey wasn't coming over. She'd invited her on the spur of the moment because Daphne had sounded so down, but now, as Lacey hugged her and kissed her neck from behind while she scooped sour cream into a bowl, she would've liked time alone with Daphne to chat and make sure she was truly okay.

"Your guacamole is delicious, babe," Lacey said after sticking her pinkie finger in the dish and licking it.

Nina smiled. "Thanks. Can you get the bean-and-feta dip out from the fridge? I'm not sure that even goes with Mexican, but it's so tasty and easy to make."

"It's perfect, like you." Lacey ran ice through the blender in preparation for the first batch of margaritas. "What time is Daphne coming?"

"Any minute," Nina replied as she sliced limes.

"How about we have a test run?" Lacey poured the drinks into margarita glasses and handed one to Nina. "Let me know how I did."

Nina sipped the drink and savored the pinch of tequila as it slid down her throat. "Mmm. You did good."

"Daphne's here," Noah called out from the living room.

"Thanks, honey," Nina replied. "Could you get the door for her?"

Daphne walked into the kitchen, greeted them, and handed Nina a bottle of Cuervo Gold. "I wasn't sure what brand to choose, so the guy at the package store said this is good in margaritas."

"Thank you." Nina took the bottle and placed it in on the counter.

"What flavor do you prefer, Daphne? Regular or mango?" Lacey held the empty glass. "I have regular here."

"Since I've never had any kind of margarita before, I'll go with whatever you recommend."

Nina looked at Lacey, then at Daphne. "Have you ever had tequila?"

"Nope." Daphne pointed both thumbs at herself. "A verified tequila virgin right here."

"This should be fun," Lacey muttered and smirked as she poured the drink.

"What does that mean?" Daphne said.

"She's just kidding." Nina shot Lacey a glare. "But sometimes tequila affects people in different ways. How do you usually do with vodka?"

"I usually drink wine or beer, but to answer your question, the last time I had vodka was when I crashed my ex's wedding reception."

"Now that's a fun way to spend a Friday night," Lacey said as she handed Daphne her drink.

Was it Nina's imagination, or had she detected a small note of sarcasm in Lacey's tone?

"Bottoms up," Daphne said. The second she took a sip, her eyes and mouth puckered in unison.

"It grows on you," Nina said with a reassuring squeeze of her arm. "Especially by the second one."

"I bet you'll like the mango," Lacey said. "If you're still standing after this one."

"She'll do just fine." Nina admonished with her eyes again, then led Daphne to the dining-room table. "Here. Have some chips and dip with that."

Noah joined them at the table and started riffling through the chip bowls.

"Oh," Nina said, playful but firm. "Are those hands clean? And secondly, put the chips on your plate. We're trying to have a civilized taco night here."

"Yes. I washed my hands," he said. "When are we eating? I'm starving."

"Have some salsa. There's bean dip, too. The meat will be cooked in no time."

"Can I help with anything?" Daphne licked her lips. "Hmm. Salty."

"My mom gets salty sometimes, too."

"Ah-ha-ha. I get it," Daphne said too loudly for the room, and when she clapped him on the back, he smiled brightly.

"Very funny." Nina smirked at Noah, then smiled at Daphne for encouraging him.

"So much for a civilized taco night," Lacey mumbled, but Nina caught the remark.

"We're using actual silverware and dishes. That's about as classy as taco night gets around here." Nina directed the comment solely at Lacey.

She pulled out a chair for Daphne to join Noah at the table as Lacey prepared the taco meats on a stovetop grill. Remorseful for feeling temperamental toward Lacey, she pressed herself against her back and whispered, "Can I help you with anything?"

Lacey whispered over her shoulder, "Not here in front of everyone."

She exhaled. Apparently, Lacey hadn't even noticed. Nina gave her a playful pat on her behind and joined the others at the table.

While Noah breathlessly regaled them with his latest adventures at school, Nina thought she'd noticed Daphne stealing glances in Lacey's direction. At one point, Daphne caught Nina catching her, so she forced her concentration back to the table conversation.

"I'm so proud of Noah," Nina said. "It's only been a couple of months, and already he's made some new friends and joined the STEM club."

"That's cool," Daphne said. "Girls are in that club, too?"

Noah rolled his eyes. "More girls than boys are in it. So annoying."

"Excellent," Nina said. "Boys and girls should be working together as equals in all settings."

"Sports, too?" Daphne asked.

"Of course," Nina said. "I heard that our town's high school football team has a female wide receiver. I'm planning to take Noah to a game some Friday night."

"That sounds like a lot of fun," Lacey said as she carried a plate of grilled chicken and shrimp to the table. "But now we eat." She grabbed the pitcher of mango margaritas from the fridge and refilled their glasses.

Nina smiled a thank-you to Lacey and again thought she'd caught Daphne flashing a little judgmental side-eye in Lacey's direction. She had to be misinterpreting it. Daphne hadn't a catty bone in her body and certainly didn't judge anyone unless a person gave her just cause. And even then she probably wouldn't have expressed herself.

Maybe it was just Lacey. She often assumed control in a way that made others sit back and yield to her confidence. Once Nina had grown used to it, she looked forward to the occasional reprieve.

After they'd ravaged their Mexican feast, leaving no tortilla chip behind, Nina brought out a tray of desserts. "Ladies and gentleman, I present desserts de los Noah, a new recipe inspired by the one and only." She nodded toward Noah, and after the proper amount of oohs and ahhs, they dug into an amalgamation of flan, ice cream, and Noah's favorite, churros.

As her eyes rounded the table to see who was ready for coffee, she noticed Daphne nodding off. Noah giggled when he noticed it, too.

Lacey shook her head, clearly amused. "The mango ones. They'll get ya every time."

"Daphne, you okay?" Nina gently shook her arm. "Wanna go lie down for a bit?"

Daphne's eyes sprang open. "No, no. I'm fine. I should get going." When she got up from the table, she tilted to the side and grabbed the back of her chair.

"Mom, she can't drive home," Noah said loudly.

"I know, honey. Why don't you go up and get ready for bed now."

"I'm not done with my dessert."

"Take it into the family room then," she growled and gently pulled him up by his shirt.

It felt a bit like herding cats as Nina tried to corral an unsteady Daphne who was already digging in her pants for her car keys, as well as encouraging Noah, who was clearly enjoying the scene, to go in the other room.

When he finally obeyed, she turned to find Daphne heading toward the front door. She looked at Lacey and snarled, "Why aren't you helping with any of this?"

"I've had a few too many myself," Lacey replied, not looking so good. "And I think dessert sent me over the edge." She pushed back from the table and sprinted to the bathroom.

"For fuck's sake," she whispered to herself and intercepted Daphne as she reached for the door handle. "Daph, give me your keys. You cannot drive home like this."

Her response slurred out. "But I have to go to work tomorrow."

"I'll make sure you're awake early enough to get to work on time."

"Okay." Daphne headed toward the couch.

"Not there." Nina grabbed her and herded her toward the stairs. "I have a guest room with a comfortable bed."

Daphne stopped when they reached the bottom step. "Up there?" She rested her weight against Nina as she squinted toward the top of the staircase.

"Yes. We can do it," Nina said, wanting to check on Lacey but afraid Daphne would escape if left unattended. She held onto to her as they ascended the stairs.

She dropped Daphne off at the bed in the guest room, then went to get her a T-shirt to sleep in. When she returned a moment later, Daphne had keeled over on the pillow. She smiled at the partial grin still on Daphne's face. She probably should've stopped her after her second margarita, but she seemed to be having such a good time, Nina wanted her to let loose. Then they just lost count.

"Daphne." She gently shook her shoulder. "Do you want to change out of your clothes? I have a T-shirt for you."

Daphne nodded and bolted upright, her eyes slits. "Yes, yes. I need a T-shirt." She tried to remove her shirt over her head but got stuck inside it.

"Let me help you." Nina raised Daphne's arms over her head and pulled the shirt off in one motion. "Want to leave your bra on?"

"No," Daphne said, her phrases sliding out like one long word. "It's like a straightjacket. I want it off." Her arms flailed as she attempted to unclasp her bra from behind.

"Okay. Here. Stand up." Nina lifted her to her feet, put the night shirt over her head, and reached around to unclasp the bra. She then helped Daphne fully into the T-shirt, at which time Daphne threw her arms around Nina's neck.

She pressed her lips to Nina's ear, dampening it with her warm breath. "Thank you so much for helping me, Nina. Bras are the worst."

"That they are." Nina tried not to laugh, but Daphne was an adorable drunk. She was still clinging to Nina, her arms wound around her neck like a boa constrictor and squeezing her almost as tight. "Are you ready to go to sleep now?"

"Nina?" Still clinging.

"Yes?" Still holding.

Daphne looked at her, clearly struggling to focus. "Nina? You're such an amazing friend. I love you so much."

Now Nina couldn't help but giggle. "I love you, too, Daph. How about we go to sleep now? It's getting late." She tried to lower her onto the bed, but Daphne resisted.

She squeezed her tighter and whispered, "I'm in love with you, Nina," in her ear.

Nina wasn't laughing anymore. She nudged Daphne back enough to study her. "What did you say?"

"I said I love you," Daphne replied, her voice louder.

"No. That's not what you just said."

"God, I'm so tired." She went limp in Nina's arms.

"Daphne, what did you…"

It was no use. Nina laid her down and dragged the covers over her, lingering in the room to make sure she was falling into a deep-enough sleep.

Nina was not imagining things. She'd heard Daphne say she was *in love* with her, not just that she loved her. They were definitely not the same thing. Maybe she was just babbling because she was so drunk. But what was that expression? Drunk words were sober thoughts?

Whatever the truth was, she certainly wouldn't get it out of Daphne that night, nor was she sure she even wanted to. Anyway she had another disaster to attend to downstairs.

She walked into the kitchen expecting to find Lacey facedown at the kitchen table but instead found her loading the dishwasher.

"Only a woman with her shit as together as yours could rally from a Mexican and tequila puke fest enough to finish cleaning up."

Lacey shrugged casually. "I feel much better now. Did you get Mary Queen of Shots off to bed okay?"

Nina laughed lightly, still a little stirred up from Daphne's confession. "Yeah, finally. I don't think I've been a very responsible hostess, letting a newbie drink three or more margaritas on her maiden voyage."

"She's a big girl," Lacey said. "She loosened up and was having fun. Besides, we didn't let her drive anywhere."

"She'll be hurting in the morning."

"The price we pay for our indulgences." Lacey smoothed out the dishtowel over the rack and turned to Nina. "Guess I'll be heading out now."

Nina studied her, appreciating how much Lacey seemed to love her. She'd held on as long as her sanity would've allowed when they'd first fallen in love, and now she was back going after what she wanted. And what she wanted was Nina. The validation was hard to resist. "Would you like to stay over? I'd feel better if you didn't drive home either."

"I'm fine now. Really."

"Daphne's given us the perfect opportunity to introduce Noah to the idea of sleepovers."

Lacey's eyes shone with delight as she swept Nina up in her arms. "I'd love to." She kissed her sweetly on the lips. "And remind me to thank your friend in the morning for being such a lightweight."

They walked upstairs together, and after getting ready for bed, Nina peeked in on Daphne, dying to know if her drunk words were indeed sober thoughts.

CHAPTER SIXTEEN

As they walked down the hall to Sophie's room, Daphne was glad Nina had wanted to come with her. She'd hoped and believed that Sophie would be finishing her recuperation at home, but that wasn't the case. As they approached the room, she sighed.

"Are you okay?" Nina said.

Daphne nodded. "It's just that she's been here for nearly two months. It's almost Christmas."

"You mentioned she's been slowly but steadily improving. Maybe she'll be going home soon, if not in time for Christmas."

"I hope so." Daphne shrugged, struggling to convince herself it was possible.

"She's going to love the present you got her." Nina pointed to the Christmas gift bag that contained a blown-up photo of Sophie and her late husband at Christmas when they were first married.

"Thanks," Daphne said.

They went in, and Sophie looked up with a half-smile of recognition. She'd regained some use of her affected side but was still partially paralyzed.

"I brought you a present, Soph." Daphne bent and gave her a kiss.

"Present? For me?" she said slowly.

"Yes. An early Christmas present. Hope you don't mind. I couldn't wait to give it to you." Daphne placed the bag in her lap and helped her remove the gorgeous antique frame containing the photo.

"William. My Willie." She hugged the frame to her chest with one arm. She then looked up with glassy eyes. "Thank you."

Daphne noticed, through her own cloudy eyes, that Nina's were pooling as well.

"That's a beautiful photo of you and your husband," Nina said.

Sophie smiled and gently stroked the glass over his face.

Sophie's son walked into the room with a tray of two coffees from a local coffee shop. "Hi, Daph. I wish I'd known you were coming." He indicated the coffee as he handed his mother hers.

"No problem," she replied. "We can't stay long. We have some antiquing to do today."

"Actually, I'm glad you're here. Can I talk to you privately for a second?"

"Sure." She followed him into the hall. "Is everything okay?"

He nodded. "As okay as it's ever going to be, I'm afraid. Even though she's made great progress, the doctors and therapists don't believe she'll improve much more, certainly not to her pre-stroke ability."

"How can they be so sure? At first they weren't even sure if she'd wake up, but now look at her."

"I know, but whatever additional progress she may make won't be enough for her to be on her own again. I'm putting her house on the market, and I just wanted to let you know before you see the sign on her lawn."

The news hit Daphne like a kid learning that Santa Claus was really just her parents. She knew Will was expecting a response of some kind, but she couldn't find words to convey her feelings.

"I'm sure it's a shock," he said. "Especially since you guys have been neighbors for so long. It's just time. She's going to be eighty-three soon, and my wife and I don't feel comfortable with the idea of her living alone again."

"Is she moving in with you?"

Daphne realized how rude the question sounded the minute it came out, not that his face wasn't a clear-enough indication.

"She's going to a facility that specializes in stroke aftercare."

"Oh. Oh, that's awesome." Daphne stammered, trying to correct herself. "I mean not that it's awesome she's going to a home, but…"

"I know what you mean. It's not that much farther than this place, so I hope you'll still feel free to visit her."

"Yes, of course, I'll visit. If you or she needs any help with anything in the meantime, don't hesitate to ask."

"Thanks. I'll take her house keys back if you have them."

"Oh, yeah. They're in the car. I'll run and get them."

"No. That's okay. I'll get them next time I go over to the house." He paused. "She'd set aside a couple of antique pieces she wanted you to have some day, so…"

"That's so sweet." Daphne smiled against her overwhelming urge to burst into tears in front of him. "My friend and I have to get going now."

She walked back into the room and saw Nina sitting beside Sophie's bed reading a magazine article to her. When she looked up, the touching scene and her beautiful eyes and warm smile didn't help her effort to maintain her composure in front of everyone.

"We should go now."

"Already?" Nina got up with a look of concern. "Anything wrong?"

Daphne shook her head and gave Sophie a hug and kiss good-bye. Something about the situation made it impossible for her to sit and talk and smile with Sophie, who knew nothing about her fate.

Out in the parking lot, Nina waited to unlock the car. "What happened in there?"

"Her son is moving her to a convalescent home. Permanently."

"Oh, no," Nina said and unlocked the doors. "I'm so sorry."

"I understand it's what's best for her, but it just sucks," Daphne said as she got in the car. "I mean one minute she's living her best old-lady life, and the next, bam! She gets a massive stroke and barely knows her own name. Ugh. I hate life sometimes."

Her heart aching for Daphne, Nina gave her thigh a comforting squeeze. What else could she do for her? She knew Daphne cherished their friendship, but in many ways, Sophie was like her family, too. "Do you still feel like antiquing today?"

Daphne nodded. "If I don't, I'll just go home and be miserable."

"Good," Nina said as she started the car. "I'd much rather you be miserable with me than alone. Dinner's on me today."

"You don't have to do that. I'm not even hungry."

"Well, you're not *not* going to eat on my watch." Nina grabbed her hand and weaved her fingers between Daphne's. She actually wanted to scoop her up and pull her into the tightest embrace ever, but that usually resulted in people who were teetering on the edge of a breakdown having one then and there. Instead, she drove toward their first destination.

They'd fallen into a silence as they drove, until Daphne said, "Can you show me that retail space you mentioned?"

"Which one?" Nina said, playfully. "I've mentioned about a half dozen over the last few months."

"Whatever one's still available." Daphne looked at her with determination.

"I'll text my realtor friend to see if that last one is still available." Nina couldn't contain her smile. "This one's a tiny space, but it's cute, the location's great, and the rent is reasonable."

"I'm not sure what reasonable is to someone with no money, but okay. Let's go check it out."

It didn't take long for Nina's friend Rikki, a slender statue of a woman in a sharp suit, to arrive with folders, iPad, and keys.

"Nina's told me all about your business plan. I'm so excited you're finally ready to go. You have eight hundred square feet of floor space and another two-fifty in inventory storage. I'm assuming only you will be working in the space?"

Daphne nodded.

"Good." Rikki waved her arm as she guided them around the room. "As you can see, there's no break room unless you want to plop a table in the middle of your storeroom. But then that eats up space for your merchandise. Given that you're a collector, I'll assume you'll need all the space available."

"The location is fantastic," Nina said. "But this strip mall has a few empty store fronts. Why is that?"

"This area is ripe for a turn-around," Rikki said. "The stores that closed weren't strong anchors anymore. I mean, Radio Shack?"

"True," Nina said.

"My agency just leased a space in here to a vegan café," Rikki said. "That's going to do very well at this location. You add a classy, quaint, antique shop, and it's only going to drive the popularity of all the properties up." She looked at Daphne expectantly.

Nina nudged her in the back. "Do you have any questions?"

"Me? Uh, no," Daphne said. "Not now. I think you've covered everything for the moment."

Rikki looked at her watch. "Dang it. I'm late picking up my kids."

"Give me the lock," Nina said. "I'll take care of it. I think Daphne would like to take a look around again."

"You don't mind?" Rikki said.

"No problem at all."

As soon as Rikki closed the door behind her, Nina had a strange sensation—almost like she was a kid who'd sneaked off to do something she'd been specifically instructed not to. Maybe it was because she wasn't often alone with Daphne. Her mind flashed to the last time they were alone in her guest room.

She'd meant to broach the subject of Daphne's drunken statement the next day after she'd sobered up, but by then the shock of the moment had passed, and it seemed more convenient to let it go than to slice it open for examination.

"Let me take another look at that storeroom," Daphne said, and Nina followed her lead.

❖

Daphne stood in the back and stared at the empty, dusty shelving, imagining what it would feel like if the place were hers.

How amazing would it be to walk into Trash to Treasure Antiques and Collectibles each morning instead of that atrocious call-center cubicle? But that would mean she was the boss...of everything... responsible for everything. She so wanted it to be real, but the enormity of the change left her weak in the knees.

"I'd give anything to see what you're envisioning," Nina said.

"Huh?"

"You look so intense, like you're watching the future play out in a movie preview."

"I wish I could get even a peek at how the future plays out. The whole thing is so surreal."

Nina seemed to be creating her own narrative. "I'll tell you what I see: a woman who's finally come into her own...a businesswoman, an antique expert, a person who's happier than she's ever been because she's independent and in control of her career and her life."

Daphne leaned close as though trying to see the same picture. "Who is it?"

Nina laughed and gave her playful shove. "You, dummy. Well, future you."

"Maybe stuff me in a time machine and set the dial for a hundred years from now."

"I'm not even going to entertain those kinds of comments anymore, Daph. Self-deprecation is endearing to an extent, but you better mix that with some self-confidence, or your ass will be permanently enshrined in a customer-service chair at Sky-Hi Airlines. Is that what you want?"

"That is the complete opposite of what I want. But I'm terrified of quitting my job and then failing. Don't most new businesses fail?"

"Statistically, that's what they say," Nina said. "But are you just a statistic?"

"No," Daphne said meekly.

"I can't hear you," Nina said.

"No," she said louder.

"No what?"

"No, I'm not a statistic. I'm gonna do it. As soon as I'm ready, which will be soon."

Nina smiled. "I know you'll do it when you're ready. And I'll be the first one in line cheering you on." She then pulled Daphne in for a hug.

Daphne held on, resting her cheek on Nina's shoulder. Out of nowhere, a wave of emotion crashed over her, saturating her with happiness for the store, sadness for Sophie, and a burgeoning love for Nina.

Nina gently pushed her back. "Hey." She studied her eyes. "Now why are you crying?"

Daphne laughed through her tears, feeling like a fool. "I don't know. I'm just a hot mess. I guess I'm feeling overwhelmed again."

Nina dried Daphne's tears with her sleeve. "It's okay to cry if you need to. You've experienced a lot of fluctuation lately. But things will work out, Daph. Whatever happens, you're strong enough to deal with it. And I'm here for you in any way you need me to." She held Daphne's face up in her hands. "You know that, right?"

Daphne closed the small space between them, coming in so hot with a kiss, their teeth banged together. It was a minor glitch that they got over instantly as Daphne kissed her passionately and with an uncharacteristic assertiveness that likely surprised Nina as much as it did her. It roared through Daphne, igniting her desire like a flash. She should've contained it the moment she felt herself giving in to the desire.

As though sensing her faltering, Nina grabbed hold of her head and held it as her tongue began exploring Daphne's mouth. What was happening? A volcanic-like eruption of emotion and passion in Nina, too?

Nina wrapped her hands around Daphne's ass and pushed herself closer. They were both breathing heavily, and Daphne tingled as her underwear grew wetter by the kiss. Nina pushed her against the counter and gripped her breasts, running her thumbs over her nipples straining through her shirt and bra.

Daphne whimpered as Nina rubbed her thigh between Daphne's legs. Still, their mouths stayed on each other, licking and sucking as though they contained the last bit of pulp from a succulent fruit.

❖

Forbidden fruit, Nina thought, as their dry-humping almost brought her to orgasm. Once again she was succumbing to the overpowering sensuality of another woman, but this time it was different. With Lacey, it had felt wrong and dirty as she'd explored her new, startling desires while still married to Zack. This time, beyond her sexual hunger for Daphne, Nina felt a connection to her soul. Her heart seemed to desire Daphne's as much as her body craved hers. She was consumed.

Daphne grasped fistfuls of Nina's hair and jerked her head back. "I'm so in love with you, Nina," she whispered.

As she was about to confess her love for her, too, Daphne ran her tongue down her neck, and she shivered from Daphne's hot breath on her skin. She reached for Daphne's hand, about to shove it inside her pants.

"Hello?" The realtor called out as she came back inside.

Nina and Daphne launched back from each other and attempted to straighten out their hair and clothing as they rushed out of the back room.

"Oh. You're still here," Rikki said, her gaze darting between them.

"Yeah, uh-huh," Nina said. "Daphne wanted to see what kind of inventory storage the space has."

"Oh?"

"I think I want to lease it," Daphne said.

Nina and the realtor whipped their heads toward her in unison.

"You do?" Nina said.

"Fantastic," the realtor said before Daphne could respond. "I'll call you tomorrow, and we can go over the application and all the details. I have to pick up my kids now. I just forgot this." She held up her iPad case. Then she ushered them out along with her and locked up.

Nina started her car, and as she adjusted her seat belt and rearview mirror, a text from Lacey popped up on the console. She quickly cleared the screen but not quickly enough to prevent Daphne from seeing it.

"So what are you going to tell Rikki when she calls tomorrow?" Nina asked as she backed out of the parking space. "You can let it go to voice mail I suppose, but you'll have to answer her eventually."

"I'm telling her I want it," Daphne replied, staring straight ahead.

"Really?" Nina finally looked at her.

"Yeah. Why? You don't think I can do it?"

"What the hell, Daph? I've been saying you can do it for months. I've wanted to scream that it's about time and that you're ready to give it a go, but I didn't want you to have a meltdown."

"I wouldn't say I'm ready, but a moment ago it seemed like the right time."

"It is the right time. You're getting consistent traffic on your website, and having a commercial space people can walk into and actually see your merchandise is the final step."

"This might be a trivial concern, but what am I supposed to use for money to get this going?"

"You're leasing, not buying, so you won't need a lot. First month's rent, security deposit, and a few grand extra to tidy up the place. A small-business loan will more than cover it."

"I stroll into a bank and ask for a loan, just like that?"

"Well, not just like that. We'll tighten up that business plan we drafted. Look, financial institutions are eager to loan to women and minority business people. It'll look good on paper if they ever need a government bailout."

Nina offered an encouraging smile as she drove, but Daphne continued to avoid eye contact. It almost seemed like she'd completely shut down emotionally, and with all that had come at her recently, Nina was afraid to risk opening the floodgates by asking what was wrong.

"I'm sure you're really nervous about this decision, but trust me. You're going to be so happy you gambled on yourself in the long run. And I'm here to help you any way I can."

Daphne finally turned to Nina. "Shouldn't you answer Lacey's text?"

Nina froze. They clearly couldn't ignore the kiss this time. "Daphne, I'm sorry. I don't know what…"

"You don't owe me an apology. I'm the one who kissed you."

"Well, I kissed you back, and I shouldn't have."

"What would've happened if Rikki hadn't forgotten her tablet?"

Nina exhaled heavily on that one. "I don't know." That was a lie. She knew exactly what would've happened.

"Why did you let me kiss you?"

"I don't know." As soon Nina heard herself say it, she knew how stupid and phony she sounded.

Daphne stared at her. "For a woman who's hardly ever unsure about anything, two 'I don't knows' in a row have to be some kind of record."

"I kissed you back because I wanted to. I shouldn't have, and what's more, I shouldn't have wanted to."

"I don't feel like antiquing today. Can you just take me home?"

Nina's heart started racing. "Daph, let's not let this ruin our friendship. I don't want to lose you. I mean your friendship."

"I don't want to lose yours either. That's why I need you to take me home. Now."

Nina was quiet as she figured out where she needed to turn to comply with Daphne's request. Should she have mentioned how badly she hadn't wanted to drop her off? A mild panic rose in her. She should say something. But what?

"I can't imagine what you must think of me," she finally said.

"What do you mean?" Daphne's head was resting against the passenger window.

"In spite of what it looks like, I'm really not a serial cheater. However, given my recent track record, I don't quite know how to convince you of that, other than to say that until I met Lacey, I'd never been disloyal to anyone."

Daphne shrugged. "The whole thing with Zack and Lacey I can sort of understand, even if I don't condone cheating of any kind. But now that you have Lacey, what's your excuse? Why would you risk your relationship by kissing someone like me?"

"Why are you saying it like that?"

"Like what?"

"Like you're inferior to her, which you are so not."

"Even if that were true, Lacey's the woman you've wanted all along. I don't get why you're messing around with me."

Nina opened her mouth to speak but stopped short of another "I don't know" because that answer was no longer acceptable to either of them. Why *was* she doing it? Did she have actual romantic feelings for Daphne, or were her actions some sort of pushback against Lacey's pressure to commit so soon?

"I guess I need to examine that question," Nina said.

"Yeah. I'd say so."

They remained quiet for the rest of the ride home, Nina because she felt she'd already said more than enough.

When she pulled into Daphne's driveway, she half-hoped for an invitation in to continue their dialogue in a more positive direction, but Daphne's expression, like she'd just been dumped at the prom, signaled that would not be happening.

"Will you let me know how you make out with Rikki tomorrow?"

Daphne nodded and got out of the car. "Thanks for everything," she said and closed the door.

Once Daphne was inside, Nina slammed her palms against her steering wheel.

When Daphne closed the door, she leaned against it and allowed herself to cry, to really sob—a full-on, slide-down-the-wall-and-ugly-cry-into-her-hands release. The weirdest thing about the situation? As helpless and despondent as she felt, she'd never felt more alive. She was a giant kettle of emotion bubbling over with love, lust, sadness, hope, and complete terror. Everything was going wrong and right at exactly the same time, and all she'd wanted to do was run into her bedroom, lock the door, and the draw the shades down against the world. But instead she just sat on her floor bawling into her arms folded across her knees.

Where had she gotten the nerve to tell the real-estate agent she wanted to lease that space? To even dare to think about venturing out into the world as an independent businesswoman? What had gotten into her?

Nina. Nina was what had gotten into her.

And now after tasting the sweetness of truly living, she'd never be able to return to the uneventful life of an introverted underachiever that she'd mastered without even trying.

The thought made her stop convulsing. Her eyes finally quit clouding with tears. After wiping her cheeks and nose on her sleeve, she got up and made a plan.

But this time, she'd have to move ahead without Nina.

CHAPTER SEVENTEEN

Nina reclined in her office chair, taking a moment for herself before leaving to meet Lacey for lunch downtown. She'd been trying to avert an ironic public-relations nightmare with the central California branch, whose hourly employees were threatening a walkout to protest their subpar health-insurance benefits. She'd rubbed her face in frustration so many times that morning she'd need to touch up her makeup before she left her office.

As an upper-management exec, Nina shuddered at the idea that her company, a health-insurance provider, was shortchanging its own employees on part of their benefits package. She was embarrassed for the company and especially embarrassed for herself as a high-level representative of it. Even though she wasn't responsible for overseeing employee benefits packages, she truly felt for them and found it immensely difficult to prepare a statement for the media justifying the company's policy, if it came to that.

This might end up a liquid lunch with Lacey.

As she freshened up in the washroom, she checked her phone, as she'd been doing for the last two weeks. Nothing from Daphne, and that bothered her. They'd never gone this long without talking—several days maybe, but never a week or more. Daphne had been visibly upset with her when she'd dropped her off after their storeroom kiss, so Nina had laid low, waiting to hear from her. Had that been a miscalculation? Maybe Daphne was waiting for her and wondering the same thing.

To hell with it. Enough was enough. She grabbed her phone and texted, *"Hey, you. What's going on in Daphne's world?"*

As soon as she hit send, she said out loud, *"Daphne's world?* Jesus. Could you have been any cornier?" She shook her head at that, at her work dilemma, and at the conversation she'd been meaning to have with Lacey about her increasing frequency of sleepovers.

Yep. Definitely liquid at this lunch.

❖

Sitting at the bar at Salerno's, an upscale Italian restaurant, Nina salivated as she eyed the dirty martini the bartender was mixing her. After the first heavenly sip, she returned her eyes to the entrance for Lacey. She also watched for Daphne's return text to pop up on her phone. Daphne was a reliably consistent text returner, usually within fifteen minutes. Instead of a text, Daphne called her.

Nina leapt off the bar stool and took the call in the hall near the restrooms. "Hi. What's going on? How's Sophie?"

"About the same, unfortunately. She was just transferred to Masonicare."

"I'm so sorry," Nina said. "How are you doing?"

"I've had a busy couple of weeks. I signed the lease the other day."

Nina was floored, questioning whether she'd heard her correctly. "For the retail space?"

"Yeah. I was clearly temporarily insane when I did it, but Rikki was so helpful. She hooked me up with the small-business-loan officer she deals with. They're moderately confident it'll go through."

"That's...that's terrific." Nina forced herself to sound enthusiastic, but inside she was steaming. She'd been Daphne's number-one cheerleader since day one. She'd ridden her regularly to get serious about believing in herself and pursuing the dream she'd let languish on her vision board for years. And now that she was ready to go, Daphne had completely cut her out.

"I can't believe how relatively painless the whole process has been," Daphne said. "Of course, it's not set in stone yet. I can't do anything without final loan approval, but Rikki's been amazing."

"You know Rikki's taken." Nina heard her words but couldn't stop them from gushing out like cheap beer from the stomach of a fraternity pledge. "With a guy. She's bi, just so you know."

Silence.

Finally, Daphne said, "What does that have to do with anything we're talking about?"

"Uh…I have no idea, but it needed to be said."

"It really didn't, but anyway. How's Lacey?"

The transparent insincerity in Daphne's voice made Nina feel instantly better about momentarily flying off the verbal rails. "She's great. I'm meeting her for lunch in a few."

"Fantastic," Daphne said. "Have a great day."

The tension between them was murkier than Nina's dirty martini, but she wasn't about to let Daphne out of the conversation so easily.

"Wait a minute. Don't rush off. What can I do to help? You need a business plan for the loan process."

"I looked up small-business-plan templates on the internet, and Rikki helped me fill in the blanks. But thanks for asking."

Nina's ticked-off meter was approaching full tilt. Daphne's new cool, self-assured demeanor was bordering on rudeness. Had Nina created this monster?

"Well, would you like to go out for a glass of wine to celebrate?" Nina looked up and noticed Lacey signaling to her from the bar. She held up her index finger to her as she anticipated Daphne's eager "yes."

"We should probably wait for the official approval first," Daphne said with anything but eagerness in her voice. "But sure. We can sometime."

Sometime? Nina clenched her teeth, then switched her irritated tone to playful. "Waiting's for suckers. I'm so confident in your future success that I say we just do it tomorrow night. My treat. You free?"

"Let me check, and I'll get back to you."

Nina was back on irritated as she fumbled for a sharp retort. She also noticed Lacey tapping at her Rolex from the edge of the bar. "Yeah, no problem. Okay. I have to run now."

She squeezed the end button so hard she could've cracked the screen. Heading over to Lacey, she tried to shake off her thoroughly perplexing, frustrating chat with Daphne. Was Daphne over her? Whatever "over" entailed in their ambiguous relationship.

"Hey, babe." Lacey kissed her cheek and ushered her to a table for two near a window. "I don't have too long. Who were you on the phone with? A client?"

"No. Daphne. She's decided to lease that retail space I told you about."

"Good for her," Lacey said as she seemed more focused on perusing the menu. "She could use something to keep her occupied."

"That sounds kind of catty."

Lacey looked up in surprise. "I didn't mean it that way. But come on. She's kind of a sad sack. Running her own antiques business will be great for her."

A streak of fierce protectiveness rose to the surface. "If you don't mean to be catty, why do you always seem to have a dig queued up for her?"

"She's just..." Lacey grimaced.

Her expression raised Nina's hackles. "She has the biggest heart of anyone I know."

"Really? Anyone, huh?"

"You know what I mean—of any of my friends. You should see the way she looks after her eighty-year-old neighbor."

Lacey nodded almost dismissively. "Let's not spend our whole lunch together bickering about Daphne." She waved the server over and looked down at the menu. "I think I'll get the beef-tips special. How about you?"

Nina poured the rest of her drink into her mouth. "I'll go with the grilled-shrimp salad."

"Want to split the fried calamari? They do it New York style."

Nina shook her head. "I'm not that hungry." She looked up at the server. "I'll take another dirty."

"We'll do the calamari, too," Lacey said as she handed over the menus. "You have to eat more than a salad if you're double-fisting martinis at lunch."

What the fuck? Now she was controlling what Nina would have for lunch, too?

"I've had a rough morning, Lacey. I'm perfectly capable of handling a two-martini lunch."

"What's going on? Have they walked out yet?"

"Not yet, but they're close. And Lancaster's personally selected me to come up with an offer by the end of the day, or it's going to happen."

"Personnel negotiations isn't even your job."

"No kidding. Should I tell the CEO to go pound sand?"

"Not if you want a future there. What are you going to give them? Doesn't have to be much. They're not even unionized."

"I want to give them what they want," Nina said. "They want more choice in their plans and a larger network. They're not unreasonable requests. But Lancaster's being an asshole about it. He thinks they'll be grateful for a one-percent premium reduction."

"I appreciate what you're trying to do, but you certainly don't want to start a precedent of treating worker bees like they matter. That's the quickest way I know of getting blackballed in the industry."

"I can't tell whether you're being ironic or entitled," Nina said. "But I'm so fed up with walking that tightrope. I hope they do walk out in San Fran. I hope they walk out, and the whole West Coast profit margin tanks this quarter."

Lacey looked concerned. "Are you angling for a severance package or something?"

"You know what? I don't think that would be so bad. I can take it and do something else with my life. It would be nice to feel inspired about my career again."

"How about going back to living on a budget? Does that inspire you?"

"God, Lacey. Life's not all about money. I lived on a budget in the early stages of my career. It wasn't horrible."

"Looks like Daphne's rubbing off on someone."

Now it just felt like Lacey wanted to be antagonistic. "If seeking purpose and fulfillment in your job is being like Daphne, then maybe I want to grow up to be just like her."

"Maybe she'll hire you as a cashier in her little knickknack store." Lacey sipped her drink and looked out the window.

"What's your problem, Lacey? You have something you want to say?"

Lacey turned back to her, vulnerability in her eyes. "If you want me to be honest, I think your friend is too needy. You always manage to make her the topic of discussion, and then I have to listen to you go on and on about how you can fix her, like you have a blueprint for a new and improved Daphne and want to be the engineer."

By the grace of the gods, the server delivered her second drink. Lacey's statement knocked the wind out of her, and once she'd caught her breath, she sipped her martini until the truth of it stopped stinging so much.

"One of things I love about you, Nina, is your compassion and fiery eagerness to help others, but I'm starting to feel like the third wheel in your life…again."

Nina scooped up Lacey's hand in hers. "Baby, I'm sorry. I didn't know you felt that way. I'll be more mindful now. To be honest, she's doing great on her own. The realtor is helping her through most of the process. I haven't even talked to her for a while."

Lacey looked down, almost like she felt ashamed. "I'm sorry. I hope I didn't sound like a jerk. I guess I'm still a little hypersensitive about, you know…"

Nina released her hand when the server brought their lunch entrees. "Don't apologize. Maybe lunchtime dates aren't always such a hot idea, given we're both stressed at our jobs."

Lacey laughed, seeming relieved. "That's not untrue. Let's talk about our weekend plans."

Nina smiled and picked at her salad. Now was absolutely not the time to bring up space and time boundaries.

❖

Daphne had signed the lease and received the keys during the week but was finally able to head over to her new shop on Saturday, eager to begin preparing it for the as yet unscheduled grand opening. Unlocking the door and walking in with her carrier of cleaning supplies was a bittersweet experience. The times when she'd allowed herself to imagine her dream leaping off her vision board and taking form in the real world, Sophie and Nina were walking in on either side of her, as joyous and brimming with pride as she was.

But, as in so many instances, reality simply couldn't live up to the power of the dream.

As she swept the floor, she surveyed the walls that needed painting and the display space that needed to be redesigned. She also needed a sign for outside above the door. The small-business loan would fund those projects. But when would she hear back on that? With no past business experience, she had no way of assessing whether she should be nervous. Nina had told her that one of the biggest keys to a contented life was not worrying about anything until you had a concrete reason to.

Nina. They'd been avoiding each other since their storeroom misadventure, an experience Daphne had continually replayed in her mind despite her efforts to forget it. What was the point? It was only driving her crazy. Nina clearly wanted Lacey.

She'd been trying to occupy her mind by dealing with the shop and visiting with Sophie, but now that some time had passed, she wondered if she could get past her feelings for Nina for the sake of their friendship. She missed her, and she wished she'd just texted Nina and asked if she'd wanted to help her get things in the shop in order. Even though that only meant giving the place a good scrubbing, Nina would've been enthusiastic to help in any way.

She flipped her empty bucket over, sat on it, and stared at her phone. She was being a fool. Was she really going to let stupid feelings ruin a solid friendship? She was about to become a full-fledged, legit businesswoman. Shouldn't she have the emotional maturity that went along with it?

With that she sent Nina a text.

Almost immediately Nina called her.

"Hi there, busy lady," Nina said. "What's been going on?"

"Not much other than trying to organize things in the shop. I got the keys this week, and I'm here now cleaning."

"You are? How long will you be there? I'd love to come help you."

"That's okay. I got it. You're so busy with Noah and Lacey, and you've already helped me so much. I can manage cleaning and disinfecting on my own."

"You're missing like the best part of this experience," Nina said.

"What's that?"

"Having a friend help you means you get done twice as fast, and then we can go for a drink."

Daphne laughed. As usual, she instantly felt uplifted whenever she heard Nina's voice. She frowned when she searched her memory for any other friend in her past who had inspired that same reaction. Sophie? Sort of but…Nope. Only Nina. She needed to get over this crush because her friendship was too important to lose over something like that.

"Let me know the next time you're free, and we'll do just that," Daphne replied.

"What about today?"

The question took Daphne off guard. "Well, yeah, today works. But haven't you already planned your day?"

"Actually, no. I had a remote meeting this morning, but Zack has Noah this weekend, and Lacey's in Vermont visiting her family until tomorrow night."

"Why didn't you go with her?"

Nina sighed into the phone. "I'll be there in thirty and explain."

When they ended the call, Daphne smiled, feeling infinitely better about all things.

❖

By the time Daphne had taken her first bag of trash to the dumpster in the parking lot, Nina had arrived with sushi takeout and a four-pack of local beer. They exchanged an awkward hug and stood at the counter eating.

"I hope I didn't break your rhythm coming in here and forcing a food break on you," Nina said.

"There's no such thing as forcing sushi on me," Daphne said. She'd decided that while she couldn't *not* notice Nina's perfect lips and mouth and dazzling white teeth, she didn't have to allow them to derail all rational thought. She'd simply acknowledge them and then force her brain back on track.

"And how lucky are you that this restaurant is only a few doors down," Nina said.

"Now I know where all my profits will go after I start earning them." Daphne sipped cold beer from the can. "So why didn't you go away with Lacey?"

"Mmm, yes, that." Nina wiped her mouth as she chewed. "I'd had a conversation with her about a week ago about space and boundaries and such. It didn't go over well."

"What did you say?"

"After choosing my words carefully, I let her know that I wasn't fully comfortable with her spending almost every night at my house. I mean, Noah is just getting used to the idea that Mommy dates a woman now instead of Daddy, and Lacey seemed to be moving things along at a pace I wasn't comfortable with."

"That sounds reasonable," Daphne said as her heartbeat quickened. "I mean, if you don't count the year of your affair, it's been only a few months. That's total U-Haul syndrome."

"Right? But she's counting that year. She says that, altogether, we have a year and a half as a couple, and that's plenty of time to know if this has happily-ever-after potential."

"Obviously you're not counting the year."

"I'm not. It was an incredibly confusing, tumultuous time for me, and I'd temporarily lost all understanding of who I was and what I wanted. I wasn't on an equal playing field with her then. From my point of view, Lacey and I started off fresh over the summer."

"And you haven't been able to get her to understand that."

Nina shrugged. "I don't think it's my job to make her understand. It's how I feel. My life has never been as unencumbered as hers. When we met, I had a husband. I still have a son, and that's never going to change. I'm afraid that one of the main things that attracted me to her has become an obstacle."

"The fact that she's pushy?"

Nina looked at her like she'd answered a math question with a color. "No. That she's assertive and confident in what she wants."

"Oh. Yeah. That makes more sense. That is pretty sexy in a woman, huh?"

Nina glared at her. "You are definitely not helping."

Daphne giggled. "Sorry. So how did you leave it?"

"She decided to take the weekend and visit her family without me. I haven't figured out if it was simply a break she felt we both needed or a spectacular display of passive-aggression."

"It's probably just a little break." Daphne reflected on how she'd recently needed to do the same thing with Nina. "Sometimes you need one, if things start to get a little murky."

"Yes, yes," Nina said, nodding. "You're absolutely right." She tapped her beer can into Daphne's and took a sip, holding it in her mouth before swallowing. "Speaking of that, can I talk to you about something?"

A rush of heat swept up Daphne's face. Ugh. This was happening and not even with the buffer zone of texting. "Sure." She grabbed a napkin and dabbed at the droplets of beer that dribbled out during her response.

"You know what I'm going to say, don't you?"

Daphne nodded. "Let me start by saying I owe you an apology. I'm sorry." She began to stammer. "I, um, I know I should've said it to you sooner, but I just hoped we could—"

"Make believe it didn't happen? I think we tried that, and it only made things more awkward."

Feeling ashamed for her role in the kiss, Daphne bowed her head.

"But here's the thing," Nina said. "You don't owe me an apology. You don't have anything to be sorry for, Daph. It happened. We know it was a mistake, but if there's any blame, it belongs to both of us. I'd like to put it behind us for the sake of our friendship. What do you think?"

"Um, yeah, I agree, for sure," Daphne said, although the "mistake" part stung. "I admit that I avoided you for a while, but that was partly because I thought you were mad or disappointed in me. I felt like a total idiot."

"So did I." Nina chugged the rest of her beer. "I guess that's one of the pitfalls of having lesbian friends who are cute." She laughed, but her reaction seemed forced, like she was grasping for anything to lighten the mood.

"Yeah, that's it." Daphne pretended to be righteous. "I've never had a gorgeous friend before, so it was all your fault."

"You're pretty damn cute, too. Don't think that was a loophole." Nina chuckled. "When you think about it, we're both kind of virginal in a way. We've both been with only one woman each. It's like we just went through this delayed coming-of-age moment together."

"Uh, since I'm thirty-eight and you're over forty, yeah, that's really delayed…like those ten-year-olds sitting in strollers you see at the mall."

Nina almost spewed out her beer. They shared a hearty laugh that made Daphne feel so much better about the situation. It was a watershed moment. She truly felt like she was coming into her own in terms of self-discovery and honesty in her feelings. It was so freeing—finally.

"You know what? I don't think it'll take long to get this place up and running." Nina's tone was back to business. "We should have it all cleaned up by tomorrow. Have you heard back on your loan yet?"

"Not yet. That's what I wanted to ask you. Does it usually take this long?"

"It can, especially since you're a first-timer. Have you asked Rikki about it?"

Daphne shook her head. "I didn't want to bug her. It's not even her responsibility."

Nina patted her shoulder. "Don't stress, Daph. I'm confident you'll get the loan. All kinds of administrative red tape can cause any number of delays, especially with new businesses."

Daphne's outlook suddenly collapsed. "What if I'm rejected?"

Nina grabbed her hand and shook it. "What did I say about saying 'what if' in business? We don't."

"It's either what is or what isn't." Daphne repeated the mantra blandly.

Nina cupped her hand to her ear. "What was that? I didn't quite hear you."

Daphne smiled in spite of herself. "I said it's either what is or what isn't. There are no what-ifs in business."

"Atta girl. Now come on. Let's stop goofing off here and get to work. We have to scrub this dump into an antique shop."

Daphne stuffed the last piece of shrimp tempura into her mouth and gathered up the empty containers. "Thank you."

"It's nothing," Nina said. "I was dying for sushi."

"I didn't mean for lunch."

Nina smiled. "Is it safe to friend-hug again?"

Daphne giggled. "Yes. I think we're copacetic."

Chapter Eighteen

After they'd finished their work at the shop, Nina invited Daphne out to dinner to celebrate. They'd each gone home, showered, then met again at an expensive restaurant in New Haven, a favorite of Nina's since moving from Fairfield County. Daphne would pitch a fit when Nina grabbed the check at the end, but it would be easy enough to put out that fire.

"Have you ordered the signage for above the door yet?" Nina said as she glanced at the specials.

Daphne shook her head. "That's one of the items I'll need the loan to buy."

"Do you plan to use the exact logo from your website for it?"

"I probably should, huh? I do love it."

Nina nodded. "You're getting steady website traffic now, so I'd stick with it. You know, brand recognition."

"I have a brand?"

Nina laughed. Daphne's sweet naïveté only seemed more endearing the more she witnessed it. "Wait till you have an actual store people can walk into."

Daphne smiled as she sliced into her caprese salad.

"How about the interior design?" Nina said. "You're not going to leave it the way it is?"

"No. I've been messing around on the computer on one of those virtual-design websites. I think I've come up with an awesome layout."

"Oh, I can't wait to see it. Can you send me the link?"

Daphne seemed reluctant. "I wanted to get it done and have everyone see it for the first time at the grand opening."

"Even me?" Nina batted her eyelashes. "Surely your bestie gets the privilege of a sneak preview."

"I suppose I should show you, in case it's utter trash. But that's another thing I can't start without the loan. Do you think Rikki can refer me to contractors in the meantime?"

"Absolutely. She deals with only the best." Nina smiled. She made a mental note to give her friend Rikki a call to ensure she was looking out for Daphne.

Daphne smiled. "You've done so much for me; I might as well put your name on the business."

Nina sipped her cabernet and picked at her Caesar salad. "All I've been doing is offering business advice and sharing my contacts. That's not such a big deal between friends."

"Don't minimize your contributions, Nina." Daphne beamed with appreciation. "I don't just mean about the business stuff. I could spend the rest of my life thanking you and never feel like it's enough."

"Daphne, effusive thanks are not necessary. Look, I'm all about women helping women. Sadly, it doesn't happen enough in this world. You know that mentor program for college girls I started?"

Daphne nodded.

"That's been the best part of working as an executive for Global Health." Nina tore a piece of bread in half and dipped it in olive oil.

"You should become a college business professor," Daphne said casually.

Nina looked up, about to chuckle at the suggestion, but something halted her reaction.

"Have you ever thought about it?"

"Never."

Daphne smiled. "I don't know where you could possibly fit it into your schedule, but you'd make an amazing teacher."

Nina pondered the idea briefly. "I don't know if that would be a good fit for me, but thank you. It's a nice compliment." Nina felt her phone vibrate and assumed it was Lacey. She took a quick glance and saw a text from Noah. "Excuse me. Let me reply to my son. He just texted to say he loves me." She felt her smile spread across her face. "At least someone's texting me that."

"You haven't heard from Lacey?"

Nina shook her head. "Not since first thing this morning. I texted her over two hours ago."

"She's probably just wrapped up in family stuff."

She appreciated Daphne's clichéd attempt to downplay the implications, so she gave a confident nod. The whole situation with Lacey bothered her, but surprisingly, she wasn't missing her like she'd thought she would. Lacey had been right. They needed some time apart after a period of too much, too soon.

When their entrees arrived, Nina's heart smiled as she watched Daphne dive into her house-made gnocchi with marinara. How was a woman with such a ravenous appetite able to stay so slender? The answer was simple. She worried the calories off each day.

"Crap," Daphne muttered as she dabbed at a blob of sauce on her shirt with a cloth napkin, smearing the red splotch.

"This must be why I never see you wearing white," Nina said, trying not to laugh.

Daphne rolled her eyes at herself. "I think I stopped right around the time I became too big for bibs."

Nina was struggling to appear sympathetic. "That job might be too big for just a napkin."

"I'll be right back," Daphne said and headed toward the restrooms.

Nina watched her sleek, angular shape until she disappeared around the corner. Daphne. She was klutzy, insecure, awkward, and shy. In some circles she'd be known as a complete mess. Yet she brought a glow to Nina's heart every single time they were together. She was also smart, funny, and had the most compassionate soul of anyone she'd ever met. Despite her painful lack of confidence, she subtly exuded the brightest, most hopeful aura.

As Daphne came back around the corner and headed to the table, Nina perceived her moving in slow motion, her legs in those tight black jeans taking long strides as she curled one side of her sandy blond hair behind her ear. Nina winced when she actually heard herself sigh out loud. She began emitting short spurts of breath as she realized what was happening to her.

Currently, at that very moment, she was crushing on Daphne. Hard.

❖

On her drive home from the restaurant, Nina wondered how she could've been so stupid. She hadn't become such fast friends with Daphne for no reason. They'd made out hot and heavy in the storeroom, for God's sake. Not exactly the appropriate way friends celebrate one friend's success. She'd felt a connection to Daphne from the start and had been slowly falling in love with her. To her credit, she'd had the good sense to say no to Daphne's suggestion of drinks back at her house, even though it was still relatively early, and Daphne lived only fifteen minutes outside downtown New Haven. Who knew what could've resulted?

She turned up the radio as her thoughts came on fast and furious, racing through her mind at a pace that made them almost indecipherable. Now what? She groaned out loud and kept driving.

Minutes later, a call from Lacey came up on her car's Bluetooth, scaring the crap out of her. "Hey, babe," she said out of habit.

"Sorry I didn't get back to you sooner, babe," Lacey said." The service up here is terrible. Your text finally came in when I got back to my parents' house."

That was a rather elaborate explanation. "Where were you all day?"

"I spent the day hanging with my old friends. We hit a few breweries."

"Nice. Was Barb there?" For some reason, Nina found it necessary to bring up Lacey's first girlfriend ever, who she was with some twenty years ago. Jealousy seemed like an odd emotion to crop up then.

"Yeah. Our whole crew was there," Lacey said, sounding snotty. "Why ask about her specifically?"

"Wasn't she your first girlfriend?"

Lacey laughed mirthlessly. "How about 'I miss you' or 'come home' or 'I wish you were here' instead of lame questions about a relationship I had a lifetime ago?"

"How about I stop asking lame questions and you lose the attitude?"

"Nina," Lacey said softly. "What are we doing?"

"What do you mean?" Nina still felt attacked.

"I haven't seen you in a week. We've barely spoken, and I'm a hundred miles away. We finally have each other on the phone, and this is the best we can do?"

Out of nowhere, Nina burst into tears as she was driving down the interstate, silently at first, but then she broke into loud sobs.

"Nina? Are you okay? What's the matter?"

"I don't want to fight with you, Lacey, especially while you're so far away."

"Okay, baby. Let's not fight. I'll be home Wednesday, and we'll talk it out then."

"Wednesday? I thought this was just a weekend getaway."

"It was originally, but it's hard to get in quality time with family and friends in two days. Are you out with Noah now?"

"He's with Zack. I'm driving home now from dinner with Daphne."

"Oh. What did you do today?"

"I had a remote conference, and then I helped Daphne at her shop."

"Hmm. That's a lot of Daphne."

"She had a lot to do. The space was vacant for a while. And I don't think dinner afterward is so unusual."

"I have an idea," Lacey said. "Why don't you come up here with me until Wednesday? I'd love for my family to meet you... unless you feel that's trampling over more boundaries."

"I'd like to meet them, too, Lace, but this week isn't good. I have to go to New York for a meeting of international execs on Monday."

"I don't suppose it can be rescheduled?"

"Absolutely not. Executives are flying in from Germany and the UK tomorrow. The only acceptable reason for rescheduling international exec meetings is death, and by death, I mean one of ours."

"I get it, Nina," Lacey said, slipping into droning indifference. "No problem. We'll do it some other time."

Nina bit her tongue, choking back the hundreds of snide quips she could've uttered in response to Lacey's unreasonable attitude. Instead, she went with, "Enjoy the rest of your stay, and we'll talk when you get home, okay?"

"Okay. I love you, Nina."

"I love you, too." Nina ended the call and negotiated the exit ramp, trying to negotiate the confusion in her head. Although they were experiencing a bump in their relationship, Nina loved Lacey. She'd never doubted that. But was it possible, dare she use the word normal, to be in love with one woman while extreme friend-crushing on another?

She wanted a nice, smooth "yes" to that query, but her business savvy told her that was one negotiation she wouldn't win.

The next morning Daphne woke feeling restless, unsettled. Her life was on a fast track to change, and she felt like she was running alongside the club car trying to keep up. Over the last couple of years, when anything bothered her or she just felt like venting about life, she'd pop over to Sophie's to hang out in her nurturing company. They'd drink and laugh, and inevitably, Sophie would feed her something delicious and pile the rest in a container for her to take home. Now, without warning, that consolation was over.

As she headed down the nursing home corridor to Sophie's room, she realized that spending almost all day and night with Nina only reinforced the fact that she was falling more in love with her each time they were together. At first it had been a lark, some innocent bit of intrigue her life sorely needed, but now it wasn't so much fun anymore to be near to her, smell her enticing perfume and scented lotion, or watch her luscious lips move when she talked, laughed, or sipped a drink.

Worst of all, she clearly couldn't trust herself to manage her impulses when she got too close to Nina. She shook her head. How long would it take to get over the embarrassment of that incident?

She tapped on Sophie's open door and walked in. After showing her a cactus inside a ceramic cat, she placed it on the TV stand.

"Hi, Soph." She gave her a kiss on her cheek and a gentle hug.

"Hi, Daphne," Sophie said slowly, her face working on a smile.

Daphne dragged a chair next to hers, and they looked out the window onto the courtyard. "How are they treating you? They taking good care of you?"

Sophie nodded. "Hard work."

"They're working you hard, huh? Well, that's how you'll get better."

"Bullshit," Sophie replied. "I'm old."

Although it was sometimes difficult to read Sophie's facial expressions since the stroke, Daphne recognized her playful curmudgeon temperament when she heard it.

"Is your therapist a hot guy at least?"

"Girl. Hot girl." She shrugged and smiled.

Daphne laughed. "What time is your next therapy session? I'll hang around."

"Your girlfriend. How is she?"

"I don't have a—oh, right. You mean girlfriend in the way little old straight ladies mean it. My friend, Nina, is fine." She paused, nostalgic for the times around Sophie's kitchen table with coffee or Manhattans or wine. Even with their generation gap times two, Sophie always covered her with the sense that everything would work out in the end. "Actually, I kind of wanted your advice on that, if you don't mind me bugging you about it."

Sophie bobbed her head once.

"I'm gonna go ahead and take that as a green light," Daphne said. "So, Nina. You once told me that she and I should date, and then I said 'oh, no, Soph, we're just friends. We don't like each other like that.' Well, now I do like her like that. In fact, I like her so much that it's starting to feel weird sometimes hanging out with her doing simple, innocent things like going shopping or Taco Tuesday or—"

"You're in love?"

"Sophie," Daphne exclaimed. "No. I'm not in love…" She fixed her attention out the window at the birds and squirrels trotting and scampering across the grounds. She then sighed loudly. "Damn, Soph. Even with half your brain barely functioning, you can still figure me out. Or am I that transparent?"

Sophie smiled. "You're in love."

Daphne looked down and picked at the threads around a hole in her jeans. "I'm in love. But I don't know what to do. She's my best friend—present company excluded—and she's in a relationship. I don't want to lose her friendship, but I'm afraid I might, if I can't contain my secret feelings for her."

"Tell her."

"How can I tell her? She loves me but just as a friend. She seems crazy about Lacey." Daphne looked around and lowered her voice as though Nina might be hiding inside a linen cart or something. "Between you and me, I don't think that relationship is all that solid, but you know, it's not my place to suggest that to Nina."

"Tell her you love her."

Daphne was growing frustrated not knowing if Sophie was responding on stroke autopilot or if she truly was trying to drive her point home. "I can't, Sophie," she finally blurted. "I'm afraid."

Sophie reached across and placed her hand on Daphne's arm. "Stop being afraid. Own your life. You blink one day and you're in here."

It was the most Sophie had spoken since suffering her stroke. When Daphne cleared the tears from her eyes, she studied the intensity in Sophie's face, how her glassy eyes conveyed the message with more clarity than her carefully chosen words.

She was quiet for a while, trying to formulate a response that could come close to matching the poignancy in Sophie's spot-on assessment. Daphne had finally felt ready to initiate the first steps toward a new career, so what was stopping her from taking the same leap of courage in her romantic life? Duh. Lacey.

Luckily, the dietary aide rolled in the lunch cart and diverted her thoughts to the aroma of some sort of soup permeating the room. After the aide arranged the table tray in front of Sophie's chair, the gourmet masterpiece was revealed: lentil soup, mashed potatoes, applesauce, and coffee, a feast fit for a queen—one whose reign had clearly come to an end. Daphne checked her gag reflex.

"Do you need any help eating?"

Sophie shook her head, laid her napkin across her lap, and picked up the spoon with her fully functional hand. She ate slowly, offering Daphne her applesauce, which she politely declined.

"It sure as hell isn't your homemade pierogies and skillet-seared kielbasa, is it?"

Sophie shook her head in clear disgust. "They say I'll choke."

"Aside from the peculiar food combination, that soup actually smells pretty good."

Sophie shrugged as she dipped her spoon in the mashed potatoes.

"Thank you, Sophie," Daphne said, suddenly feeling overwhelmed with emotion.

"For what?"

"For being my first genuine best friend. If you were forty years younger, I'd probably be in love with you, too." Daphne served her a goofy smile.

"Not while I'm eating," Sophie said, then smiled.

Daphne laughed. "I'd be the best and worst thing to happen to you. I'd ruin you for other men."

Sophie placed her spoon down and carefully raised her middle finger at her.

"Is that part of your therapy?" Daphne asked.

They both laughed, and it felt good to hear Sophie make that sound. She must really be getting better, Daphne thought.

CHAPTER NINETEEN

After receiving the strange call from a sign-delivery company saying she needed to authorize an installation, Daphne rushed down to the shop, searching for hidden cameras to see if she was indeed being punked, as she'd suspected.

She pulled in a few spaces away from the truck that had the large outdoor signage swinging from a crane arm and two guys up on ladders ready to install it above the entrance.

The one operating the crane greeted her as she approached. "Haya doin'? This is the sign you ordered?"

"It's the sign I wanted," she said. "But I didn't order it."

"Are you Daphne...?" He glanced over the paperwork on his clipboard.

"Carsen. Yes. I'm her."

"My paperwork says you ordered it, and you're signing for it, so just give me the word, and my guys'll install it, and we can get to our next job."

"I'm sorry. I'd love to give you the word, but I didn't order it. And more importantly, I don't know how I'd pay for it once it's installed."

He looked at his guys on the ladders, then at her like he, too, thought he was being punked. "It's already paid for. All you gotta do is sign here."

Suddenly, a loud bang from inside her shop stripped her away from crane guy. She trotted up to the entrance and cupped her eyes to look inside. "What the fu..."

She charged in and found a full-figured gal in a tool belt wearing a bandana that tamed wild curls. She looked up from a pile of decimated counter. "How's it going?"

"It would be going a lot better if I knew what the heck was going on around here."

The woman looked around the room. "Looks to me like you're opening up a store."

"I was until my business loan got denied."

The woman shrugged. "All I can tell you is a woman named Daphne Carsen hired me to demo this retail space and install new product shelving and a sales counter."

"I'm Daphne Carsen, and why is everyone telling me I've done things I have no recollection of doing nor the money to do them with, I might add?"

"Whoa. That's a mind fuck—excuse me, freak. The money went into my account, and the plans were emailed to me. Do you want this or not?"

"Uh, yes, I do. And you seem quite capable," Daphne said, staring at the woman's tree-branch arms.

"Then here I am doing the job. I'm Olive, by the way. Olive Yousamich, general contractor." She wiped a hand on her jeans and extended it to shake.

"Nice to meet you, Olive. If you'll excuse me, I'm just gonna go make a phone call."

"Sure thing" She gave a two-finger salute, picked up her sledgehammer, and resumed her demolition work.

Out on the sidewalk, Daphne stepped past the sign installers and dialed Rikki's number. "Hi, Rikki. It's Daphne. I'm sorry to bother you, but I have people here at my shop hanging signs and smashing old counters to bits, and I have no idea why. Wasn't my business loan rejected?"

"Yes, it was," she said. "But I guess you have a guardian angel looking over you."

"Even I'm not naive enough to believe in those. Who was it?"

"I'm not at liberty to say."

"Aha," Daphne exclaimed. "You could've said it was an anonymous benefactor. Now I know who it is." She ended the call and immediately dialed Nina's phone. When Nina answered, she spat, "Since when did you get into the silent-partner investing business?"

"I'm fine. How are you?" Nina said.

"Nina, what did you do?" Daphne's emotions were in such a whirl, her voice cracked as the question made its way out.

"You sound a little tweaked out. Are you okay?"

"No, I'm not, especially now that I know how little faith you have in me. And isn't there some realtor code of ethics that says you don't go around telling people your client's business loan was rejected?"

"How could you say that, Daphne?" Nina's monotone reply reflected genuine hurt. "I believe in you more than anyone, so much so that I simply provided an alternative channel through which you could get your business off the ground."

"Because poor, pathetic Daphne can't accomplish anything on her own. How much is the loan for, eight?"

"I borrowed ten to give you some breathing room."

"I'm coming by tonight with the first payment." She was about to end the call but couldn't resist. "And I hope you plan to live to a hundred, because that's probably when I'll finally finish paying it off."

"Yes. As a matter of fact I do plan to live that long," Nina said, matching Daphne in decibel level. "And you better, too, you brat. By the way, was there a 'thank you' queued up anywhere in that tirade?"

The lid on Daphne's pressure-cooker mood finally blew in the form of a low, rumbling laugh. She leaned against the glass and, when she stopped laughing, exhaled as she slid down to the sidewalk. "Thank you. Thank you so friggin' much."

"That's better. Next time try leading with that."

"Nina, it's so much money."

"It's really not in the grand scheme of things. Rikki says that contractor is the best in the area, and your signage came out amazing. Go take a look."

Daphne walked around to the front of the building and gazed up at the sign that loomed over her like the marquee of a dream. Then it hit her. "Wait a minute. How did you know…"

Nina sauntered around from the side of the building still holding her phone against her ear and a bouquet of roses in her other hand.

Daphne melted in a smile as she shoved her phone into her pocket. When Nina approached she received the flowers but held them at her side as she hugged her and dampened her ear with her tears. "How can I ever thank you for all this, Nina?" She was trying to pull back to address her, but Nina wouldn't release her grip. "I swear I'll repay every penny if it takes me the rest of my life."

Nina finally let her go and looked adoringly into her eyes. "That's what I'm counting on, Daph—not the paying-me-back part, but the part about being around for the rest of our lives."

Daphne studied her. Why was she being so sentimental now? "You goof. We're friends forever. Nothing's going to change that."

"Not even falling in love?"

"What?" Daphne heard her perfectly clearly, but the insinuation crashed into her brain like another chunk of felled countertop.

Nina was staring at her shoes, then looked up, shyly. "I told Lacey it wasn't going to work with us."

"Why not?"

"Because I realized I was in love with someone else. She didn't even need to ask who."

Daphne stood speechless, trying to appreciate Nina's beautiful face through clouds of tears.

"Now if you're not interested in something more and want to keep it just friends," Nina said, "I can totally respect that. All I ask is that you're honest about—"

Daphne dropped the roses, flung her arms around Nina's neck, and kissed her passionately. Nina's arms then curled around her waist and up her back as she returned Daphne's passion with what felt like ravenous desire.

They stood on the sidewalk and made out like obsessed teenagers at a bowling alley until Daphne noticed the sudden silence of construction noise around them. When they finally separated, the sign crew and Olive, standing at the entrance, broke into applause.

Daphne grinned bashfully as she bowed her head.

Nina elbowed her playfully and caressed her back. "I think you have some business to attend to."

The crane operator held up the clipboard. "Now will you sign for the installation?"

Daphne and Nina laughed, and Daphne ran over to scribble her signature on the work order.

After everyone on site had a plastic cup of celebratory champagne Nina had waiting in a cooler in her car, Nina and Daphne left so they could both go home and prepare for their first official date, which was happening that night.

They sat at a table beside a wall of windows in a fancy, revolving restaurant overlooking downtown Stamford. Piano keys tinkled from across the room as the lights from the city cast an amber glow across Daphne's face. Nina wanted the atmosphere to be special and unique, as it would be the restaurant they'd forever remember as the location of their first date.

Nina drew her gaze away from Daphne's soft features, the curve of her smile in profile as she viewed the city below, to top off her first glass of pinot grigio.

"Thank you," Daphne said. "I love how you always know exactly what to do, like it's instinctual or something."

Nina smiled. "All I did was refill your glass."

"Are you kidding? You picked the most amazing restaurant, selected the perfect wine, and your makeup is flawless. I'd wear it more if it would come out like yours."

"You don't need any more makeup, Daph. Your natural beauty is the only accent that face needs."

Daphne's wheat-field complexion bloomed with the colors of a winter sunrise. "Well, if you're sure, then I won't bother with makeup tutorials."

"Positive." She paused, noting how easily Daphne capitulated. "Do I come off as bossy? Not like sexy assertive but pain-in-the-ass bossy?"

Daphne giggled. "No, not at all. Why would you even ask?"

"Noah called me that earlier tonight—he always calls me that—and I got to thinking maybe he's right. I mean, look. I just refilled your glass without even asking. I literally opened your physical store without asking. Wouldn't that turn off someone as laid-back as you?"

When Daphne slipped her hand under Nina's so gently, a shiver fluttered up her arm.

"First off, you're not too bossy," Daphne said. "I'm totally going with option one: sexy assertive. I'm just in awe of how you know exactly how to go after what you want without ever second-guessing yourself out of it. I've dreamed of being that self-confident. And second, you're being generous when you call me laid-back. Nina, I'm not. I come off that way because I'm usually paralyzed with self-doubt."

Hearing Daphne explain her self-perception, Nina could've started bawling at the table. But she took the effective-leader approach. "Okay. That was a former version of you. You're a businesswoman now. You're the one who came up with this plan a long time ago on your vision board. You've always had this passion in you, and now it's finally coming to fruition."

"All thanks to you."

"It's been a team effort, Daphne. Business success and failure is almost always a team effort. All you needed was a mentor."

Daphne looked up and smiled ironically. "Like the kids you volunteer to help?"

"Those aren't kids, honey. They're young women who are going to take the world by storm, and I couldn't be prouder of that program."

"I know. You brag about that more than you do your son."

Nina's cheeks prickled in embarrassment. "I do brag about it a lot, don't I?"

"I was serious when I said you should become a college professor. You'd be so great. I mean your program is awesome, but you're able to reach only a few girls a year."

Nina sighed as the server brought their entrees. "I've been giving it a lot of thought since you suggested it."

"Really?"

Daphne's smile killed her. And she just loved the way the sandy-blond threads of hair dangling from her upswept date 'do framed her sweet face.

"Yes, really. Like major contemplation."

"So what's the plan? I know you have one," Daphne said as she blew on a steaming forkful of gnocchi.

"I'm exploring my options," Nina said, tantalizing Daphne with her cagey cool. "Connecticut University has an impressive MBA program, and I may look into teaching a night course in the fall."

"Hearing that makes me so happy." Daphne leaned back in her chair and spread her napkin across her lap.

"And you want to know something else? I'm positive all that deep contemplation never would've occurred had you not planted the seed."

Daphne grew demure as she lowered her gaze to her plate.

"You look exceptionally pretty tonight," Nina added, as if poor Daphne wasn't already writhing in self-consciousness.

"I do?" As she was lifting the fork to her mouth, a single gnocchi rolled off and onto the silky royal-blue button-down that made her eyes seem to scream, "Hey, now."

Nina contorted her face to suppress her laughter. "Not that I don't adore you in your messy buns and hoodies, but your swing at elegant beauty always ends up a homerun."

Daphne finished what she was chewing and leaned closer. "Nina, you are the sweetest, most romantic person I've ever met. No wonder why Zack is still a dick to you. He's gotta be sick over losing you."

"I could say the same thing about Savannah letting you go, Daphne. You know that old expression, 'One woman's trash is another woman's treasure.'"

"I'm living it." Daphne pushed her dish aside and sipped her wine. "I can't tell you how wonderful it is to be sitting here in this beautiful restaurant having dinner with you. But honestly, I would've been ecstatic having pizza and cuddling with you at home."

"That's our next stop," Nina said. "Honestly, if I have to sit here and stare into your soulful eyes and watch you lick your luscious, saucy lips much longer, I'll probably combust."

A naughty blush tinged Daphne's cheeks. "I'm assuming that means no dessert."

Nina bit her lip as a warm tingle shot through parts of her not suitable to discuss during elegant dining. "Not here, anyway."

Nina had spent a lot of woman-hours mentally crafting how she'd set the scene for the first time she made love with Daphne. She'd envisioned scented candles, chilled wine, and a little seventies soul pumping out of Alexa as they soaked in the bubbly bliss of her indoor hot tub, only a few steps away from her king bed draped in silky sheets. Just anticipating the scene inspired a physical response.

But when they left the restaurant and stood on the sidewalk waiting for the valet, the moon and wind and tree branches played shadow games with them. They gazed at each other, a giggle here, a sigh there. Daphne's fingers brushed across Nina's waist, and she kissed her softly. She teased her with a flick of her tongue until Nina forgot they were out on a sidewalk.

On the way home, they groped each other in the car, Nina swerving over the line a few times when she sneaked her hand between a gap in Daphne's royal-blue button-down shirt. Finally, on the porch, as Nina keyed in the numbers to unlock her door, Daphne's arm reached around her, and her hand slid inside the front of Nina's pants, nearly making direct contact with the part of her that had been dying for Daphne's touch all evening.

By that point, any elaborate seduction ritual she'd planned was moot. Nina barely had time to turn down the covers on her bed, as she preferred to focus on opening that royal-blue shirt, plucking at one button, slowly, agonizingly, at a time.

Daphne breathed heavily against her face when Nina released her from her shirt and then her breasts from the bra as she swirled her tongue behind Daphne's ear. Daphne seemed to be holding in a volcanic eruption as she trembled under Nina's touch.

After they stripped off each other's pants, Nina laid her down and pressed herself against Daphne's hot skin. The way Daphne clawed at her back as she ran her lips across her neck and collarbone told Nina that an eruption was imminent—for herself, too, as the feel and sound of Daphne's escalating arousal made her throb with desire.

Daphne writhed beneath her, clearly ready for whatever Nina had planned. No longer able to resist, Nina slowly traced a path down Daphne's taut body with her lips, stopping to explore and taste her sweet skin along with way.

Daphne's groans grew louder with every stroke, every lick Nina teased her with. "Don't hold back, baby," Nina whispered. "You sound so sexy."

And soon Daphne's moans escalated into shouts of ecstasy as she shuddered from Nina's touch. When Nina crawled back up to hold Daphne, her cheek grew wet from the tears rolling off Daphne's face.

"Hey," she whispered in concern. "Is everything okay?"

"Yes, yes," Daphne whispered, then wrenched her arms around Nina like a vise and pulled her tightly to her chest. "I just never knew love could feel like this."

Seeing the tenderness on Daphne's face, Nina started choking up, too. *No, no, no. There's no crying in the middle of hot, primal sex.*

But Nina couldn't stop herself. She laughed as her own tears began to trickle down her face, and she moved over to share the pillow with Daphne. She kissed some of Daphne's tears away and smiled. This was the kind of love she'd wanted to feel all her life.

❖

Finally recovering from the minor embarrassment of crying after the kind of sex that could rock the earth off its axis, Daphne knew it was time for redemption. She'd lost herself in secret fantasies of this moment numerous times throughout her friendship with Nina, and now she was squandering valuable time emoting over how insanely in love she felt.

Now, more than anything, she wanted to taste Nina, to find out if she'd become as addicting as she'd always imagined. She propped her against a pile of pillows and teased her before diving into her sweet spot. Nina stroked Daphne's hair gently, but as her tongue bored faster and deeper into her, Nina grabbed her head and moved her pelvis in rhythm with Daphne's tongue. She was loud and wild, and Daphne thought she might orgasm again just listening to Nina climax.

Having had only Ann Marie as a partner, she'd never known sex could be so magical, so utterly satisfying. Maybe Nina's complete lack of inhibition, which was highly erotic on its own, inspired that realization, or maybe she'd simply never fallen so intensely, completely in love before.

As she held Nina and Nina gently explored her chest and shoulders with her fingertips, Daphne was certain it was an exquisite combination of both.

CHAPTER TWENTY

The next morning when Nina woke up in Daphne's arms, she couldn't remember having fallen asleep. It felt so natural to lie there together, nothing between them as their skin pressed against each other's. Was she moving too fast, letting her heart grip the reins after ending things with Lacey only a couple of weeks ago? She didn't care. It had been ages since she'd experienced her emotions with such clarity.

Other than being Noah's mother, she couldn't remember when she'd felt so sure about anything, even in her professional life when she'd had to make important decisions swiftly and without faltering. That was her, in the business world. Since Noah was a baby, however, romance had taken a backseat to all her other obligations, as her ex-husband had so often pointed out.

But now as Daphne lay in her arms, loving her back, the drawbridge between Nina's heart and mind was closing and seemed like it would stay down permanently.

"Daphne, baby," she whispered as she gently shook her shoulder. "We have to get up. I have to get Noah at my mom's."

"Okay," Daphne replied, her voice strained as she stretched.

"You can borrow something of mine to wear."

"I can just wear my same clothes home. No biggie."

"Oh." Nina hesitated. "Well, I thought you might like to hang out with Noah and me today, maybe meet my mother?"

Daphne propped herself up on her elbow. "Really?"

Nina nodded. "I mean, if you want. If you think we're shifting into high gear too fast, just let me know. I've never fallen in love with my best friend before, so I'm unfamiliar with the protocol."

Daphne giggled as she lay back down in the crook of Nina's arm. "We've had this problem before, but I guess now it isn't so much of a problem if we're lying naked together in your bed."

Nina melted into Daphne's tepid eyes. "We are, aren't we?"

"We are." Daphne kissed her shoulder. "But it still feels so unreal."

"Last night was amazing," Nina said. "I've never felt like that before."

"Like what?"

"Hmm, how can I describe it?" Nina stroked the side of Daphne's arm. "I honestly don't think my mind, heart, and body have ever been so beautifully in sync as they were when your lips and fingertips were exploring me. And your eyes seemed to unlock something in my soul." A shiver ran through her. "The way you made me feel scares me a little. I've never been so vulnerable, but there's something so pure, so gentle about you that I just let myself go."

Daphne was silent. Had she seriously fallen back to sleep while Nina purged her entire heart to her? "Daph?"

A sniffle and a few droplets of tears on Nina's chest were her reply.

"Aww, don't cry, honey. Why are you always crying?" Nina lifted Daphne's chin and kissed her sweetly.

Daphne sniffled again through laughter. "They're happy tears," she said, wiping her cheeks. "I've never been this happy before."

Nina giggled at Daphne's unbearable cuteness and practically squeezed her into asphyxiation. She glanced at her alarm clock. "You know…we don't need to jump out of bed this minute."

"I was hoping you'd say that." Daphne lightly dragged her fingernails up Nina's forearm.

The joking subsided as Nina kissed her and ran her hand down the middle of Daphne's chest. Even with her hair a mess and last night's light mascara all smudgy around her eyes, Daphne's beauty hit her so hard, Nina could barely breathe.

When Daphne let out a purr of arousal, Nina mounted her and began to grind into her as she nibbled at her neck, hungry as a vampire. And the harder she devoured her, the louder Daphne moaned.

Nina opened her eyes, not wanting to miss a single second of their ridiculously wild synergy, the way their bodies fit together as if they'd been molded for that precise purpose. As Daphne's fingers dug into her back, she realized their connection went beyond the physical. It was greater than anything she'd ever known outside of motherhood. She started tearing up at the overwhelming surge of emotion. That is until Daphne grabbed hold of her hips, and they began rocking against each other in rhythmic thrusts until the friction of their harmony carried them away.

On the car ride over to Nina's mother's house, Daphne's stomach was undulating like the tide during a hurricane, even more so than last night when she'd showed up for their first date with a bouquet of roses and a box of gourmet chocolate-covered strawberries. If she thought it was difficult to impress a woman who had it all, how was she supposed to win over a ten-year-old boy? She already had, in a way, but as his mom's bestie, not her…gulp… lover? Partner? Girlfriend?

"So," she said as her leg kept frantic time to a Taylor Swift female-independence anthem Nina had blasting. "What are we going to say to Noah? What should I say?"

"Well, I suggest you start with 'hello' and see where it goes from there." She smirked, never taking her eyes directly off the road.

"That's not funny, Nina. I'm pretty sure it's easier to win over a teenage girl's father than someone's kid."

"I'm going to assume you're speculating and have no recent frame of reference."

"Stop joking. I'm really nervous."

Nina reached over and quelled her hyperactive leg. "Listen to me. Noah already likes you. He once told me he liked hanging out with you better than Lacey. If that's not a seal of approval, I don't know what is."

"That does make me feel a little better. But do we have to tell him today that we've changed the nature of our relationship? That might be too much for him."

"No, we don't," Nina said. "I was going to suggest that we let his discovery happen naturally. The more time we spend together, the more comfortable he'll feel having you around."

"Would he just reach the conclusion that we're a couple on his own?"

"Probably. He knows I identify as a lesbian now, thanks to Lacey. She sort of forced me to have a discussion with Noah early on that I wasn't sure was necessary. He's very inquisitive. When he wants to know something, he's not the least bit shy about asking. And I'm honest with him. So if it's okay with you, we can just take things at a pace we're all comfortable with."

"Sounds like a plan." Daphne smiled in relief, watching the trees whip by as they drove down the country road heading to Nina's mother's house. She cracked the window to smell the freshness of budding trees and woodsy greens. Spring was her favorite season, as it always promised new beginnings.

When Nina braked at the stop sign before an old wooden bridge crossing a river, Daphne threw the gearshift into park. "C'mon. Let's get out and take a quick selfie."

Nina hesitated—but only for a moment. "It's quite a backdrop, isn't it?"

"Gorgeous. But it's got nothing on you," Daphne said, surprising herself with her elevated flirt game.

They bolted from the SUV and converged at the beginning of the bridge. After turning to accommodate the glare of the midday sun, they posed for a few selfies.

As the river churned and splashed behind them, Daphne drank in another sip of Nina's beauty, and smiled. "So does this mean we're like...official?"

Nina smiled back as she brushed away wisps of Daphne's hair tousled by an interloping breeze. "Daphne, my heart knows what it wants. For the first time in my life, I have no doubts."

She stretched her arms around Nina's waist and tugged her close. "I have no doubts either, Nina. I love you."

Nina cooed with apparent delight. "I love you, too, baby. And it's officially official because we're both fully sober."

They attacked each other with kisses as they giggled, and Daphne nearly raised her off the ground as she wrapped her in the tightest of hugs.

❖

When they arrived at her mother's house, Nina was pumped full of excitement. Daphne was meeting her mother for the first time, and she couldn't wait. She shuddered a little at how the whole thing might go down. She'd come out to her mother when she'd decided to divorce Zack, but after all that, she'd never got around to introducing Lacey to her.

She thought about Zack and Lacey and how much both of those relationships had shaped who she'd become. For someone so confident in her abilities and decisions, they'd both given her pause to reexamine that confidence and realize it bordered on the edge of arrogance. She was humbler now, a characteristic she'd learned about from Daphne, who'd modeled it in so many ways.

After all the emotional upheaval she'd experienced to get here, she realized Daphne was a much bigger player in her epiphany than she'd realized.

She shut off the ignition and turned to Daphne, who looked semi-paralyzed with fear. "If you don't relax, my mother will think I kidnapped you and dragged you here against your will." She slipped her hand under Daphne's hair and gave her neck a squeeze and tickle.

Daphne looked around in an apparent attempt to take in the entire property. "Your mother's house looks like a country club. Does she rent it out for destination weddings?"

Nina sighed playfully. "Well, my dirty secret's out now. I hope it doesn't color your impression of me."

Daphne laughed. "If being raised filthy rich is the only secret you kept from me, that's a fabulous place to start."

Nina swiveled toward her and took her hand. "I'm not cashing that check you gave me, Daphne. I won't cash any check you give me for that loan, so you might as well save yourself the time writing them. That money came from a trust fund my father left me when he passed. Whether we end up together down the road or not, I don't want you to repay me."

Daphne's eyes floated in a lake of vulnerability as she placed her other hand over their clasped fingers. "Nina, I know all this is new between us, but I don't want to talk about not being with you down the road."

"I don't either. I just said that so you wouldn't feel obligated to me."

"Since I met you, all I've felt is my love for you growing bigger than I could handle at times. I can't even imagine what could happen to reverse the course. And I don't want to."

"Mom." Noah bounded out the front door and ran toward the car, holding something inside his coat.

"Hey, buddy." She jerked her head toward the house, and she and Daphne got out of the car. "Before I ask what you're hiding from me, can you say hi to Daphne?"

"Hi." He offered Daphne a charming grin, then resumed working on Nina. "Mom, Mrs. DeVito was over for coffee before."

The mention of Nina's mother's cat-lady widow friend from the country club seized Nina's heart in a momentary panic. "Noah, what's in your jacket?"

"Mom. Please," he said, solemn as a judge. "I swear I'll take care of him and clean his litter box."

When he produced a tiny orange kitten from inside his coat, Daphne squealed and lunged toward him, her fingers like mechanical claws angling for a prize.

"Oh, my God," she said as she smothered the poor thing's head in kisses.

"Two against one," Nina mumbled to herself as she rubbed her palm against her forehead in resignation. "I assumed you've already named him."

"Mike Wazowski," Noah replied with the brightest of smiles.

Daphne cracked up laughing, clearly up on her *Monsters, Inc.* characters.

Nina arched an eyebrow. "I was hoping that having to watch that movie three hundred times would have some redeeming outcome."

"I'm so jealous," Daphne said, cuddling the kitten against her face.

"Can I have my cat back?" Noah said.

"Hold on. One more kiss."

"Can we go inside now?" Nina said, darting her gaze between the both of them.

Daphne sat rapt in the closed-in sunporch overlooking the expansive backyard bordered by a lake. As Nina's mother carried a dish of watercress-and-lobster-salad finger sandwiches to go with the other gourmet hors de'ourves on the table, Daphne half expected Ina Garten to walk in with her, trailed by a camera crew.

When she finally joined them at the table, Daphne immediately noticed where Nina's stunning good looks came from. But when Nina squeezed her thigh beneath the tablecloth, Daphne snapped out of her googly-eyed stare.

"So, Daphne," her mother said. "I'm so delighted to finally meet you after hearing Nina speak about you so often."

Daphne smiled, her mouth full of finger sandwich.

"I love the story of how you met," she said. "My mother's lamp could've been lost from our family forever were you not so honest."

"Well, it's not so difficult choosing honesty when you see your car and half of your license plate splashed across the TV screen." She nearly choked on the wad of sandwich in her mouth when she noticed both mother and daughter looking slightly aghast at her quip. "I meant I never would've taken it in the first place had I known it wasn't spring-cleaning junk."

Nina's mother looked only partially relieved.

"Daphne's into antique salvaging, Mom," Nina said. "She's opening her store soon."

"Oh, that's right. Nina told me all about that. I'm looking forward to browsing around when it opens."

"The grand opening is a week from Saturday," Daphne said. "If you're free, please come. I'm making sort of an event out of it."

"Mom, I have to get the recipe for your lobster salad," Nina said. "I've volunteered for refreshment duty."

"Lobster?" Daphne said. "I was thinking doughnuts and coffee."

"Not when my mother makes all these killer apps."

Nina's mother smiled. "Aren't you the sweetest friend."

Nina's face blanched as white as the hand-embroidered lace tablecloth. "Uh, Ma, remember our phone call the other day?"

Her mother smiled as she seemed to puzzle it out in her head. Then suddenly, "Oh, yes. I do recall. You two are lovers now."

Nina groaned, apparently as mortified as Daphne felt. After they'd kicked each other black and blue under the table, Nina finally spoke. "Yeah, we usually say partner or significant other, or, heck, even girlfriend will suffice."

"Oh, for heaven's sake." Her mother daintily bit into a small asparagus puffed pastry that Daphne reasoned could've easily fit into her mouth whole. "Well, you people can get married now, so maybe I'll just call her Daphne until I can refer to her as my daughter-in-law."

"Mom," Nina exclaimed as an adorable blush apple-glazed her cheeks.

"I'm teasing," her mother said. "I know you just started dating. But judging by the way you're practically sitting in each other's lap, I suppose it won't be too much longer."

"Mother. Since when are you so chatty? Don't you usually like to sit and look regal and refined in the company of new guests?"

She picked up the cocktail sitting by her hand. "This is my second old-fashioned of the day." She sipped it and barely swallowed before adding, "You two weren't the only ones nervous about this impromptu luncheon."

After that, Daphne relaxed and reveled in a beautiful afternoon with Nina's immediate family, feeling as enthusiastic to be part of it as the new kitten must have.

The Friday before Nina's vacation, her boss requested a one-on-one conference call. The request was odd for many reasons, not the least of which was that it was a gorgeous spring afternoon, ideal for hitting the links. Also, Nina had always been so efficient at her job, the boss had the luxury of never having to contact her directly.

Nina sprang up from her reclined position in her chair when Spencer Lancaster's video conference call came through on her laptop.

"Spencer, so great to see you. Hope all's well down in Charleston."

"Good to see you, Nina," he said, barely cracking a smile. "Listen. I won't keep you because nobody likes Friday-afternoon conferences, but I just wanted to get to the bottom of something I noticed happening in the New England region."

"Oh? What's that?" Nina pinched her chin between her thumb and forefinger, feigning curiosity.

"Breast-ultrasound claims are going through as preventative care. Did you authorize that change?"

He was being cagey for some reason. If anyone was going to authorize a change in procedure claim status, it would be Nina.

"Well, since it's Friday and nobody likes late-afternoon conferences, I'm going to go ahead and say yes, it was me."

He laughed a little as he scratched at his goatee, clearly indulging Nina's sardonic tone. "I can understand a few appealed claims here and there, but the latest quarterly report indicates that all claims submitted for ultrasounds accompanying mammograms have been paid out. Why is that, when our national policy designates them as diagnostic, not preventative?"

"Based on my understanding of preventative care, Spencer, these specific ultrasounds serve the same function as mammograms, so not covering them has been an oversight on Global's part."

"Nina, you're a highly regarded member of Global Health Insurance's upper management, but you do not have the authority to change policy on procedure designations. This has to stop."

"Spencer, do you know anything about the purpose of mammograms?"

"Of course I do."

"Well, it seems that your full understanding stops there. Women with dense breast tissue, and who've had prior biopsies, require more than just a mammogram to ensure they don't have early stage breast cancer. They need the ultrasounds to ensure the mammogram didn't miss any irregularities, as they're known to do on occasion. You can't pay for one and not the other. They're two procedures toward the same goal."

"Nina, our policy stands. Mammograms are covered under preventative care. Ultrasounds are not. That's that. I trust I'll see a substantially lower number of claim payouts next quarter. Yes?"

"But they're both a means to the same end, Spencer. How do you cover one and not the other?"

"Ultrasounds are coded as diagnostic. You can't pick and choose when they should be considered preventative."

"But in this instance, they absolutely should be."

"That's not something you or I can arbitrarily decide. It has to be taken up with the board as well."

"Okay. Well, I'm going to do that."

"Fine. Go ahead, but in the interim, they're not covered, and I need you to make sure the New England division stops paying the claims."

Nina gnawed on her bottom lip a moment to prevent herself from saying something to Spencer she'd regret. The bureaucracy and the red tape were becoming untenable. She was an executive at a Fortune 500 company, but the weight of the realization that her success and standing in the corporate world was predicated on how well she denied others reimbursement for medical care was becoming a burden too heavy to shoulder.

"Now you have yourself a splendid weekend, Nina." His smile seemed both genuine and sinister. It gave her the chills.

"Yes, you too, Spencer. I'll make sure to handle what needs to be done."

"That's why we have such faith in you, Nina."

Nina ended the call in frustration, then smiled when she remembered her date with Daphne.

Tomorrow was the grand-opening extravaganza of her antique shop, and Nina couldn't wait to bask in the joy and sense of pride Daphne would surely charge the room with. But first, they had tonight.

❖

That night Daphne had brought dinner over to Nina's house. With the opening of her antique shop the next morning, her anxiety would've had her fidgeting at the table if they'd gone to a restaurant, or skulking through each room of the house if she'd stayed in and tried to go to bed early. She'd thought of a different, more appetizing way to burn the excess energy, but it was Nina's weekend with Noah, so it was Plan B.

She walked into Nina's house with her bags full of prepared food, and to her surprise and delight, Nina dashed toward her with hugs and kisses before she could lay her supplies down.

They landed against the counter, entwined in each other's arms.

"What are you doing?" Daphne asked when Nina stopped smothering her in kisses. "Are you okay?"

"I am now," Nina said. "I had the worst day, and it's so much better since you walked in."

Daphne sighed. What a moment, seeing Nina so vulnerable with her emotions, relying on her to be the rock for a change. Daphne had never been the rock before. She and Ann Marie, or Savannah, were so young when they got together, Savannah, with her domineering personality, had always handled important matters. Now here she was being the emotional support for one of the strongest, bravest women she knew. By default, that must've made her a strong woman, too.

"Do you want to help me cook, or would you rather relax with a glass of wine while I get everything together?"

"The wine is a no-brainer," Nina said, waving an empty wineglass in front of her. "What's in those bags?"

"All the fixin's for personal pizzas," Daphne replied as she refilled Nina's glass and poured herself one. "I have everything we need and every imaginable topping. Except pineapple. This isn't Hawaii."

Nina sprawled in the chair as she sipped her wine. "You look awfully cute in a domestic role. Can I just watch you make them?"

"I'd planned to come over wearing only an apron but..." Daphne leaned over and kissed Nina's sticky wine lips.

"Good call." Nina nodded toward Noah standing in the archway. "But let's not take that idea off the table."

"I'm hungry," Noah said.

"Can you say hi first?" Nina said.

Noah padded into the kitchen and gave Daphne a quick hug without being encouraged. Daphne pretty much melted as she locked eyes with Nina.

"This is 'make your own pizza' night," Daphne told him. "You pick your toppings and put it all together."

Noah's face lit up. He dashed to the sink, and after washing his hands, he immersed them into the blob of dough Daphne set out for him. They horsed around pretending to be Italian pizza chefs, flinging flour, shredded cheese, and toppings around on each other's flattened-out dough.

Noticing Nina's persistent giggles, Daphne yanked her up to join them, and before long, everyone's dreadful week evaporated in the warmth of family and a preheated oven.

That night Nina brushed her teeth while Daphne sat in bed, checking her phone, her forehead wrinkled with what seemed like concern.

"Everything okay, honey?" Nina said through a mouthful of toothpaste foam.

"I hope. I texted Sophie's son this morning, but he hasn't responded. I stopped in to see her after work yesterday, and she just didn't seem herself—well, even less than usual."

Nina didn't like the sound of that, but she refused to suggest anything but positivity on the eve of such an important day for Daphne. "I'm sure he'll get back to you. He probably had a hectic week like the rest of us."

Daphne placed her phone on the nightstand and smiled. "You're probably right."

Nina crawled into bed and cozied up to her. "Aren't you exhausted? You have such a big day tomorrow. You need to get some rest."

"I can't. I'm so wired. Today I walked out of a job I've had my entire adult life. It still doesn't seem real. When Sunday night comes around, I'll probably start making my lunch for the week."

"That must've been an empowering experience."

"It was," Daphne said. "Store-bought farewell cake, a gift card to Panera, and the only coworker I truly loved, Pascale, a grown man, blubbering in the corner of the kitchen."

Nina giggled. "You lived out my exact fantasy for the last two years."

"It felt wonderful knowing I never have to go back to that call-center cubby and listen to angry, frantic travelers yell at me about their cancelled flights anymore. But it's scary. I don't think I've felt the full impact yet."

"Try not to stew about that now," Nina said. "You have way bigger things on the horizon."

"I'm so nervous about that, too. But also excited."

"Just be excited, baby. It's going to be a blast." She nuzzled closer. "Your shelves are fully stocked, our advertising blitz was sure to reach a massive audience, and well, as usual, you can count on me for ancillary support."

"You just want to see if your marketing campaign was a success," Daphne said and pinched Nina's sides with a naughty grin.

"I am a little curious," Nina said. "But honestly, Daph. Tomorrow is all about you and that big, old Make it Happen vision board of yours. Be ecstatic. You're making your biggest dream on there come to life."

"I've made my two biggest items on there a reality. And if you ask me, finding true love is harder than opening your own business."

"What?" Nina feigned surprise. "For you it was easier than stealing a lamp from a divorcee."

"Ha-ha. I see what you did there."

Nina reached around and pulled Daphne's head toward her for a kiss. "I've always believed in true love. I was just never looking in the right direction for it. Until now."

Daphne slid down on the pillow to meet Nina face-to-face. "I just wish Sophie could be there with us tomorrow."

"Maybe she can. Try her son again first thing in the morning."

Daphne nodded. "So you never finished your work story. What happened with your boss?"

Nina sighed. "What always happens. I get a curt, condescending little speech that ends with him saying 'Run it past the board.'"

"I'm sorry, baby." Daphne squeezed her closer.

"Meh. That's why they pay me the big bucks. Anyway, tomorrow I get to live vicariously through you and the debut of your sensational new career."

"Ooh, that sounds kind of vampirish. I have a succubus for a girlfriend," Daphne said, pecking at Nina's lips. "That's hot."

CHAPTER TWENTY-ONE

After a night of tossing and turning, maybe actually sleeping for an hour or two before dawn approached, the alarm jarred Daphne awake—and that jarred Nina awake.

"Sorry, babe," Daphne said.

"What's the matter?" Nina touched her chest above the V-neck opening in her T-shirt. "You're all clammy."

Daphne lay as still as a corpse, her heart drubbing against her rib cage. Her throat was parched, and she couldn't stop shaking. "I think I'm having a panic attack."

Nina hovered over her. "What? Why?"

"Nina, I quit my job yesterday." Daphne forced herself to swallow.

"Yes, I know. We talked about this last night."

"How could I have been so impetuous, so reckless?"

"Honey, you aren't either of those. You left the airline to pursue your dream of being a business owner. Remember the vision board?"

Still prone and motionless, Daphne nodded and licked her dry lips as she tried to tap out a rhythm on the inside of her arm to calm her raging nervous system. "I also remember having a stable job with a regular income and health insurance."

"Do you also remember feeling miserable, suffocated, and uninspired?"

Daphne nodded. "Is it too early for a shot of tequila?"

Nina checked the clock. "Seven thirty? Yeah, I'd say so." She patted Daphne's arm. "Honey, you're just having an attack of nerves. Why don't you get out of bed and move around a little. Maybe that'll help."

"Nope," Daphne said, shaking her head. "I'm gonna stay here for another minute. Or hour. Or day. Whatever."

Nina repositioned herself beside her, reaching under the covers for her hand. "Listen, Daph. What you're feeling now, nervous—"

"Terrified."

"Okay." Nina continued in a soft, soothing tone. "What you're feeling is normal. You're taking a huge leap in your life. Starting something brand-new is going to freak anyone out a little. You're like the bravest woman I know," she said, shaking their clutched hands for emphasis. "And even if this antique shop fails, you'll always have under your belt the accomplishment of facing your greatest fear."

Daphne's stomach plummeted even further. "What do you mean, if it fails? You said it won't."

"Well, uh, I was just…All right, look. That was a worst-case scenario. Of course it won't fail." Clearly frustrated with herself, Nina ran her hands over her face. "Listen to me, Daphne. Are you listening?"

Daphne nodded and forced her scattered attention on Nina's firm, reassuring expression.

"Think of it this way," Nina said, fully composed. "When our baggage is too heavy, airlines make us lighten our load so we can fly. And we do it. We may complain a little, but we do it so we can fly. Think about that."

When Nina leaned down and kissed her on the forehead, Daphne closed her eyes and let the warmth and comfort from her lips radiate through her body.

"You want to fly, Daphne, and I want to see you do it. Let go of the fear." She released her grip on Daphne's hand and stood up.

Daphne gazed up at Nina's confident posture, those fiery eyes full of encouragement and something clicked. She flung the covers aside and rose triumphantly to her feet. She faced Nina, grabbed her shoulders, and kissed her on the lips. "Thank you."

Nina wrapped her arms around Daphne's waist and pulled her in like a warm wave, drenching her with confidence. "You got this, baby," she said softly against her ear.

Daphne nodded and rested her forehead against Nina's for a moment. "I'll jump in the shower, and then we'll get this show on the road."

As the tepid water ran over her face, Daphne realized that all of Nina's advice and pep talks had seeped in. Her once-debilitating thoughts of inevitable failure were slowly dissolving and sliding toward the drain in the sudsy water. Meeting Nina felt like a gift from the universe—the wind beneath her wings or the hard-core kick in the ass she'd needed to embrace a new journey without letting fear drive her off her path.

She was ready for this dream to come true.

❖

They arrived at Trash to Treasure Antiques and Collectibles a half hour before opening. Daphne had stocked the shelves during the week, so they only needed to complete some cosmetic touches. After lighting sandalwood candles inside and fastidiously repositioning items such as a Soufflenheim pottery roaster, a vintage French glazed pottery pitcher, and an antique French lidded jug and goblets, she headed outside to festoon the front.

Noah climbed and stretched to help hang banners and loved using the rented helium tank to fill the balloons, under Nina's supervision. When he came outside clutching a handful of gold and silver balloons, Daphne said he could string them up wherever he saw fit.

Nina then appeared, flashing a close-lipped grin. She consulted her watch, then said, "Good luck, baby," in a helium-possessed voice.

Daphne desperately needed the ensuing laugh to cut the tension thrumming in her temples. "Why does your goofy side always surprise me?"

Nina took another hit from the open balloon. "I go to great lengths to keep it a secret." She winked, then nodded toward the parking lot to a couple of women headed straight for the shop. "It's showtime."

Daphne smiled as a surge of eagerness tingled through her, and they all bolted inside and assumed their positions out of the fray toward the back of the store.

About fifteen minutes later the shop was buzzing with patrons. Nina gave Daphne a nudge to step out into the room and make her presence known in case anyone had a question. She reminded her of one of the first rules of small business: let the customers know that they're worth more than just a sale. After approaching several safe-looking older women, Daphne had her schmooze groove on point—and it was so effective that it resulted in her first sale.

As the shop steadily filled with people, Daphne wasn't able to keep as close an eye on each new customer. But Pascale was tall and lanky enough to stand out.

"So, this is what you left me for," he said, his arms spread out like eagle wings.

"Pascale," Daphne squealed as she accosted him with a hug.

"The place looks great," he said, taking it all in. "I'm proud of you, kid. Now where are the lonely, middle-aged chicks with enough disposable income to splurge on pricey antiques?"

"Whoa. You're finally off the Gen-Zers. It's a day for miracles."

"Not off. Just willing to expand my horizons." He ran his hand through his wavy brown hair like he was a brooding underwear model.

Daphne smirked. "Well, even the tiniest amount of personal growth is worth noting. Thank you so much for coming today."

"No problem. And just because you're not working with me anymore doesn't mean we're not gonna be friends. You better stay in touch." His eyes seemed to get misty with sincerity.

"Pascale? Are you getting choked up?"

He cleared his throat. "No. You are."

"Listen," she said. "If we don't get together for beer and pizza at least once a month, I'll be furious with you. And I still expect rude texts about Galena and the other hot messes at Sky-Hi."

"Goes without saying."

Daphne was about to reply when someone from behind accidentally bumped into Pascale, lurching him toward her.

"Oh. Sorry, buddy," the woman said. "This pedestal is heavier than I thought."

"Olive, so good to see you," Daphne said. "This is Olive, the contractor. She's the one who single-handedly whipped this place into shape."

"'Sup?" she said to Pascale.

"Pleasure to meet you." He gently took Olive's hand and kissed the top of it.

"I don't think you can do that without asking these days," Daphne mumbled out the side of her mouth.

"Well, look at you, all black-and-white-movie debonair," Olive said to him, beaming.

"I guess you can," Daphne said to herself.

"Your craftsmanship is flawless," Pascale said.

"Oh, jeez." Daphne slipped away from them with ease as they'd clearly forgotten she was standing there.

Noticing that Nina had receded into the shadows, she searched and found her at the entrance to the storeroom. Sipping her coffee, Nina gave her a smile over the lid of the cup and a thumbs-up. Daphne wheeled around toward the front of the shop, relishing that singular, fleeting epoch when everything—the stars, the planets, the ebb and flow of the universe—felt aligned in harmony.

And then it happened.

Like a funnel cloud descending on a defenseless prairie town, Savannah Locke swept into the store flanked by two young, dashing gay boys. Flying monkeys. The thought flashed in and out of Daphne's mind. Savannah had developed a klatch of hangers-on since hitting the YouTube big time and, as a result, never traveled sans an entourage.

Daphne stepped behind an antique coat rack on which hung vintage clothing items, and peered around a musty-smelling London Fog raincoat for signs of the mad Dr. Francesca-stein, gastric-bypass surgeon to the wannabe stars. Savannah had apparently not brought her.

"What are you doing?"

She flinched at Nina's voice emanating from behind, then whirled around. "Do you know who that is?"

Nina studied Savannah for a moment. "I'm tempted to say a white Billy Porter, but I know it's not."

"That's Savannah, my ex." Daphne's eyes remained fixed on her as her angst thwarted her effort to be low-key.

"Is that so?" An evil grin spread across Nina's face. "What are you waiting for? Go say hi and show her around your fabulous new shop."

She studied Nina in surprise. "Yeah?"

"Yeah," Nina replied with a resolute nod.

"Yeah," Daphne said. Light was suddenly dawning. "Yes. That's exactly what I'll do."

Nina patted her butt like a football coach, and Daphne sauntered over to Savannah, who was browsing the small assemblage of antique costume jewelry.

"Hello, Savannah," Daphne said, her voice smooth as crushed velvet. "Welcome to my world of antiques."

Savannah swung around like a well-rehearsed diva. "Why, Daphne, hello. This is your place?"

"Give me a break, Savannah. You know it is." Daphne did a double take at the resting bitch faces on the boys bookending her like they were security guards. *As if.*

Savannah rolled her eyes. "Okay, okay. Maybe I'd heard you were finally opening up the store you were always going on about."

Daphne bristled. Savannah had always been snarky and condescending, even before she'd had the tiniest reason to be, but now she was just plain awful. "So you had to come by and cast a spell of negativity on it, assuming it'll fail."

Savannah's frown actually seemed genuine. "Daphne, I'm sorry you think so low of me. I realize we ended on a rather sour note, but I'm here because I wanted to be among the first to come out in support of your new endeavor."

"Really?"

"Yes, really." Savannah's tone was totally unaffected with pretense. "We were together for half our lives." She rolled her eyes, then slipped back into diva mode as she picked up a gaudy early twentieth-century-style rhinestone bracelet. "I love this," she said, letting it dangle between her fingers. "Are there earrings to match?"

Leave it to Savannah to swoop in like a fairy godmother and upstage Daphne with an uncharacteristic show of authentic kindness.

"Hmm. I don't believe so," Daphne said. "A lot of times with estate sales, you get what you get."

"I'll take it anyway," Savannah said with a shrug. "I'd like some room accents as well. Do you have anything in the fifties art-deco style?"

Daphne felt the air filtering back into the room. "I think I do. Check over in the décor section in the corner." She pointed toward the back of the room, where Nina stood.

"Back there, near that tall, dark, and handsome woman? Your salesgirl?"

"Better." Daphne gave a satisfied smile. "My girlfriend."

"Oh," Savannah said with a mild blush. "Oh. Well. Everything's certainly coming up roses for you." She smiled and placed her hand on Daphne's shoulder. "I'm glad."

"Thank you," Daphne said, finally feeling free to be herself around Savannah. "And thank you for your support."

She left Savannah to her browsing, and as she started walking toward the back of the store, she watched Nina slip into the back room.

"Can you believe this?" Daphne said once they were in privacy. "She's actually here to wish me well."

"A credit to your sweet nature, no doubt." Nina tapped her playfully on her nose.

"I still say part of her is here to see if this business will go down in flames."

"Then overcharge her."

Daphne giggled and threw her arms around Nina's neck. "I'm having the best day."

"You're clearly in your element." Nina gave her a tender kiss. "And since you have this totally under control, I'm gonna sneak out and pick us up some lunch. Noah can stay and handle floor sales for you."

"No. Don't go. Let's order from Uber Eats."

"This is a special occasion," Nina insisted. "No room-temperature fast food allowed. I want to get us something special. It'll be a surprise. I promise I won't be long."

Daphne slipped her arm around Nina's waist and walked her all the way through the shop to the front entrance, slowing her pace as they passed Savannah.

That one felt good.

As Nina drove into the convalescent-home parking lot, she smiled, pleased with herself as she envisioned the look on Daphne's face when she wheeled Sophie into the antique shop for the festivities. Her excuse that she was going to pick up a special celebratory lunch for them was sheer brilliance.

She walked into the facility and approached the reception desk, all brightness and cheer. After the young woman there finished clicking her lavender gel nails on her computer keyboard, she looked up and greeted her.

"Hello. I'm here to see Sophie Gorski. Actually, I'd like to sign her out for the afternoon, if that's possible."

"I'm sorry. Who did you say?"

"Sophie Gorski."

As the young woman clicked a few keys, Nina watched the color drain from her face. "Um, I'm afraid you can't."

"Why not? She's my friend."

"Well, um, Mrs. Gorski passed away last night."

Now it was Nina's turn to feel blanched. "What?" she said in a whisper, then managed an "Are you sure?"

The receptionist raised her pointy nail to the computer screen and read it. "Yes. The funeral home picked her up an hour ago."

Nina stared into the air over the receptionist's head, trying to recover from the shock.

"I'm sorry, ma'am." The young woman's soft voice lulled her back to reality.

"Oh, um. Thank you. Thanks," Nina said and trudged off across the polished tiles toward the door.

"Un-fucking-believable," she shouted to the sky as she crossed the parking lot.

She sat in her car for a moment, trying to process the gravity of the situation. How could the universe be so cruel to Daphne? On the happiest day of her life, she'd have to hear the worst possible news. She licked her lips, trying to stay calm. She sure as hell wasn't going to be the one to tell her.

Half in anger, half in desperation, she tore out of the parking lot and headed back to the store. When she returned, Daphne came running to the car excitedly.

"Hi, love." She poked her head inside the driver's window for a kiss. "I'm so glad you're back. We're starving. My appetite's come back now that I'm not petrified anymore," she said with a giggle.

Lunch? Son of a bitch.

"Uh…" Nina extended the syllable as she tried to fabricate an excuse on the spot. "I forgot to get lunch. I had to make a sudden pit stop at home, if you know what I mean." She rubbed her stomach for effect.

"Oh, honey." Daphne was all sympathy as she whispered, "You had to poop? You should've just gone here. It's private back there."

"Er, uh…I can't go in public." Nina rolled her eyes at the humiliating hole she was digging herself into. "How about sushi? I'll run over and grab it."

"Sure. That sounds good. Let me get back inside. I left Noah in charge of the cash register." She stretched open her eyes in mock panic.

"Okay. I'll be back."

Nina got out of the car and strolled a few doors down to the Asian take-out place where she and Daphne were becoming regulars. How was she supposed to go back into the shop and act like everything was peachy now that she knew what she knew? She'd never seen Daphne so enthusiastic about anything. This was her day. Nina was not about to cast a shadow over it.

❖

By seven o'clock, Daphne's banner day was winding down. She'd counted the receipts several times, and each time, to her disbelief and delight, she'd grossed almost four thousand dollars. In one day. She understood the windfall was from all the grand-opening hype signs in the area, that it was a gorgeous spring day, and that Nina had flooded social media with advertisements leading up to the event. She also remembered she'd have to include overhead costs, but her sales were promising. If she could maintain that amount monthly, plus what she did in website sales, she wouldn't end up having to sell her house and move into the back room of the store.

The bell over the door announced Nina's return after driving Noah to his friend's house to spend the night. Daphne walked out from the back and noticed Nina's expression and her pale complexion.

"Is your stomach still bothering you, babe?"

"Huh?" Nina said with a quizzical look. "Oh, right. Um, yeah, I'm fine. So how do you think things went today?" She plunked herself down on an antique stool.

"Way better than I expected. Almost four thousand."

"That's incredible."

"It totally is," Daphne said as she slid between Nina's legs to give her a kiss. "And I have you to thank for it." She kissed her again, more sensually, but Nina wasn't responding as expected. She was not herself. Clearly more than gastro-intestinal distress was going on.

Her heart started palpitating as her mind wandered into the worst possible place. Nina planned to break up with her. Yep. She'd outgrown her already but was hanging in there until Daphne's journey to independent businesswoman was complete. And now that it was, boom. She was out of here.

She lifted Nina's chin. "Nina, what's wrong? Please tell me."

Nina sighed heavily, still staring into Daphne's eyes. "I have some bad news, Daph."

"I knew it." Daphne withdrew from her. "You want to break up with me."

"What?" Nina sprang up from the stool. "No, that's not what—"

Daphne's phone vibrated and sang from her back pocket, and in her moment of desperation, she grabbed it and saw that it was Sophie's son. When she answered it, Will's voice sounded cold and vacant.

"Hi, Daphne. It's Will. I'm calling to let you know Mom passed early this morning."

The news compounded her agitation that Nina was dumping her. A light gasp escaped her mouth as she clutched the edge of the counter for support.

"Daphne?" he said.

"I'm so sorry, Will," she said as her voice cracked in sorrow. "I'm…I don't know what to say."

"I know. It was a blessing though. She was ready to see my dad again."

"I think she was, too." Daphne inhaled slowly, trying to hold it together as tears streamed down her cheeks.

"I just wanted to say thank you for being a good friend to her over the last few years. She treasured your company."

"She was the best friend I could've asked for, Will. I hope she knew that."

"I'm sure she did. I'll text you when her arrangements are made."

"Okay." After she ended the call, she pinched her fingers up to her eyes as her grief broke through. She walked into Nina's arms and sobbed into her shoulder.

"I'm so sorry, baby," Nina whispered as she rubbed her back.

After feeling sufficiently purged, Daphne pulled back. "Okay. I'm ready for your bad news now."

"You dummy," Nina said, wiping Daphne's tears with her thumbs. "That was the bad news."

"You're not breaking up with me?"

"God, no," she said excitedly. "You're not getting rid of me that easily now that you're a successful antique dealer."

Daphne threw her arms around Nina's neck. "I don't want to get rid of you. I'm so crazy about you."

"I am, too, honey. I've never wanted anyone more than I want you. I can't even imagine us breaking up, much less being the one to do it."

"What a relief. I'm so glad to hear you—Wait a minute. How did you know about Sophie if I just found out now?"

"I wasn't going to get lunch today or to poop. I went to the convalescent home to get Sophie so I could bring her here and surprise you. Needless to say, that plan was a colossal flop."

Daphne chuckled in spite of herself. "And you embarrassed yourself saying you almost crapped your pants just to save my feelings?"

Nina nodded. "Yup."

Daphne gushed. "That's the sweetest thing ever, Nina. You're my hero in so many ways." She gave her a lingering peck on the lips.

"If that's not love," Nina said. "I'm sorry about your friend, Daphne. If I can do anything at all…"

Daphne smiled. "Just keep being you."

CHAPTER TWENTY-TWO

Daphne sat on her front porch sipping a glass of Sophie's favorite cabernet sauvignon as she watched the new people move into her house. Sometimes she wondered why she made some of the choices she did, this exercise in morbidity being one of them. But it was a last bit of closure as she processed saying good-bye to her friend, a ceremonial sendoff for Sophie, who was, as they say, in a better place.

She watched the two young boys chase each other around the front yard in their shorts, shirtless in the hot summer sun, screeching and laughing as they wrestled each other to the grass. Their arrival should effectively end her nights sleeping with the windows open. She took a large gulp of wine as she reminisced about the many times she'd crept home across their lawns stuffed with Sophie's delicious Polish cooking and wine.

She closed her eyes and recalled with a smile how it had felt when Sophie gave her the most poignant hug of her life the day Savannah moved out of the house and drove away with Francesca in the passenger seat, their shame, or lack of it, concealed behind matching Jackie O-style sunglasses.

From day one, Sophie had been convinced that Daphne's love life wasn't the sinking, *Titanic*-size disaster Daphne felt it had become. Sophie would listen to her vent, but only for a little while, refusing to let her plummet like a stone into a well of self-pity. A Polish immigrant who came from nothing, Sophie didn't play like that.

Daphne smiled and stopped hating this quaint little hetero family of four and their yappy little hybrid dog in honor of Sophie. She'd have been delighted to know that a young family was settling into the home she'd created with her husband and son a lifetime ago.

Yeah, Sophie would be delighted. But Daphne wasn't. Fuck that. Those kids were loud.

As she stood up to go inside, Nina's car pulled into her driveway.

"This is a nice surprise," she said as Nina walked up to the porch. "I thought you had reports to finish."

"You sounded so sad." Nina produced a single rose packaged in cellophane from behind her back and handed it to her with a kiss.

"Thank you," Daphne said. "It's beautiful, and you're the sweetest."

They sat down together on the top step.

"Are you going to refill that glass or what?" Nina asked.

Daphne laughed and filled the glass for her. "I don't know why I'm sitting out here. I should've closed my windows, blasted my AC, and binge-watched something until the moving truck left."

"That's probably what I would've done," Nina said after another sip. "But you're definitely more in tune with your emotions than I am—especially the dark, scary ones."

"I just hate the idea that other people are in Sophie's house. I know she hadn't been there in months, but as long as she was alive, I could pretend she was coming home. It was stupid, but it was something to hold on to. Now there's nothing."

Nina rested her shoulder against Daphne's for a quiet moment. "You never know. Maybe you and the missus over there will strike up a friendship."

"Eh, she made a point to wave before, so she seems nice enough. But she'll never be Sophie."

"I think I'm starting to fully understand the scope of your love for antiques."

"What do you mean?" Daphne had never given it too much thought.

"You love to cherish things in your life. And you hate with a vengeance to let go of what you love."

Nina's observation was profound. Intense. And absolutely spot-on. She stared at her as if a dark secret had been exposed. "How are you not a psychiatrist?"

"I'm on target, aren't I?"

Daphne nodded as she gathered her thoughts. "Remember when we were first getting to know each other, and I told you I'm an only child?"

"Of course. Your brother passed when he was a teenager."

"I was only eight when he died, but I remember the whole year he was sick like it was yesterday." She paused as the ghostly memories of his loss fluttered through her. "So many things changed. So many things I took for granted."

Nina draped her arm around Daphne's shoulder as she talked.

"Afterward my mother couldn't throw out any of his stuff. She stored most of it in boxes in the basement, but one spring the sump pump broke, and our cellar flooded. Most of his things were ruined. We tried to dry the contents, but his NFL collectible cards that he adored, this red-corduroy stuffed bunny my grandma gave him as a baby, and most of his drawings were all destroyed. In a way it was like losing him all over again." She forced a smile. "So, yeah, I think you nailed it, Dr. Colombo."

Nina gave her shoulder a squeeze. "Maybe this antique shop is some symbolic way of making sure you never lose anything precious again."

"Crazy reason to open a business, huh?"

Nina shrugged. "It makes complete sense. There are as many reasons for starting one as there are businesses. But yours is about as tragic and poetic and beautiful as they come."

Daphne rested her head on Nina's shoulder, so at peace in her presence.

"Do you know what makes one business owner more successful than another?" Nina asked.

Daphne shook her head.

"Passion. And if your inspiration is any indication, your venture will be a huge success."

After they exchanged a tender kiss, Daphne dropped her head onto Nina's shoulder again and watched the airy cumulus clouds pass overhead, hoping Sophie and her own brother knew how much they were missed.

❖

Nina followed Daphne into the house and then the kitchen after offering to help whip up something light and healthy for dinner. Standing out back looking after the chicken on Daphne's small grill, she contemplated when the appropriate moment would be to share her good news with her, the original reason she'd dropped by that afternoon. She hadn't anticipated their conversation would swerve quite so far onto the unpaved paths of grief and loss, but it was okay. The universe clearly had another purpose for Nina that day.

When she went inside, Daphne had set the table with a large bowl of dressed salad greens with quinoa, feta cheese, and cherry tomatoes. Plus a chilled bottle of white to complement dinner.

"Do you mind if we eat in here?" Daphne asked. "I don't want the neighbors to assume things about me."

Nina was surprised. "That you're a lesbian?"

"No. That I'm sociable."

Nina placed a hand over her chest as she laughed. "You gave me a minor heart attack."

Daphne poured their wine and sliced a loaf of French bread. "This isn't much of a Saturday-night dinner." She looked up from her plate. "Maybe we should've gone out."

"This is perfect. It's all about the company tonight." Nina leaned over and kissed her. "Let's drink to Sophie."

Daphne smiled and raised her glass. "To Sophie." The crash of some sort of large item rumbled in from the neighbor's driveway. "And to new beginnings."

"Hope that wasn't an antique," Nina said, and they exchanged naughty grins. "Speaking of new beginnings." She reached into her pants pocket and handed Daphne a business card.

Daphne's eyes bulged as her mouth formed a circle of surprise and delight. "Nina Colombo, Adjunct Professor, Connecticut University? Are you kidding me? How did you keep this a secret?"

Feeling humbled, Nina bowed her head. "I wanted to surprise you."

"Mission accomplished." Daphne jumped up, landed in Nina's lap, and linked her arms around her neck.

"I didn't have the balls to quit my job or anything like you," Nina said. "But I'll be teaching Business Ethics with a focus on women in business every Monday night for the fall semester. If all goes well and I find it's a good fit, who knows where it can go."

"I've always wanted to sleep with a college professor." Daphne gave her a warm smooch. "I'm so friggin' proud of you," she said, enveloping Nina in a hug.

Nina pulled back and stroked the hair off Daphne's forehead. "I never would've done this if it weren't for you."

"Me? I just mentioned it to you once or twice in passing."

"You planted the seed," Nina said sincerely. "I've loved being a mentor, but for some reason, it never occurred to me that I could be a college instructor and reach groups of young people instead of just a few a year. Until you and your vision board."

"Wow." Daphne beamed. "Who knew that thing had such power?"

"It wasn't just that. As I watched you take that enormous leap into something so new and so uncertain, you lit a fire inside me."

"Uncertain?" Daphne clenched her teeth in pretend panic. "You said it was a sure bet."

Nina giggled. "Will you stop? The shop is doing fine. Sales are on a slow but stable trajectory for a new business."

"I've had to dip into my savings twice, but I'm not panicking. Someone really smart and really sexy once told me you just have to dig your stilettos in and hang on for dear life during the first year of any new business."

"Sound advice." Nina glanced around the kitchen and examined the vision board still occupying almost an entire wall. She smiled at the large checkmark in glittery gold marker that sliced through the number-one item, the antique shop. "Would you like more unsolicited business advice?"

"It's never unsolicited from you. I'd love to spend a whole day rooting through that brilliant brain of yours."

"In that case, you could ease a great deal of your financial worries by consolidating households. I mean, why pay for one mortgage when..." Nina waited to see if Daphne would catch on.

"Wait." A glimmer of understanding flickered in her eyes. "Consolidating households? Like..."

As she spoke, Nina stood up, uncapped the gold glitter marker, and drew a check through item number two, Marry the Love of My Life. "Is moving in with her the same thing?"

"Are you asking me to move in with you?"

"It makes more sense," Nina said playfully. "My house is a lot bigger than yours."

"And my new neighbors are noisy," Daphne said, inching closer.

"And clumsy," Nina added as she slid her hand around the back of Daphne's head and drew her in for a sensual kiss.

"Is that the only reason you want me to move in? Pragmatism?"

Nina rolled her eyes. "I should say yes, just because you're being a wiseass. But the truth is, I can't think of a more gorgeous way to start each new day than to open my eyes every morning and see your face."

Daphne's radiance was almost blinding. "This has been the single most spectacular dinner of my life."

Nina took that as a "yes."

The next morning, Daphne carried the OJ and prosecco over to Nina's for Sunday breakfast. No point in losing a wonderful tradition. It just needed some updating. Sophie would've wholly approved.

They had gathered around the table for a feast of Belgian waffles, at Noah's insistence. Nina pulled the second set of fluffy golden squares from her waffle maker and slid them onto Daphne's plate. When Daphne began drizzling syrup across them, Noah looked at her in dismay.

"What's the matter?"

"You don't want butter on them?" he asked.

"I don't know," Daphne said. "I don't usually put butter on waffles. Should I?"

"You have to when they're homemade," he replied. "They're dry."

"I beg your pardon," Nina said with a grin.

"Just kidding," he said as he slowly pushed the butter across the table like it was a train car.

"Would you stop playing and just give it to her," Nina said with a glare. She folded her arm, spatula still in hand, and watched.

When the butter dish finally arrived at the station in front of Daphne, she lifted the lid and found a dainty, oval-cut diamond engagement ring sticking out of it. With a combination of shock and confusion, she stared at Noah.

"Will you marry my mom?" He tried to keep a straight face, but a smile itched the corners of his mouth.

Nina got down on one knee, plucked the ring from the butter, and wiped it on her napkin. "What he said," she offered shyly.

Daphne clapped both hands against her mouth as strange squeals of happiness emanated from behind them.

"Sorry about the butter," Nina said. "Noah said I should trust him."

"No, no. It's magnificent," Daphne said, almost breathless. "It'll help the ring slide on."

"You can say no if you think it's too soon," Nina said from her knee. "I mean, we don't have to do any—"

"Yes, yes, yes," Daphne shouted as she leapt from her chair and swept Nina up into an embrace. She kissed Nina so hard she thought she might leave marks on her cheeks and lips.

"I've never been happier, Daphne, not since this guy was born." She pointed at Noah, now more involved with his waffles than with their deal. Lifting Daphne's left hand, she slid the ring onto her finger. "This is one merger I know will be an epic success."

Daphne held onto Nina, muffling her whimpers of happiness into Nina's shoulder, practically squeezing the air out of Nina's diaphragm. She then thought of her vision board. "That moves number three up in rankings on my board."

"Greece," Nina said with an air of recognition. "What a perfect locale for a honeymoon."

As Daphne continued to study and gush over her engagement ring with its vintage look, a thought struck her. "Nina, this ring looks familiar. Where did you buy it?"

Nina played it cool with an arched eyebrow. "From a guy I know."

Daphne's eyes fell from Nina to the ring again. "This isn't…" The rest of the sentence caught in her throat.

"Will said Sophie would be thrilled at the idea of me putting it on your finger."

"Oh, my God," Daphne said, almost in a squeak. As tears spilled down her cheeks, she wrapped her arms around Nina again.

"You are my treasure, Daph," Nina whispered in her ear. "Forever."

About the Author

Jean Copeland is a multi-genre lesfic author and educator from Connecticut. Her novel, *The Revelation of Beatrice Darby*, won an Alice B. Readers Lavender Certificate and a Goldie award for debut author. Her other novels, *The Second Wave* and *The Ashford Place*, received Rainbow Awards honorable mentions.

When not writing novels, Jean enjoys blogging and chatting with the women on *The Weekly Wine Down* podcast. Her urban fantasy novel, *Spellbound*, co-written with Jackie D, is available everywhere.

Books Available from Bold Strokes Books

Death Overdue by David S. Pederson. Did Heath turn to murder in an alcohol induced haze to solve the problem of his blackmailer, or was it someone else who brought about a death overdue? (978-1-63555-711-4)

Entangled by Melissa Brayden. Becca Crawford is the perfect person to head up the Jade Hotel, if only the captivating owner of the local vineyard would get on board with her plan and stop badmouthing the hotel to everyone in town. (978-1-63555-709-1)

First Do No Harm by Emily Smith. Pierce and Cassidy are about to discover that when it comes to love, sometimes you have to risk it all to have it all. (978-1-63555-699-5)

Kiss Me Every Day by Dena Blake. For Wynn Jamison, wishing for a do-over with Carly Evans was a long shot, actually getting one was a game changer. (978-1-63555-551-6)

Olivia by Genevieve McCluer. In this lesbian Shakespeare adaption with vampires, Olivia is a centuries old vampire who must fight a strange figure from her past if she wants a chance at happiness. (978-1-63555-701-5)

One Woman's Treasure by Jean Copeland. Daphne's search for discarded antiques and treasures leads to an embarrassing misunderstanding, and ultimately, the opportunity for the romance of a lifetime with Nina. (978-1-63555-652-0)

Silver Ravens by Jane Fletcher. Lori has lost her girlfriend, her home, and her job. Things don't improve when she's kidnapped and taken to fairyland. (978-1-63555-631-5)

Still Not Over You by Jenny Frame, Carsen Taite, Ali Vali. Old flames die hard in these tales of a second chance at love with the ex you're still not over. Stories by award winning authors Jenny Frame, Carsen Taite, and Ali Vali. (978-1-63555-516-5)

Storm Lines by Jessica L. Webb. Devon is a psychologist who likes rules. Marley is a cop who doesn't. They don't always agree, but both fight to protect a girl immersed in a street drug ring. (978-1-63555-626-1)

The Politics of Love by Jen Jensen. Is it possible to love across the political divide in a hostile world? Conservative Shelley Whitmore and liberal Rand Thomas are about to find out. (978-1-63555-693-3)

All the Paths to You by Morgan Lee Miller. High school sweethearts Quinn Hughes and Kennedy Reed reconnect five years after they break up and realize that their chemistry is all but over. (978-1-63555-662-9)

Arrested Pleasures by Nanisi Barrett D'Arnuck. When charged with a crime she didn't commit Katherine Lowe faces the question: Which is harder, going to prison or falling in love? (978-1-63555-684-1)

Bonded Love by Renee Roman. Carpenter Blaze Carter suffers an injury that shatters her dreams, and ER nurse Trinity Greene hopes to show her that sometimes hope is worth fighting for. (978-1-63555-530-1)

Convergence by Jane C. Esther. With life as they know it on the line, can Aerin McLeary and Olivia Ando's love survive an otherworldly threat to humankind? (978-1-63555-488-5)

Coyote Blues by Karen F. Williams. Riley Dawson, psychotherapist and shape-shifter, has her world turned upside down when Fiona Bell, her one true love, returns. (978-1-63555-558-5)

Drawn by Carsen Taite. Will the clues lead Detective Claire Hanlon to the killer terrorizing Dallas, or will she merely lose her heart to person of interest, urban artist Riley Flynn? (978-1-63555-644-5)

Every Summer Day by Lee Patton. Meant to celebrate every summer day, Luke's journal instead chronicles a love affair as fast-moving and possibly as fatal as his brother's brain tumor. (978-1-63555-706-0)

Lucky by Kris Bryant. Was Serena Evans's luck really about winning the lottery, or is she about to get even luckier in love? (978-1-63555-510-3)

The Last Days of Autumn by Donna K. Ford. Autumn and Caroline question the fairness of life, the cruelty of loss, and what it means to love as they navigate the complicated minefield of relationships, grief, and life-altering illness. (978-1-63555-672-8)

Three Alarm Response by Erin Dutton. In the midst of tragedy, can these first responders find love and healing? Three stories of courage, bravery, and passion. (978-1-63555-592-9)

Veterinary Partner by Nancy Wheelton. Callie and Lauren are determined to keep their hearts safe but find that taking a chance on love is the safest option of all. (978-1-63555-666-7)

Everyday People by Louis Barr. When film star Diana Danning hires private eye Clint Steele to find her son, Clint turns to his former West Point barracks mate, and ex-buddy with benefits, Mars Hauser to lend his cyber espionage and digital black ops skills to the case. (978-1-63555-698-8)

Forging a Desire Line by Mary P. Burns. When Charley's ex-wife, Tricia, is diagnosed with inoperable cancer, the private duty nurse Tricia hires turns out to be the handsome and aloof Joanna, who ignites something inside Charley she isn't ready to face. (978-1-63555-665-0)

Love on the Night Shift by Radclyffe. Between ruling the night shift in the ER at the Rivers and raising her teenage daughter, Blaise Richilieu has all the drama she needs in her life, until a dashing young attending appears on the scene and relentlessly pursues her. (978-1-63555-668-1)

Olivia's Awakening by Ronica Black. When the daring and dangerously gorgeous Eve Monroe is hired to get Olivia Savage into shape, a fierce passion ignites, causing both to question everything they've ever known about love. (978-1-63555-613-1)

The Duchess and the Dreamer by Jenny Frame. Clementine Fitzroy has lost her faith and love of life. Can dreamer Evan Fox make her believe in life and dream again? (978-1-63555-601-8)

The Road Home by Erin Zak. Hollywood actress Gwendolyn Carter is about to discover that losing someone you love sometimes means gaining someone to fall for. (978-1-63555-633-9)

Waiting for You by Elle Spencer. When passionate past-life lovers meet again in the present day, one remembers it vividly and the other isn't so sure. (978-1-63555-635-3)

While My Heart Beats by Erin McKenzie. Can a love born amidst the horrors of the Great War survive? (978-1-63555-589-9)

Face the Music by Ali Vali. Sweet music is the last thing that happens when Nashville music producer Mason Liner, and daughter of country royalty Victoria Roddy are thrown together in an effort to save country star Sophie Roddy's career. (978-1-63555-532-5)

Flavor of the Month by Georgia Beers. What happens when baker Charlie and chef Emma realize their differing paths have led them right back to each other? (978-1-63555-616-2)

Mending Fences by Angie Williams. Rancher Bobbie Del Rey and veterinarian Grace Hammond are about to discover if heartbreaks of the past can ever truly be mended. (978-1-63555-708-4)

Silk and Leather: Lesbian Erotica with an Edge edited by Victoria Villasenor. This collection of stories by award winning authors offers fantasies as soft as silk and tough as leather. The only question is: How far will you go to make your deepest desires come true? (978-1-63555-587-5)

The Last Place You Look by Aurora Rey. Dumped by her wife and looking for anything but love, Julia Pierce retreats to her hometown, only to rediscover high school friend Taylor Winslow, who's secretly crushed on her for years. (978-1-63555-574-5)

The Mortician's Daughter by Nan Higgins. A singer on the verge of stardom discovers she must give up her dreams to live a life in service to ghosts. (978-1-63555-594-3)

The Real Thing by Laney Webber. When passion flares between actress Virginia Green and masseuse Allison McDonald, can they be sure it's the real thing? (978-1-63555-478-6)

What the Heart Remembers Most by M. Ullrich. For college sweethearts Jax Levine and Gretchen Mills, could an accident be the second chance neither knew they wanted? (978-1-63555-401-4)

White Horse Point by Andrews & Austin. Mystery writer Taylor James finds herself falling for the mysterious woman on White Horse Point who lives alone, protecting a secret she can't share about a murderer who walks among them. (978-1-63555-695-7)

Femme Tales by Anne Shade. Six women find themselves in their own real-life fairy tales when true love finds them in the most unexpected ways. (978-1-63555-657-5)

Jellicle Girl by Stevie Mikayne. One dark summer night, Beth and Jackie go out to the canoe dock. Two years later, Beth is still carrying the weight of what happened to Jackie. (978-1-63555-691-9)

Le Berceau by Julius Eks. If only Ben could tear his heart in two, then he wouldn't have to choose between the love of his life and the most beautiful boy he has ever seen. (978-1-63555-688-9)

My Date with a Wendigo by Genevieve McCluer. Elizabeth Rosseau finds her long lost love and the secret community of fiends she's now a part of. (978-1-63555-679-7)

On the Run by Charlotte Greene. Even when they're cute blondes, it's stupid to pick up hitchhikers, especially when they've just broken out of prison, but doing so is about to change Gwen's life forever. (978-1-63555-682-7)

Perfect Timing by Dena Blake. The choice between love and family has never been so difficult, and Lynn's and Maggie's different visions of the future may end their romance before it's begun. (978-1-63555-466-3)

The Mail Order Bride by R Kent. When a mail order bride is thrust on Austin, he must choose between the bride he never wanted or the dream he lives for. (978-1-63555-678-0)

Through Love's Eyes by C.A. Popovich. When fate reunites Brittany Yardin and Amy Jansons, can they move beyond the pain of their past to find love? (978-1-63555-629-2)

To the Moon and Back by Melissa Brayden. Film actress Carly Daniel thinks that stage work is boring and unexciting, but when she accepts a lead role in a new play, stage manager Lauren Prescott tests both her heart and her ability to share the limelight. (978-1-63555-618-6)

Tokyo Love by Diana Jean. When Kathleen Schmitt is given the opportunity to be on the cutting edge of AI technology, she never thought a failed robotic love companion would bring her closer to her neighbor, Yuriko Velucci, and finding love in unexpected places. (978-1-63555-681-0)